TELL THE WOLVES I'M HOME

KATLYN A. SKINNER

For fourteen year old Katlyn.
We did it.

"Gabriel drew his sword and lunged for Laurel. He..."

A paper wad flew across the room.

"Gabriel drew his sword and lunged for Laurel. He knew he had no choice now but to kill his own brother. He let out a cry of both rage and sadness as he..."

Someone snickered behind me.

"He let out a cry of both rage and sadness..."

Chairs scraped against the floor.

"He let out..."

A group burst into laughter.

"He..."

Mrs. Hale yelled at everyone to quiet down.

I sighed a little in defeat, closing my book.

She should know by now that it was useless to try and get them to be quiet. It was seventh period on the Friday before spring break. Everyone was too excited to care about school anymore. As far as the students were concerned, spring break had already started. There was chatter everywhere of plans for the following week.

Paper planes and wads of tin foil from lunch soared across the tiny classroom. Everyone was anxious and buzzing.

It pained me to think I had to wait to find out if Gabriel really did kill his own brother, but I'd much rather hold off until I was somewhere quieter. A paper wad pinged me in the face. Someone laughed, but instead of giving them the satisfaction of looking up, I ignored them completely and glanced out the window at the open field outside. The grass rolled up the hill toward the trees, guarding the edge of the woods. I felt a longing to be out there right now, to be running through those trees.

Sharp pain hit my teeth. I reached up and pressed my index finger against my canines to see if it was a fluke. No luck. I dug through my backpack, took out a pack of gum, and shoved several pink sticks in my mouth. Chewing always seemed to ease the ache. The pain had been off and on for a few days now. I needed to remember to tell Aunt Claire about it when I got home.

I slumped in my chair, miserably. I wished I could be as excited as everyone else about spring break, but I knew what I had to look forward to next week. My aunt's monthly business trip was the same week. Which meant I would have to spend the entirety of my spring break alone…with Rob.

I loved Aunt Claire. She was a great mother figure: smart, caring, and she had a way of looking at the world like there was magic in it, but my aunt had one flaw. She had the worst taste in men…and rushed into relationships too quickly, having had countless boyfriends and a total of three husbands.

Then there was Rob.

He seemed like a good guy at first, taking my aunt

out on fancy dates, showering her with gifts, and he even showed a general interest in me, which none of the others ever did. He was a handsome, well-respected lawyer in town. I had nothing but hope that things would work out for them.

He fooled us both.

Once Rob married my aunt and moved in, he showed his true colors. Suddenly he became possessive and controlling toward her. He wanted to know where she was at all times. She stayed home more and made excuses to her coworkers and friends when they'd invite her out. Violent fights ensued when my aunt finally put her foot down after Rob suggested she quit her job.

But their fighting wasn't as scary as the attention Rob showed me when Aunt Claire wasn't looking. What should have been innocent touches between an uncle and niece, lingered a bit too long. Once I caught on, I never let him get too close. He wasn't stupid, but I think part of him loved playing this cat-and-mouse game. He relished every time he'd catch me alone and cop a feel before I'd escape.

My aunt knew she had to get out of this relationship, but once she'd made her intentions known, Rob promised she would get nothing if she left him. He was a lawyer, after all. He made sure his name was on everything. He could take our house, our car, and all my aunt's money, and he had made a "generous" donation to my aunt's employer and my college tuition.

He had us. Without him, we would be broke and homeless. So we had to go on pretending like nothing was wrong and I had to keep this secret from Aunt Claire. I knew if she found out she would take being homeless over what Rob was doing to me. I couldn't let her sacrifice everything.

She started stashing away money to open her own business and soon, with a few loans from the bank, he wouldn't be able to touch us. But she couldn't do any of that if we were homeless and without a job. I squirreled away money myself by working at a local bookstore downtown. The faster we saved, the faster we could escape Rob.

Aunt Claire worked for a floral chain literally called "Florals." They were a franchise with lots of shops all over the country. She'd been working at our local one since high school and had been manager since before I was born.

It was mandatory for all managers to attend these monthly meetings, choosing different states and hotels to hole them up in. She was only gone for a few days every month, but this one also included a flower convention and the managers decided on the spring and summer flowers for their displays.

I thought Rob would have found some way to put a stop to her going, but I think he liked being alone every now and again. Whether it was to torture me or some other agenda, I didn't know. I was usually at Molly's or working overnight at the bookstore.

I was thinking of all the ways to avoid being at home with Rob next week, but I supposed if all else failed, I could lock myself in my room with snacks and pretend I wasn't there.

Something jabbed my side, making me jump.

"Hazel? Are you listening? Stop popping your gum for five seconds."

I glanced over to my right at Molly, irritated that my train of thought was derailed. I popped my gum again and smiled, pleased to see annoyance on my best friend's face. She sat in the desk beside me, her sketchbook open.

"Sorry."

I looked out the window again as I folded up all my thoughts and shoved them in the back of my mind to figure out later.

"You okay? Is it…?" She raised her eyebrows.

"No," I said curtly.

Molly knew all about my living situation, but she promised never to tell anyone if I never kept it from her.

I switched subjects.

"No, it's just my teeth. They've been killing me lately."

I didn't want her to worry about me while she was at camp. It cost her a lot of money to go.

She furrowed her brow, like she was deciding whether to believe me.

"Okay, but you promised me." She folded her arms.

I grabbed her shoulder. "I promise. He hasn't touched me."

This was a partial lie. I never told her that sometimes he caught me as we passed each other on the stairs and would cop a feel while Aunt Claire wasn't looking, or how he'd reach under the table during dinner to lay his hand on my knee and smile that sickening smile, like it was all a game.

I couldn't tell her any of that because it was fine. I would never let him go too far. He would never have me the way he wanted, and since all his attention has been on his cat-and-mouse game, he didn't focus his twisted attention on Aunt Claire.

The final bell rang, and everyone ran outside to freedom while I took my time, like a criminal heading for death row. John, the only other employee working with me at Conner's Book and Coffee had begged me to let him have my shift tonight. His live-in girlfriend was nagging him that he wasn't making enough money for her shopping addiction. Never mind that she didn't have a job of her own to pay for it. Normally I would say no, to hell with his girlfriend, but he'd somehow found a way to get Conner to switch our shifts so he could work today.

Molly seemed to momentarily forget my sour mood. She practically skipped beside me, telling me all about her plans for camp.

"There's going to be a waterfall and hiking. Singing, dancing, and cute guys. I can't wait." She smiled for a second, but then it faded.

"Are you going to be okay while I'm gone?"

I scoffed. "Sure I will. I'll be working at the bookstore all week, getting in some extra hours."

She stopped walking, but I kept going. I didn't need her pity and I didn't want to ruin her excitement.

I turned around.

"And I've got this great book I've been dying to finish." I hoped I sounded convincing.

She jumped forward and hugged me. She was at least three inches taller than me, so I was squished against her chest.

"You're really brave, you know that?" she said.

I shrugged into her, my cheek still pressed into her chest.

I didn't feel brave.

She continued. "And I promise as soon as I get home, you're coming straight over. Camp ends Thursday, so we'll still have the rest of the week together."

"I can't wait," I mumbled into her shirt.

Molly truly was my best friend, but not only that, she was my only friend. I gave off an odd vibe with other people, I guessed. The things they stressed about seemed so trivial compared to what I had to deal with, but even before the stress of Rob, I found people to be a bit hard to understand. A lot of them probably thought the same about me. I preferred books to people. It had been that way since I was old enough to read. Books were my escape. Fantasy was better than reality.

Molly, however, didn't seem to care that I avoided people whenever possible. Or that I didn't agree or disagree that some boy was cute or that some girl's hair was way too red or that her outfit didn't match with her shoes. She didn't care that I loved books more than social interaction. She just liked that I listened, and when I did speak, she genuinely cared about what I had to say. She knew how to have meaningful conversations, things worth talking about. I sometimes found it surprising that Molly could have been best friends with anyone, but she chose me. And in the end, I chose her too.

We walked to my house first. She skipped ahead of me up the porch, took the key from under our welcome mat, unlocked our door, and walked in like she lived there.

"We're home!" she yelled. No one answered.

She turned toward me. "Meet me at my house later tonight. I don't leave for camp until tomorrow morning and I have a surprise for you."

"Okay," I replied, "but couldn't you just give it to me now?"

"I would, but I don't have it at the moment. Anyway, I gotta get home and clean the house and pack. Mom's one condition for letting me go was to make sure the house was clean before I leave." She walked out onto the porch and turned to look at me.

"So, see you tonight then?"

I nodded. "Yeah, I'll head over after my run."

I waved as she jogged down the steps and toward her house, which was only two houses down.

First thing I always did when I got home was check the garage for Rob's car. The spot where his maroon-colored Mercedes sat was empty. I relaxed a little. He was still at work.

I raced upstairs and changed into my running clothes. I usually tried to head out before Rob got home, and I knew he'd probably be here soon, but my teeth started to hurt again. I went to the bathroom, hoping maybe I'd see something in the mirror.

I stood in front of it and opened my mouth, getting as close as I could over the sink. Nothing seemed weird. No cavities or any teeth out of place. I pressed on each tooth, trying to find the source of the pain. When I reached my canines, I let out a yelp as a drop of blood started to form on my finger.

"Geez." I breathed.

I opened my mouth again and gasped. My canines had grown.

I rested my knees up on the counter and leaned in closer to take a better look. Sure enough, they were at least a quarter of an inch longer and much sharper. I grinned wide so I could see all my teeth, staring at how strange my canines looked compared to the rest. I ran my tongue across them.

"Oh great," I whispered to myself. "I'm a freaking vampire now."

How I could joke in such a bizarre situation was beyond me, but I didn't really know what else to do. I smiled again and suddenly they started to grow smaller. I covered my mouth with my hand.

This was just too weird.

I took a step off the counter and inspected my face in the mirror. Was anything else different? I couldn't tell. I still had the same long, wavy brown hair. The same hazel eyes that I was named after. The same bushy eyebrows that always made me look a bit too intimidating, and the same six freckles on my nose that I kept track of since I was twelve.

"Hey, kiddo."

I jumped as a male voice sounded from the bathroom doorway.

Shit.

It was Rob. I hadn't heard him come in.

I turned toward him. Rob wasn't a bad-looking man. In his late thirties, tall, a little on the chubby side with broad arm muscles to match. He had long, dirty-blond hair that was always in a bun and a small goatee and mustache. He definitely fit my aunt's type in the looks department. She was always into the reformed hippy type. He was dressed in his usual business suit. White shirt, red tie, tan slacks, and black dress shoes. And right now, those shoes were standing in the doorway, my only exit. I was trapped. His gaze skimmed across my body, taking in my tank top and shorts, which now felt far too revealing.

"Uncle Rob." I spoke politely and nodded. "I was just leaving."

I tried to walk past him, but he wouldn't budge.

"You really don't have to call me Uncle Rob. Uncle just makes me feel so...old."

He leaned against the doorframe and ran his hand down my arm.

I grew hot with anger. I was tired of this game he played. I was tired of tiptoeing past him.

My body started to ache, like I'd been running too

long the day before and now I was paying for it. My knuckles hurt, as did my chest and legs.

What is happening to me?

"Just let me by, Uncle Rob. I just want to go for a run." I pushed for the door again. He wrapped his arm around my waist and pulled me to him, hard.

"What did I say?" He hissed in my ear. "It's just Rob." He buried his face in my hair and breathed deeply.

I flinched.

"Get off!" I screamed, pushing him away, hard.

Where did all this strength come from?

I tripped and fell on the floor, banging my head against the tub. Rob, seeing me fall and hit my head, gave a nervous laugh and asked if I was okay. Reaching for me, he crouched and pulled me toward him, pinning me under his weight.

"Hey, it's okay. You're okay," he said as he tried to soothe.

I wanted to scream, but instead, something else burst from my lungs: a growl. A deep, snarling, animalistic growl that startled the both of us. He rose slowly, eyes wide and mouth agape. As soon as he was off me, I took off running. I had no idea if I was running from Rob or myself, but it carried me downstairs and outside.

I didn't stop there. I kept going. Past our only streetlight in town, past the fast-food restaurants in the middle of town, past the bookstore I worked at, past city hall, and even past the school. I had no idea where I was running to, but I had no intention of stopping.

CHAPTER
TWO

I ran to the outline of the trees behind the school. The same ones I stared at so eagerly in seventh period, but I didn't stop there. I found a clear path and continued to run until I started to forget why I was so upset. This was always my favorite part of running. The part where my body overcame the gripping ache in my legs and chest, as well as the burning in my lungs. The pain became almost nonexistent. I felt like I could go on forever.

I followed a deer trail across a creek and past a small meadow with a boulder in the middle of the clearing. I slowed a little to admire it. It almost looked like a shrine. The boulder was shaped like a dog's head. Its nose pointing toward the sky. A ring of wildflowers surrounded the large rock, along with a blue bucket and a sponge sitting on the edge of it.

Weird. But I was in too good of a pace to stop and investigate further.

I'd run through these woods before, but only on marked trails. This was all new to me. I loved the way the ground dipped under my feet, giving me the thrill of falling as gravity took hold of my legs, and how it rose up like a hill, giving me a chance to jump over large stumps and logs. The atmosphere was different, almost alive with the activity of the woods.

I began to slow, getting a little winded. The light turned orange as the sun descended. It painted the ground and trees with a beautiful auburn-and-gold coloring. I spotted a clearing up ahead and decided to stop once I reached it. As I approached, I noticed a small lake in the middle of it. The land dipped toward it, the lines of the trees stopping where the slope started. It looked like a large bowl of water, glittering and sparkling with the setting sun.

I stared at the glistening water for a long moment and suddenly it was as if a switch had been turned off in me, or perhaps on, I wasn't sure. I smiled and ran toward the lake, kicking off my shoes and socks. I ran straight into the freezing water, letting out a small gasp at the sudden temperature change. When I was sure I couldn't run any farther, I dove through the murky water, the rush of cold hitting my face. It was so perfect after a long run that when I surfaced, I let out a loud yell.

I've always experienced what they call "runner's high" right after I finished a workout, but this was different. This was something wild, primal…simple. There was only this moment. I constantly worried for the future, never realizing how much freedom I could have if I just learned to live in the here-and-now occasionally.

A small cliff-like rock jutted out around the lake. It appeared almost fabricated in the giant bowl of water. I thought of how fun it would be to dive off it. I ran up the slope, slipping through the wet dirt until I reached the rock. I climbed over it and peered down. The water was a good twenty-five feet away, but it seemed deep enough. I prepped myself, jogging in place and shaking the cold from my hands. Then I ran and screamed, "Cannonball!" and jumped, tucking my knees against my chest. A second before I hit the water, I saw a figure standing on the other side of the lake.

The water was still a cold surprise the second time. I thought about staying under, but it was a silly idea. *You kind of need air to breathe, Hazel.* Besides, why should I care if someone saw me? My feet hit the sandy bottom before I pushed myself upward. I burst through the top of the water, taking in a huge lungful of air. Brushing the water from my eyes, I glanced around. The person I saw was now sitting by the bank on the other side of the lake, staring curiously.

For some reason I felt a little embarrassed. All my wild energy was slowly running out. I decided the only way to get rid of my embarrassment was to pretend I wasn't and just confront the person. I swam across the small lake, realizing halfway that it would have been easier to swim to the shore closest to me and walk around. By the time I reached the other side, I was gasping for air.

I pulled myself to the bank and sat down about a yard away from the stranger. Up close I could see that he was a young man, not much older than me, early twenties at most. He had ear-length, dark-brown hair and sun-kissed skin. I was completely thrown off by two ring piercings on either side of his lower lip, but what surprised me most was his eyes. Each eye was a different color. His left was blue, while his right was a light brown.

He gave me a crooked smile.

Wasn't I supposed to say something? Why wasn't he saying anything? I told myself the only reason I was staring was because of his strange-colored eyes and exotic lip pierc-ings, but the way my stomach felt like it was going to make its home in my throat made it clear that wasn't the only reason.

He was absolutely gorgeous.

I was drawn to him. It was the weirdest thing I had ever felt. He was a complete stranger but everything about him was familiar. Some deep part of me, the part that had made its appearance when I growled at Rob, the part that still growled softly in my head now, was overcome with happiness. All I wanted to do was laugh, giggle, and jump for joy.

There were no words. I felt like we'd been staring at each other for an eternity. He smiled like we were old friends, and I tried to remember how to breathe. My heartbeat was so loud in my chest I wouldn't have been surprised if he heard it.

Finally, FINALLY! He broke the silence.

"I've got a towel if you need one." He lifted a folded dark-green towel.

I gave a small embarrassed "thank you." The spell was broken. He cocked his head as if he were a confused puppy. In fact, that was exactly what he reminded me of, an adorable puppy.

"I don't see many people come this far," he said. "Then again, I've also never seen anyone randomly jump into a small lake in the middle of the woods before, so you must not be most people." He laughed.

I suddenly felt the need to explain myself. He prob-ably thought I was this wild-and-reckless girl who did whatever she felt like, but that wasn't me. I wasn't the type to run through the woods and jump into lakes on a whim. I was predictable, a girl who kept her nose stuck in a book and never took risks, because she had to, if only to stay under her uncle's radar.

I spoke quickly, tripping over my words.

"I followed a deer trail about halfway here and…" I paused, remembering why I had run so recklessly in the first place. "I guess I just lost track of where I was going," I finished flatly. "And as for the jumping into the lake, I got hot from my run and I didn't think anyone else was around." I sounded annoyed.

"So, do you always do reckless-and-wild things when no one's looking?" He was still smiling.

I narrowed my eyes, putting up my caution walls. How had I ever thought he was familiar? This was some random guy, cute maybe, but still a stranger, and I was alone with him in the woods. Not to mention it was getting dark. I stood up, brushing away the leaves and dirt from my soaked shorts.

"Why are you out here? I mean, not to sound rude, but it seems so odd that two people would run into each other in the middle of the woods."

He stood up as well, brushing the leaves off his jeans. "Not so odd. I live about a mile up the slope in my family's lodge." He pointed to the left of him. "I'm here almost every day." He continued smiling, a hint of smugness on his face.

"Oh," I replied, feeling a bit stupid. "Well thanks for the towel."

I handed it to him quickly. Our fingers brushed against each other and I felt a shock run up my arm, spreading through the rest of my body. I jerked back and stared at him. His eyebrows knitted together in confusion.

"You okay?" he asked. "You look a little flushed."

I felt…weird. Like a little sick. My body was on fire.

I didn't answer. Instead, I walked to the other side of the lake and tried to escape my embarrassment, looking for my shoes and socks.

"You gonna be okay walking back in the dark?" he called.

"Fine, thanks!" I yelled back.

"Can I at least get your name, mysterious lake jumper?"

I paused, stifling a laugh. *Mysterious lake jumper?*

"Um, no!" I called back. "If I told you, then I wouldn't be mysterious anymore."

"Well, I'll at least tell you mine then. It's Caden. I hope to see you jumping in this lake again sometime."

I shook my head, trying not to smile but failing. I found my shoes and socks in the now dim light, then hurriedly put them on and began walking quickly back the way I had arrived. I gave a short wave behind me, too embarrassed to look back.

Even though it was completely dark now, I didn't have much trouble seeing. In fact, I could see as well as I did during the day. *Strange, I was pretty sure I couldn't see this well in the dark before.* Fatigue settled in, and I still didn't feel like myself.

Maybe I was getting sick.

Did I have a fever?

I felt my forehead.

I couldn't tell. Aunt Claire was always the one who knew if you had a fever with just one touch.

I still had to go to Molly's tonight. I decided to swing by without bothering to change. I had plenty of my clothes there, and she'd have no problem letting me use her shower.

I spotted the streetlights of the school parking lot just before I reached the edge of the clearing. I didn't bring my cell phone so I wouldn't be able to text Molly and let her know I was on my way. She'd probably yell at me for forgetting my phone again. I was always doing that.

A group of guys from school cut in front of me on skateboards. I gasped as that sharp pain hit my teeth. I bared them and felt that scary growl rise up in my throat again. Luckily, the guys were already halfway down the street and too busy laughing and shouting to hear me.

I was just beginning to think the teeth growing and my growling at Rob had all been in my head, but now I was reminded that something weird was going on with me. Normal people didn't grow elongated canines and growl like some kind of animal. Maybe it was some type of rabies. I knew rabies caused foaming at the mouth and for people's brains to go crazy, but what were the chances of actually *acting* like an animal? Okay I was being stupid. Besides I hadn't even been bitten by anything. Maybe I should research it. There had to be a rational explanation. Everything would be fine. I'd just go to the doctor and they'd probably give me a shot and we'd be done with it.

I was almost to Molly's, just passing my house. The living room TV was on, which meant Rob was probably awake, sitting in his beat-up recliner, watching *Law and Order* reruns. The growl lodged in my throat didn't surprise me this time, I only swallowed it back.

I reached Molly's door and knocked.

"Who is it?"

"Hey! It's me!"

"Come in!"

I opened the door and stepped into the entry hall. "Where are you?"

"Upstairs!"

I walked up the stairs and followed the hallway all

the way to Molly's room. Her door was open. That EDM music she always listened to played as she packed for camp. She looked up as she threw clothes and shoes into a suitcase.

"Hey! Did you forget your phone again? I texted you like ten times. I'm almost finished packing and then we can hang out, but not before I give you this." She paused and looked around her incredibly messy room. "Now where did I put it?" She began hopping around—because you couldn't simply walk through Molly's room. Her floor was covered in clothes, shoes, sketchbooks, makeup, and pretty much everything she owned. She was always jumping over things.

"There it is." She snatched up a piece of paper from the top of her dresser. How she was able to find that was beyond me.

"When I was researching the camp, I came across something awesome." She stepped over another small pile of clothes to give it to me. The paper was a printout of a newspaper clipping from years ago. It was a picture of a group of kids at what appeared to be a camp.

"What is this?" I asked.

"Read the names," she replied.

I read down the list of names until I recognized two.

"Claire Morris, Bethany Morris. That's my mom and aunt." Aunt Claire stood in the middle row. She was very young and beautiful, her kinky hair a lot longer and a lot more unruly than it was now. She always insisted on putting it up into a ponytail and now I could see why.

Mom, on the left of her, could have been my twin. The same wavy hair, same smile, same size and height. This picture was black and white, but I knew from all the pictures my aunt kept that my mother's eyes were green, while mine were hazel, and her hair was a light auburn, like Aunt Claire's. Mine was a dark brown, like my father.

"Did you see him?" she asked.

I looked up at her. *Him?* I checked the names again until I hit one with my last name. *Clark Lowell.* My dad. I looked up at the back row and there he was.

My aunt only had a few pictures of my dad, but I knew him by heart. In this picture he was much younger, but there was no mistaking him. He was handsome with short, wavy hair and an earring in each ear. I could tell from his smile he was a troublemaker. I smiled, too, as if smiling back at him, trying to imagine what mom saw in him. They looked my age in the picture.

"It's your dad, right? I saw the last name and thought you'd like to see this. It was a camp on the other side of the forest, up the peak of the mountain. It's been closed for years, though, but I heard rumors that some kind of cult lives up there now and they turned those cabins into homes."

I smiled at her. She knew how much I obsessed over getting to know my parents.

"Thanks, Molly, this is really awesome."

She shrugged. "I know." She smiled, winked, then hesitated for a second, looking me up and down. "Why are you all wet?"

I glanced at my still damp clothes. "Oh, right. Yeah, I kind of went for a swim in a lake after my run."

Molly raised her eyebrows and drew them together. "What lake? I didn't even know there was a lake near here."

I almost wanted to laugh. Molly was looking at me as if I had never done a reckless thing in my life, and in truth I hadn't, not without her anyway. My thoughts flashed back to Caden's words.

So, do you always do reckless-and-wild things when no one's looking?

My heart skipped a beat. I bet he did lots of crazy, reckless things, judging by his piercings. That confusing thing inside me growled with pleasure. I'd love to be reckless, to be free of all my responsibilities. Forget them for a while, like today.

I suddenly felt the urge to tell Molly about today, but maybe not the whole growling, teeth growing part. I wanted to wait until I had more information. So, I just told her about Rob cornering me in the bathroom and then running off into the woods behind the school. By the time I got to the part about jumping in the lake and meeting Caden, her facial expressions had gone through ten different emotions, most of them anger and shock. When I finished, it was mostly just shock.

"Okay, first off, I'm going to kill Rob."

I shook my head, but she lifted her finger.

"That man is absolute trash, Hazel. I can't wait for your aunt to get those loans so she can escape that man."

I agreed with her but said nothing. She knew how I felt.

"Secondly," she continued. "You met a guy in the middle of the woods, near a lake that you just happened to randomly decide to jump into? That sounds crazy."

I laughed. She was kind of right. It sounded even crazier when I had said it all out loud.

She sat on the edge of the bed and stared at me. "Well?"

"Well what?"

"What does he look like? What happened after he saw you?"

"Oh, well nothing really. We talked. He gave me his towel. Turns out he lives in a cabin nearby, looked to be in his early twenties. The whole thing was pretty embarrassing to tell you the truth." My cheeks heated just thinking about it again. Molly had this crazy grin on her face.

"Was he cute?"

I just stared at her. "What does that even matter?"

There was no way I could lie to her because she would definitely be able to tell. My face was getting hotter. She kept smiling, waiting.

"Yes. Okay? He was insanely hot."

We had made our way to the bathroom so she could throw her toiletries in a small bag. I sat on the edge of the tub. Now she had me going and I couldn't stop.

"I don't know, Mol, he's unlike any guy I have ever seen before. He has two different colored eyes. One blue and one brown, and he has these piercings on his lower lip that would look absolutely ridiculous on anyone else, but he really pulls it off."

I was using dramatic hand gestures as I spoke, pointing at my lips and eyes. I realized too late how ridiculous I looked. I clasped my hands together and stuck them between my knees.

Molly looked amused. She raised her eyebrows and let out a long whistle. "Wow, Haze, I've never heard you talk about a guy this way before."

"What way?" I said defensively.

"As if you like him." She winked at me.

"I don't even know him."

Molly shrugged. "So? You can be attracted to someone you don't know. Take Jason Momoa for example. I don't know him, but, man, do I think he's attractive." I laughed but didn't reply.

"Does this mystery man have a name?"

"Caden."

"Cute name too. I wanna meet him." She laughed.

I shook my head as I got up and walked back toward her room. "Okay, next time I see him I'll be sure to give him your number. But for now, I'm going to use your shower and then if it's okay with you, I'm going to use your computer."

She called from the bathroom. "You think there will be a next time?"

I groaned.

She came running back into her room and bumped her hip into my side. "I've got to finish packing, but once I'm done with that, you can stay the night and we can watch crappy Hallmark movies."

I smiled. "Sounds good."

I went to her closet and rummaged through her stuff for something of mine. I didn't think any normal person would have let their best friend keep so much of her stuff in their room, but Molly never seemed to care. Not to mention, her room was usually so messy she could hardly keep track of her own stuff.

I found an old T-shirt and some raggedy green-and-red pajama bottoms and headed toward the bathroom. I closed the door, double-checking to make sure I locked it, but also vaguely realizing that I wasn't at home with Rob, and Molly was the only one home. *Better to be safe than sorry, I guess.* I reminded myself that even normal people locked their bathroom doors. I turned on the shower and undressed while I waited for the water to heat up. It felt good to be rid of those cold, damp clothes. I stepped into the shower, letting the warm water wash over my face and hair. It had been such a weird day and it was good to be able to just take a moment and think.

My body was still far too hot and I ached the same

way I had when I pushed Rob. I was probably getting sick. And I bet going for a run and jumping into a freezing lake didn't help. Maybe I should tell Aunt Claire. *I should at least tell her I don't have my phone on me. I hope she isn't worried.*

My mind wandered for a bit, before drifting to Caden. He seemed familiar. Not like we'd bumped into each other on a crowded street or in a grocery store kind of way, but in a way that was like he had always been there, like Aunt Claire or Molly. This feeling kind of reminded me of my parents. I'd never met them, but if they came back to life and walked through my front door, there would be a sense of familiarity.

Strange that he would just appear the moment all these weird things started happening to me. I've lived in this town my whole life. Why had I never seen him before? Was it just a coincidence? He said he came to the lake every day. He was probably about to go for a swim. Why else would he have a towel?

But wait! He was wearing jeans. I watched him brush his hands on them. Was he going to swim in them? Or maybe he liked to swim without clothes. My cheeks heated at the idea. I mean it was possible. It was a lake in a remote area and he probably didn't imagine someone showing up. There were no trails that led to it.

There was a knock on the door.

Shit, Rob. But then I quickly remembered I was standing in Molly's shower, not mine. I poked my head through the curtain.

"Yeah?"

"Hey, I'm done packing, hurry up."

"I'm almost done!" I replied.

Molly had packed away all her shampoo and body wash, but she had left a small bar of soap. I had no choice but to wash my hair and body with it. I realized I'd spent more time thinking in the shower than actually washing. I turned off the water and quickly dried off, throwing on my pajama pants and oversize T-shirt, then wrapped the towel around my head.

I walked into Molly's room, but she wasn't there anymore.

"Hey! I'm downstairs!" she called.

I headed down and walked past the living room toward the office, just underneath the stairs. Molly sat at her mom's desk, looking at her laptop.

"Here, take a seat. You aren't going to believe this." She patted the stool next to her computer chair. I sat down.

"Okay don't get mad, but while you were finishing up in the shower, I decided to look Caden up."

"Molly!"

"What? I wanted to make sure this guy wasn't some kind of serial killer. And anyway, I didn't expect to find anything. You only gave me his first name, but then I did find something and it's…well, look." She pointed to the computer. I leaned in and began reading the article.

Eighteen-year-old Caden Ulrika was found alive after his family home burned to the ground. Firefighters were amazed to find him still breathing, lying naked in the snow. Caden's parents, Melissa and Jason Ulrika, and thirteen-year-old sister, Kara, were later found among the charred wreckage. Officials aren't sure what caused the fire, but as of right now, it appears to have been an electrical problem. "The cabin was wooden, if this was an electrical problem that caused the fire, the house would have been in flames within minutes.

The boy was lucky to survive," says Fire Chief Palo. Caden suffers from third-degree burns on his left side and a copious amount of smoke in his lungs, but he is recovering at an alarming rate and should be able to leave the hospital within a few days.

I stopped reading and scrolled down to the picture in the left-hand corner. There was Caden, his hair a little shorter and no piercings to speak of. He was wearing a goofy smile. His two-colored eyes, one a light-golden brown and the other an ocean blue, showed no sign of grief or stress. It must have been before the fire. It saddened me to know that his happiness and carefree smile would someday be ripped away from him.

Scrolling down farther was a family photo. Caden even younger still, maybe thirteen, holding his little sister on his back, his parents smiling behind them as they leaned into one another. They all thought they had their whole lives ahead of them. Just like my parents.

I felt Molly touch my shoulder. I hadn't realized I'd been crying till I felt a tear roll down my cheek. I sniffed, wiping it away.

"So that's him then." Not a question, but I nodded anyway.

"Poor guy has had it tough. This was four years ago. I also found another smaller article about him that I thought was a little strange. It says while they were treating him, one of the doctors noticed that his canines were a bit larger than normal. She even wrote it in her report and everything, but later she said it must have just been a trick of the light because when she looked again, his teeth were a normal size. She was a total quack, I think."

I had my hand over my mouth, trying to suppress my shock. "Yeah," I said meekly.

"What? What's wrong?"

Apparently, I wasn't doing a very good job of hiding my emotions.

"Nothing, it's just…" Man, I really wanted to tell her the truth, but I was freaking out and honestly, I didn't want to freak her out either. "He's had such a hard life. I feel really bad for him."

"Yeah, you both have a lot in common. Losing your parents and all."

I nodded absentmindedly.

"Are you going to see him again?"

I looked at my best friend. Was I? Maybe not for the reasons she was thinking, but if he had the same physical problems as me, then maybe he would know more about it than I did. Maybe he could tell me what the hell was going on with me and how to fix it.

"I don't know, maybe."

Molly gave me a big smile. I rolled my eyes at her as I took the towel off my head and shook my hair out.

"Hey, mind if I use your phone to call Aunt Claire?"

"Sure." She handed me her phone. I dialed my aunt's number. It rang a few times before a groggy voice answered.

"Hello?"

Crap. I glanced at the clock on the computer. The time read twelve thirty in the morning.

"Oh crap, I'm so sorry, Aunt Claire. I didn't realize what time it was."

She cleared her throat. "No, sweetie, it's fine. I'm glad you called. I sent you a dozen texts. Are you okay?"

"I'm fine. I just forgot my phone at home. I'm at Molly's"

"You always forget your phone. That's not normal teenage behavior, you know. I'm glad you're okay, sweetie, but please try to remember to have it on you while I'm away, and call me every day, please. You sure Molly's parents are okay with you staying the whole week there?"

I glanced at Molly, her eyebrows raised.

"Yeah, it's all worked out and I promise I'll call you every day. I'll swing by the house tomorrow and grab my phone."

There was a pause and then a yawn. "Well, okay, you can just text me if you want…but call me if anything happens, okay? Anything, Hazel, I mean it. I'll be back Friday night."

I sighed. I always felt bad about lying to Aunt Claire.

"Yeah of course. I'll text you tomorrow, love you."

"Love you, too, sweetie." She hung up.

I handed Molly her phone back.

"You told your aunt you were staying at my house all week?" She folded her arms across her chest.

"Yeah, sorry, I forgot to mention it."

"You told me you would be okay while I was gone."

I shrugged. "And I will be. I just didn't want my aunt to have to worry about me all week."

She got up from the desk chair. "Yeah, well I worry about you too. You be sure to text me every day this week as well. Now, come on, I'll make some popcorn and you can pick out a movie. Mom's working the night shift and should be home any minute. She usually likes to wind down with a good Hallmark movie anyway, so we'll just stay downstairs and watch something together." She smiled and started toward the kitchen.

I honestly couldn't say how I got so lucky to have a best friend like Molly.

THREE

I woke with a start, my body on fire, my heart pounding violently. It took me a few seconds to remember I was in Molly's room. She was still asleep. The clock on her nightstand displayed ten twenty in the morning. I got out of bed quickly, realizing the sheets were drenched in my sweat. I hoped Molly would forgive me for that. That all-over body ache had returned.

I quickly rummaged through the closet and found a pair of ripped jeans and a black Jack Daniel's T-shirt. No clean underwear or a bra to speak of. I knew I'd have to swing by my house to get them and my phone before I set out. I picked up my wet running clothes and put on my shoes. I then woke Molly to let her know I was leaving. She waved her hand at me and groaned out that she would text me later. I smiled. She was unconscious once more. Molly's parents were in the living room downstairs, watching the news. I waved at them as I walked out the front door.

There was a bit of a bite to the air. This time of year,

the temperatures usually didn't rise till around noon. I jogged toward my house, trying to keep warm. When I reached the porch, I looked for the key under the mat. It was missing, so I used the one behind my aunt's favorite fern. The porch looked like a small exotic rainforest with all the plants placed around and hanging from the ceiling. It would be incredibly hard for someone to find a key in the mess if they didn't know where to look.

I unlocked and opened the door as quietly as possible. Stepping over the threshold, I looked around for Rob. My house was very similar to Molly's, as most were on our street, except it was flipped. The stairs to the upper floor were to the left instead of the right. The first-floor hall still led to the kitchen, which was slightly bigger and made the living room smaller, and instead of an office under the stairs, there was a door to the garage.

I'd lived in this house my whole life and never had a real attachment to it. While it held fond memories of my aunt and me, it also held unpleasant ones, too, and since Rob had moved in, it now held a lingering sense of disquietude every time I entered. I always had to be on guard, never knowing when Rob might appear and try to corner me. I couldn't wait to get out of here and actually have a home I felt safe in.

No sign of Rob downstairs. I made my way to the kitchen and opened the fridge to find something for an on-the-go breakfast. As I scanned its contents for anything that piqued my interest, my focus kept returning to the steak marinating on the bottom shelf. Rob probably planned to cook it for dinner later. It looked good enough to eat now. The blood running in the glass pan, the meat red and tender. The smell of seasoning mixed with the blood made my mouth water. I felt my canines extend. The pain was less now than it had been yesterday. Shaking my head, I grabbed an apple instead. I wasn't a vegetarian like Molly, but I also wasn't some crazy person who ate raw meat. I didn't even like my steak cooked medium rare. I was beginning to feel more animal than human.

I slowly walked upstairs, avoiding the spots I knew to creak. My room, like Molly's, was also the farthest down the hall. Rob must still be asleep. The master bedroom door was closed.

My room had the same layout as Molly's, but unlike her messy room, mine was clean and organized. Where her walls were a pastel purple, a color she had chosen when she was twelve, mine were still the same white-cream color they had always been since the house was built.

A stuffed wolf sat on the neatly folded black-and-gray sheets of my small twin bed. The wolf's fur was now matted from eighteen years of love. His left ear forever hanging at an angle, as did his head, which made his chocolate-colored eyes stare downward. It was the only gift my mother ever gave me before she died.

A giant bookshelf I'd made in shop class when I was fifteen covered most of the wall on the opposite side. It was a crappy bookshelf in truth. A dark-brown chestnut color with dark ringed patches from the decaying wood, and it leaned slightly to the right. But I loved it. It was covered from top to bottom with my favorite books.

Just then, I heard a door open down the hall. Rob was awake. I closed my door very softly and listened. Rob's footfalls came toward my room. I held my breath. He knocked.

"Hey, Haze, you home?"

Shit.

"Look, we need to talk."

I stuck my phone in my back pocket and headed toward the window and opened it. He knocked harder.

"Hazel, I know you're in there."

I unhooked the screen and hopped out onto the windowsill. It was narrow, so I turned around very carefully and closed the window, hooking the screen back in place. Now came the hard part—getting down from the two-story window. The oak tree in our yard had been recently trimmed. The nearest branch was a good four feet away. I'd have to leap for the nearest one, which I'd have to hang from and then inch my way to the base so I could use the knots of the trunk to climb down.

Sure. Easy-peasy.

I took a deep breath, steeling myself and leaped, my hands hitting the nearest branch. I gripped hard, feeling the rough bark scrape the palms of my hands. I inhaled from the pain. I was losing my grip fast.

"No, no, no, no," I said aloud.

I lost the grasp of one hand, then the other. I had a split second to pray I didn't break my legs while simultaneously cursing myself for being such a coward toward Rob, but instead of hitting the hard ground, I fell into someone's arms.

He grunted.

"Holy shit. I actually caught you," a male voice said, surprised.

When I looked up, however, his amused face didn't seem all that surprised. In fact, he looked very smug. I felt the urge to wipe that smugness off his face. A defense mechanism I had developed to combat embarrassment was to get angry.

"Yeah, thanks for the catch and all, really, but what the hell are you doing in my yard?"

His smug expression never wavered. He chuckled as he set me down.

"I saw you climbing out your window, and when I noticed you were about to make a jump for that tree, I figured I'd better be close by in case you fell…and well… you did." He winked.

Was he flirting with me? That was ridiculous. I brushed my stinging hands on my pants.

"Can I ask why you were jumping out of a two-story window? Is this a cry for help?"

He gave me a wide smile. *He must really think he's funny.*

I, however, did not give him the satisfaction of letting him see even a hint of a smile from me, but if my unfriendly face and flaring temper affected him, he made no hint of it.

"You don't remember me, do you?" he asked.

I looked at him for a long moment. He was tall, broad-shouldered, with pale skin, light golden-brown eyes and a mop of curly black hair that stuck up in all directions. I had to admit he did look oddly familiar, but I'd think I'd remember those giant biceps nearly ripping out of his T-shirt.

My eyebrows drew together and my mouth hung open as I tried to find my words.

He gave me an easygoing smile.

"That's okay. We were really young the last time we saw each other. I'm David. We used to play together at the park downtown before they tore it down." He stuck his hand out.

The memories came flooding back in a rush and I let out a gasp of recognition.

"Oh my God! David!" I took his hand.

Of course I wouldn't recognize him. I hadn't seen him since we were six. Aunt Claire would sometimes take me to that park after she got off work. I remember spending whole summers there.

David had been my earliest known friend. I had a hard time developing a connection with the other kids at the park. I always beat them at every game we played. Tag, hide-and-seek, red rover, it didn't matter. I always seemed to win, and they didn't like that very much. After a while, they stopped inviting me to play with them, and I stopped hoping they'd invite me. Alternatively, I started bringing my books to the park to read. I could tell this made Aunt Claire disappointed. I wanted to tell her it was okay and that books made me happy, but I knew it wouldn't make her feel any better.

David showed up the summer after first grade. He was…odd to say the least. Like me, he didn't play with the other kids, instead he liked to dig holes in the sand at the edge of the park. He completely fascinated me. I found myself looking up from my book more than once to watch him dig. He was tall, lanky, and I never saw him wear a shirt or shoes. He didn't have any tools to scoop the sand with, only his hands. He'd always leave the park covered in sand and leaves. Then every day, he'd come back and the hole would be covered, but it never seemed to faze him, he'd just bend down and start digging again.

One day, my curiosity got the better of me and I walked over to him.

"What are you doing?"

He looked up at me, his curly hair falling in his face. He put a hand over his eyes to block out the light of the sun.

"I'm trying to dig to the other side of the earth."

"Why?"

"Have you ever heard of someone who has before?"

I shook my head.

"Exactly! I want to be the first."

He started digging again.

I noticed his mound of sand was too close to the hole and was slowly sliding back in. I bent down and began pushing it farther away. He eyed me suspiciously.

"Can I help?" I asked. "You might get farther with two people instead of one."

"Hmmm." He eyed me suspiciously but then smiled. "Okay!"

I smiled back and introduced myself. "I'm Hazel."

"David."

We spent the rest of the summer trying to reach the other side of the world. Every day we'd come to the park and every day the hole would be filled again, but it didn't discourage us, because every day we still got a little farther. Sand eventually gave way to dirt, then rock, and soon the hole was wide enough to fit us both and tall enough to go over our heads.

I remember our last day together. We lay stretched out on our mound of sand, sweaty and tired.

"I think we're getting close," David said, smiling.

I looked at his dirty face, eyes squinting from the sun. "You think so? How do you know?"

He shrugged. "I don't but this is the farthest we've ever gotten. We gotta be close. I think we'll definitely reach it tomorrow."

I smiled, excited by the idea. I hadn't realized David's dream of reaching the other side of the world had somehow become my dream too.

I took his dirt-caked hand in mine, interlacing our fingers. I was feeling giddy. "We should make a pact," I said excitedly.

"A what?" he asked.

"A pact. It's like a promise."

"Oh, okay. What are we promising?"

I looked over at the other kids playing on the jungle gym, laughing and having fun, completely ignoring us, and then I looked at the parents sitting on the benches and picnic tables, whispering and glancing at us, my aunt glaring at them with a scowl on her face.

"Let's promise to always be on each other's side. No matter what. Us against the world. Hazel and David."

David turned to look me in the eye. "No matter what?"

I smiled. "No matter what."

I held out my pinkie to him. Everyone knew the most sacred pacts were made with pinkie promises.

David intertwined his pinkie with mine, a grin on his face.

We laid our heads back down on the dirt, both of us grinning from ear to ear.

"You know you're kinda my best friend," I said without looking at him.

David turned his head toward me, and I could still see his smile from the corner of my eye.

"You're kinda mine too."

He got up and shook his whole body like a dog, trying to brush off the dirt and leaves. He looked in the direction of the woods surrounding the park. A frown suddenly lined his face.

I sat up. "You okay?"

He looked back at me. "I gotta go home now."

His face had a solemn expression, shoulders slumped.

"Oh…okay," I said.

His eyes looked bleak as he stared at the ground. He didn't glance up at me.

"What's wrong? Are you in trouble?" I asked.

He shook his head. "I don't know, maybe."

He started for the woods. When he was halfway to the trees, he looked back and gave a small wave. "Bye, Hazel."

I gave a big wave back. "Bye! See you tomorrow!"

But I didn't see him tomorrow.

I was hurt and worried when he didn't show up the next day or the next, and when summer came to an end, I'd finally given up hope of ever seeing him again. Over the next few years, I wondered what had happened to him every time I walked by the park. Then I met Molly and four years later, they tore the park down and turned it into a gas station. I didn't think much of my time with David after that.

I looked at him now, trying to compare him to six-year-old David. He'd really grown into himself. He was still tall, but by no means lanky and his hair no longer hung in his face. He was…well he was undeniably handsome.

"You've really…changed." I felt stupid as soon as I said it. Of course he'd changed. I felt bad for the way I'd treated him earlier.

He laughed. "I could say the same about you. A lot happens in twelve years."

"Yeah definitely."

There was an abrupt, awkward silence. I glanced down at my shoes and cleared my throat. "Anyway, thanks for the save."

He gripped his fingers behind his head. "Yeah no problem. What are the chances I would run into you like this, huh?"

I squinted one eye like I was trying to calculate the percentage. "I'd say one in a million."

He laughed and the tension lifted. "I was on my way

to get some coffee. Would you like to join me? Maybe explain why you decided to parkour out your window?"

I paused before answering, a little thrown off by being asked to hang out with someone other than Molly. Plus, now didn't exactly feel like the best time.

I ignored the nagging in my head, which signaled I was making excuses to get out of a social situation and was about to tell him I had other plans, when Rob walked out the front door. He sat in the rocking chair on the front porch, picking up the paper to read while pulling a cigarette from his shirt pocket. He looked like he would be there for a while.

My fear of Rob spotting me outweighed my social anxiety. I turned back to David. "Coffee sounds great."

We set off into town.

As we walked, I wasn't sure what to talk about. Should I ask him how he's been? Where he went? I didn't have much practice interacting with people I hardly knew, and that was the truth of it. I didn't know David anymore. It had been a decade since we'd last seen each other. It was a strange feeling when someone you used to be close with comes back into your life a complete stranger. While we'd been digging that hole all summer, we'd talked about everything. Our favorite things, our hopes, our fears. Mostly kid stuff, but the connection had been real and now it felt snuffed out, only a small tether held us together by our childhood friendship.

The uncomfortable silence dragged on, but David either didn't mind or didn't notice. I stared at my ripped-up hands. They really stung. Not to mention I was still burning up and beginning to feel that ache throughout my body again.

"How's your hands?" he asked.

"They sting, but I guess it's better than a couple of broken legs."

He laughed. "True enough."

David clapped his hands in front of him and then behind, back and forth. I was about to ask the first thing that popped into my head, but he spoke first.

"So why were you jumping out a window? Ex-boyfriend's house? One-night stand?"

My cheeks flamed at the thought of doing anything like that.

"No, of course not. It's my house. I was…avoiding my uncle."

"Ah," he said, giving a slow nod. "The one that was sitting on the front porch when we left?"

I gave a tight-lipped smile.

"That's the one."

David didn't push further, and I was grateful. I hoped he just thought I was a rebellious teen trying to avoid her parental figure.

If only I had it that easy.

He stopped clapping his hands, sticking them in his front pockets.

I glanced at him from the corner of my eye, trying to study him without him noticing. I saw only a hint of the six-year-old boy I used to know and then it was lost again in his adult features.

"I…"

I was about to confess how sad I'd been when he left, but I didn't want to sound silly. It had been so long ago.

I pointed at Conner's.

"This is the only coffee shop in town. If you don't count the gas station coffee, and most people don't."

He wrinkled his nose and smirked.

As we opened the door, a small cowbell on the doorknob jingled. I walked up to the counter and said hello to Conner.

"Hey, Haze. Aren't you sick of this place already?"

I laughed. "Never."

"John's in the back doing inventory. What can I get for you?"

David coughed from behind me.

"Oh." I gestured toward him. "My friend and I would like my usual, please."

"Anything for you." He gave me a wink and started to work behind the counter.

I led the way to my favorite spot, a comfy booth by the window, nearest to the books. I was in my element here and I thought David could tell. He sat across from me, smiling. I tried to look anywhere but at him, feeling a bit self-conscience suddenly.

"So, what's your usual?"

"Oh yeah, sorry about that. I know everyone has a coffee preference, but Conner makes the best caramel mocha frappe I have ever had. Do you like cold coffee?"

"I do."

"Okay good, because even if you didn't, I don't think you could possibly hate Conner's frappe."

He smiled at me.

"You come here a lot?"

I nodded. "You could say that. I work here."

"Ah, I see. Do you get discounts on all the coffee and books?"

"Of course. That's half the reason I wanted to work here."

He smiled. "What's the other half?"

I lowered my gaze for a moment, then gave a small shrug. "Money, I guess."

"That's cute."

My cheeks heated. I let out a cough and shook the front of my shirt, trying to cool off.

Conner brought us our frappes…and on the house. We both thanked him, eyeing the delicious-looking frozen beverages. Now that I was sitting down, I started feeling strange again. The outer edges of my vision blurred, and I was sweating. David said nothing as he sipped his drink. He stretched an arm across the booth, staring out the window. I took a sip of mine too, hoping it would cool me off.

"You were right. This is great," he exclaimed.

I gave him a half smile.

"You okay?" he asked. "You look a little sick."

I glanced down at my hands and decided to be honest with him.

"I'm not sure. I haven't really been feeling too great the past few days."

He nodded and gave me a strange look as he took another sip of his drink. It almost looked like he knew something, but just as I was about to ask him, white flashes shifted in my eyes, like lights flickering in and out. I pushed my thumb and index finger into my eyes and laid my head against the back of the booth.

"Hey, you gonna be okay? Should I take you home?"

I shook my head. His hand touched mine and I jerked it back out of reflex. Since Rob, I've had a serious phobia of people touching me unexpectedly. I immediately regretted my reaction. David was just trying to be nice and he sounded genuinely concerned for me.

"I'm sorry," I said, taking my fingers off my eyes to open them. I could see again, but it was like tunnel vision.

"You're right. I'm not feeling too great."

I hoped he didn't think this was an excuse not to hang out with him.

The ache was full force now. I silently prayed I would be able to sneak back into the house without Rob noticing.

"I'll walk you home," he said and began to stand.

I shook my head. "I'll be fine."

All I wanted to do was crawl into bed.

I got up and waved to David.

"It was great seeing you. Let's try and catch up another time, okay?" A part of me was a little sad to leave. I really did want to see where he'd been and what kind of person he was now. He still seemed concerned. He jumped out of the booth and snatched my phone from my pocket.

Man, he was fast.

"Hey!" I protested.

Ignoring me, he powered it on, facing the screen in my direction to unlock it. "Just in case something happens. Here's my number. If you won't let me walk you home, at least text me that you're all right when you get there. My conscience won't let me rest till I know you're okay."

I nodded, a bit dumbstruck, but too out of it to argue. As he returned my phone, he gripped my hand. I didn't jerk away. It was only a handshake. He watched me intently. I'm not sure I've seen a serious expression on his face till now. It made him look like a completely different person.

"It was really nice to see you again, Hazel. I hope…" He paused. "I hope you feel better soon."

What an odd way to say that. Then my vision started to go in and out of focus and I felt a bit nauseated. I could only muster a nod as I made a sprint for the door, then outside, where I hurled in the bushes.

Sorry, Conner.

I walked home as quickly as I could. My phone started to buzz. Aunt Claire. I answered, even though I really shouldn't have. It was taking a lot of my concentration just to walk, but I needed to tell her what was going on. I don't think I'd ever been this sick before. What if it got serious and I ended up in a hospital? I'd want Aunt Claire to know.

"Hello?" I answered in almost a whisper. My throat was still sore from throwing up. I really needed some water.

"Hazel, honey, are you okay?"

"I'm not feeling well, actually. I was at the coffee shop, but I'm on my way home."

"What's wrong?"

I explained my symptoms. Fever, aching, throwing up. She thought maybe it was the flu.

"You go home and straight to bed. Do I need to come—? No, you know what? Screw this meeting. I'm coming home."

I tried to argue, but a spasm shot through my stomach and I let out a silent yell of pain. My vision went out, taking the rest of me with it as I began to fall. I thought of how bad the asphalt was going to hurt, but instead of hitting it, I fell into someone's arms…again.

I let out a gasp of pain.

I was hot before, but now it felt like I was being consumed by fire. All I could think about was the pain and the burning. I screamed, but if it was in my head or out loud, I couldn't be sure. I barely felt the arms carrying me.

Then everything went black.

A shock of cold jerked me awake. I gasped and opened my eyes briefly. I was in a bathtub full of ice water. It hurt, oh God it hurt. I struggled to get out, but strong arms held my body in the water. I let out a scream.

"Hazel, please calm down. I need to bring your body temperature down a bit. It's too high."

David.

I was angry, hysterical, and still in pain. That animalistic growl escaped my throat and my teeth extended. Before I even knew what I was doing, I bit his arm. It had to hurt, because I tasted blood, but David didn't flinch.

He just placed my head against his chest and whispered, "Shhhh, it's okay, shhhh."

I blacked out again.

I think I woke up several times, but I couldn't be sure. It was hard to tell reality from dreaming. My vision was blurring from color to black and white every time I opened my eyes. Maybe I was dreaming. I'd completely lost track of time in this in-between state. I'd never felt so detached from anything in my life, and I wondered if maybe I would die. If I did, would that be so bad? I didn't hurt anymore, but I was still hot and drowsy. It was almost nice to be here—but not really here—in and out of subconsciousness. Like sleeping in on a lazy Sunday morning.

In between spurts of consciousness, I dreamed of my parents and the life we could have had if they were still alive. I dreamed of Aunt Claire and me living in our own house, far away from Rob. I dreamed of going to college with Molly. I dreamed of Caden. In my dream, we knew each other well. We were childhood friends, like David and I had been. I watched flashes of us growing up together, I dreamed of us kissing.

FOUR

My room was cast in a bluish haze as dawn approached. It took me a moment to remember how I'd gotten there. I was in my own bed and in a pair of pajamas I hadn't put on myself. My skin was sticky, and the sheets were stained with sweat. I lifted myself into a sitting position. I was a little hot and achy, but I no longer felt as if I were dying. When I tried to swallow, I ended up coughing. My mouth was so dry. Glancing over at my nightstand I spotted a glass of water. Picking it up, I immediately downed it. I then noticed my phone on the charger, the screen was horribly cracked. I checked the time—five a.m.—then rubbed my eyes before checking my messages. There were two missed calls from Aunt Claire and a text from David. I checked his text first.

Hey, text me when you wake up. I need to know you're okay. Sorry I couldn't stay. I made sure you were

```
comfortable   and   had   everything
within reach before I left.
```

I doubted he'd be awake at this hour, but I replied.

```
I'm   awake   and   alive.   Did   you
dress me?
```

I knew I should be grateful that he got me home safe and possibly saved me from overheating, but I couldn't help but feel a little violated that a guy saw me naked while I was unconscious and unaware. I decided to text Aunt Claire while I waited for a reply from David. She was probably worried sick.

I paused, a little confused. There was a conversation in my messages that I didn't have with Aunt Claire. Someone had been texting my aunt, pretending to be me.

```
Aunt Claire: Hazel?!   Answer   the   phone!
Are you okay?! What happened?!
```

```
Aunt Claire: Hazel   Bethany,   if   you   do
not  answer  this  phone  right  now,  I
am  calling  the  police  or  an  ambu-
lance or someone!
```

```
You: Hey  sorry,  I  dropped  my  phone.
I'm   okay.   No   need   to   worry.   I'm
home now.
```

```
Aunt Claire: DO NOT SCARE ME LIKE THAT,
HAZEL. Are you really okay? Call me.
```

You: I'm fine. I can't talk right now. My voice is gone. I'm gonna try and sleep this off. I'll call you when I wake up.

Aunt Claire: I'm coming home early. I need to know you're okay. Sleep well, drink lots of fluids. There're still some cold meds in the medicine cabinet. I love you.

You: Love you too.

I stared at my phone, rereading the conversation over again. This could only be David's doing. I quickly sent him another text.

AND DID YOU TEXT MY AUNT?!

I got an immediate response this time.

Good morning, Sleeping Beauty. I'm glad to see you're feeling better. Yes, I did dress you. I couldn't leave you in those wet clothes. If it makes you feel any better, I promise I had my eyes closed the whole time ;) and I didn't want you to get in trouble with your aunt, so I texted her so she wouldn't worry.

I was angry but also a little grateful. Maybe I was overreacting. David was coming from a good place and he did pretty much save my life, but he could have taken me to a hospital instead of taking care of me himself.

```
Why didn't you just take me to a
hospital?
```

Another immediate response.

```
I didn't think it was necessary. I
knew what was wrong with you. I'm
sorry if I made you feel uncom-
fortable.
```

I really wasn't sure what to say to that. I could have died and yet David didn't feel it was necessary to take me to a hospital. This was honestly the strangest thing that had ever happened to me.

I decided not to comment on what he'd said and instead asked him another question.

```
Was anyone home when you brought me
here?
```

I waited for what felt like the longest minute of my life. I bit down on my nails nervously.

```
No one was there when I brought you
home.
```

I sighed with relief. Maybe Rob had gone out with some friends or was running errands. Whatever the case, he hadn't been home. I rolled out of bed to turn the light on, my legs feeling a bit weak. I caught a glimpse of myself in the mirror.

Holy hell. I looked awful. My hair was a tangled mess, my skin flushed and sticky with sweat, and my lips...

Was that blood? I covered my mouth with my hand. Suddenly I remembered biting David.

Oh God...oh God...he knows. He knows that I'm some kind of growling, biting, deranged freak.

I thought about texting David again and asking him about it, but I was also too afraid to bring it up.

I sat on the bed. I really needed answers.

I thought back to the article about Caden and the doctor who'd said she'd seen something wrong with his teeth. That seemed to be my only lead. If I talked to Caden again, maybe he could tell me what was going on. *Or he could also think you are totally crazy for looking him up on the internet and accusing him of growing teeth.* I shook my head. So what if he thought I was crazy? It was far more important to find out what was going on with me. I shushed the small part of me that was also a little excited at the idea of seeing him again.

I decided to go now. I knew the chances of him being by the lake were slim—it was early—but he did say his cabin was near there, and I had seen him point in its general direction. I should probably just stay in bed and rest, but I also didn't want to deal with Rob.

I texted Aunt Claire, telling her I was feeling better and that she didn't have to come home. I grabbed some clothes out of my dresser, opened my door to check for signs of Rob, then made my way downstairs and found him asleep in his recliner. I headed back up to the bathroom and made sure to lock the door in case he woke up.

Once the shower water was hot enough, I stripped and stepped in. It felt so good to rinse away the sweat. I took my time, giving myself a moment to just enjoy the peace. Once I was clean, dry, and dressed, I went back to my room to grab my phone and give myself a once-over in the mirror.

I didn't look sick anymore, in fact I looked great. There was a sparkle in my eyes that hadn't been there before and a bit of a rose-colored glow about my skin. The bags under my eyes, which had seemed permanent before, weren't there now. *You could possibly pass for pretty, Hazel,* I thought cynically, but I still felt off. My skin was too hot, my muscles still ached, and my body's sensory inputs were too sensitive.

Was the lighting always this bright in my room? And what was that earthy-wood smell? Did I just hear the microwave clock downstairs change time?

I was overthinking. I threw on my Converse and gave myself one last look in the mirror. I was just a normal girl, going for a brisk morning walk in the woods. I kept my hair down, which was odd, but I told myself it was because my hair was still wet and wouldn't dry properly if left it in a ponytail and *not* because I thought I looked my best with my hair down and was trying to impress a certain someone.

I gave myself a little nod of approval and headed downstairs. I silently went to the kitchen and grabbed a couple of granola bars for the road. I checked the fridge for any fruit but found nothing. The steak was gone but the fridge still smelled of blood and spices. I sneaked past Rob, still asleep in the recliner, and almost jumped out of my skin when he made a snorting noise as I opened the front door. Once the door was closed and I was free, I made my way toward the school.

I decided to take the same way into the woods that I had yesterday. I found the deer trail quickly and began following it. Once again, I passed by the dog-head boulder. It looked a little more detailed today. Its nose pointed up at the sky, eyes closed, almost sad looking. Once the trail ended, I kept walking straight, just as I had while running and eventually, I reached the lake. By now the sun was up and everything was bright and shiny, dew covered everything.

I walked toward the lake and stopped in front of the shore. I removed my shoes and socks, hiking my pant legs as far up as they would go, and stepped in. The water was freezing, not yet warmed by the sun, but it felt nice on my too-hot skin. Walking into the shallow part, I let my toes dig into the soft, squishy bottom as I looked at my reflection. My face stared back at me, warped by the moving water.

I wasn't sure if I should wait for Caden here or try and find his cabin. He did say he came here every day, but it was early, and I didn't know if he came here at a specific time of day or if "every day" just meant he came here often. I could just walk in the general direction he pointed and hope I found his cabin, but there was also a chance I would be hopelessly lost in a forest that went on for miles.

Luckily, I didn't have to worry for too long. Caden appeared out of the tree line on the other side of the lake. He saw me and waved. I gave an awkward wave back. I'd only met him once, but it felt like I was meeting an old friend. I was excited and nervous. My heart had once again made a home in my throat. I tried to swallow it back down as I waded out of the water. I fixed my pants, picked up my socks and shoes, then started walking his way.

I tried to think about what I would say to him. How would I ask him if he knew what was going on with me without bringing up his family's death? What if I was wrong and he thought I was totally crazy?

When I finally reached him, he had that same curious smile as last time. I was losing an inner battle with the growling thing inside me. It was happy to see him again while I was, at the same time, taken aback once more by how handsome he was. His lip piercings seemed to fit him so well and those unique multicolored eyes were mesmerizing. Eternity was stretching before us once again and just like before, Caden spoke first.

"I didn't expect to see you again so soon. It's awfully early in the morning. Did you miss my presence or was it the lake you missed?" My stomach was tied in knots, the growling thing inside me was chanting primitive possessive things like "mine, mine, mine, mine, mine!" *But he wasn't mine! Shut up!* I must have looked like a crazy person, squinting with one eye closed at the pounding in my head.

"Hazel." I spoke at last.

He cocked his head to the side in that adorable puppy-dog way.

"You asked me my name yesterday. It's Hazel."

His face brightened, like my name was a gift.

"It's really nice to meet you, Hazel."

His smile was infectious. I couldn't help but smile back.

"So, Hazel, would you want to help me with a project? I was just about to finish up today."

"Yeah, sure." I gave a small shrug.

"Great! You might want to put your shoes back on for this. We're going to take a trip into the woods."

I quickly put my socks and shoes back on. I knew that I should be a little weirded out that I was walking into the woods with a guy I'd just met, but I really felt like that ship had sailed when I decided to meet him in the woods again in the first place. We began walking in the direction I'd come in. I felt Caden glancing at me out of the corner of his eye. It made me feel awkward and I didn't do awkward. It made me blunt.

"What?" I asked.

He smiled. "Nothing. You're just really beautiful."

I felt the blush starting to form. I was apparently not the only blunt one. "Thank you," I mumbled.

We were halfway to the school, and I wondered if we were leaving the woods. Then Caden turned toward the clearing with the dog-head boulder.

"I've seen this," I said. "I pass by it on the way to the lake."

He nodded. "I've been working on it for a few months now."

I glanced at him, surprised. Now that the boulder was much closer, I could see the undeniable detail. Detail that could only be handmade.

"It's beautiful. How did you make it?"

He pulled out a bucket and chisel from behind the stone. The bucket was filled with muddy water and a red washcloth hung from its side.

"I use these, plus I have a lot of time on my hands."

"How am I supposed to help?" I asked.

He shrugged.

"In truth, I could really just use the company. You can give me your expert advice and tell me how it looks. I'm working on the other side today." He pointed with his chisel at the side I couldn't see. I walked over to where he stood. There was a rough outline of a man, or maybe a woman, I wasn't sure, kneeling on one knee, looking up with hands cupped to his or her mouth as if calling out to someone or something.

I sat down on the grass, pulling my knees up to my chest.

"Is it a man or a woman?" I asked.

"I'm not sure, actually. I'm thinking of just leaving it as both, like a metaphor for humankind."

I tilted my head and scrunched my eyebrows. "So it's a dog on one side and a…human on the other?"

He laughed a little. "It's not a dog. It's a wolf. He's howling at the moon."

"You like wolves then?" I ask.

Caden gave a small smile, one that didn't quite reach his eyes.

"Yeah, I guess you could say that."

For some reason I felt the question made him sad, so I changed the subject.

"So, I'm assuming you finished school. What do you do besides sculpt random boulders in the woods?"

He began chiseling the boulder.

"I actually help the community at Crescent Peak. Odd jobs here and there. Gardening, cooking, fixing, selling, you name it."

"It used to be a camp at one point, right?" I thought of the photo of my parents going to a camp at Crescent Peak. "Do lots of people live there now?"

He gave a small shrug. "Yeah, there's a decent amount of us."

"Us?" I asked.

He took the wet washcloth and patted the spot he was working on till it was wet.

"Yeah. Everyone's like a tight-knit family up there, I guess. My family used to live there a few years back. Most of the people like to keep to themselves. The town's a good ten miles south. To the north is the mountain and to the east and west is nothing but miles of forest."

"You don't live with them now, though?"

"Not anymore. Not since my family died."

He said it so casually, as if it was just a fact. There was a long, awkward pause as I chose my next words carefully.

"I'm really sorry," I said after a few seconds. "I read about it…in an article."

"Checking up on me?" he asked but didn't turn around.

"No," I said defensively. "Not exactly. I told my best friend about my run the other day and she wanted to see a picture of you. She's a little boy crazy."

He still didn't turn around.

"It's okay if you don't wanna talk about it. I completely understand."

Caden tossed the chisel on the ground, wiped his hands on his pants, and came and sat down beside me. "Is there a reason you came to see me today, Hazel?"

We'd never been that close before and, man, did he smell good. Like campfire and men's deodorant. I tried my best not to look at him. I felt him staring. I really wished I knew why I was so drawn to him, why it felt so right to be near him when everything else that happened in the past few days had felt horribly wrong.

I wasn't sure how to answer now. I'd come here for a reason, but now I was second-guessing myself. What if he didn't understand? What if he thought I was weird? I told myself I didn't care before, but I realized now that that was a lie. I felt awkward again. I knew if I didn't say something right now, Caden would change the subject and I would hate myself later for not getting the answers I needed.

I twisted my body to face him and crossed my legs. I spoke quickly.

"While you were in the hospital, four years ago,

after…what happened to you and your family, a doctor said that she saw your canines were much larger than the rest of your teeth, but when she looked again, they were a normal size."

He twisted in my direction, also sitting cross-legged so we both faced each other. His eyebrows furrowed.

"I guess what I'm asking is…" Then I said a little slower, "Is it true? What the doctor said? Because if so, I've been having the same problem the past few days and I was hoping you might have answers for me."

I waited silently, sure that Caden thought I was crazy, but he wasn't laughing, and he no longer looked confused. He seemed a bit surprised, if anything, but there was also a hint of an amused smile on his face, like he was realizing something that finally made since.

"Can you show me?"

I nodded slowly and leaned in close so he could see my teeth. I hoped I didn't have bad breath. Nothing happened at first. I tried to think of a trigger, something I had been thinking of the last time they extended. My mind drifted to that bloody steak that had been marinating in the fridge at home. A small pain hit my teeth—a lot less severe than the last few times—and felt my tooth with a finger. They had lengthened.

Caden didn't freak out—like I expected—but whispered, almost to himself, "It's really happening then."

"What is?"

He didn't answer. Instead he asked, "Do you know anything about your parents? About your dad?"

I was thrown off by such an odd question and a bit annoyed by the change of subject.

"My parents? I don't know. My father died in a car crash a few months before I was born, and my mother died shortly after giving birth to me. My mother's sister raised me."

He gave me a knowing, sympathetic look.

"What?" I asked impatiently.

He leaned back on his hands and let out a breath. "It's a lot to explain and you may not believe me. You didn't have any symptoms before now?"

"No." I was becoming increasingly irritated. I placed my hands on both of Caden's knees and leaned into them. "Just tell me."

Caden raised his eyebrows as if in surprise at my impulsive behavior, but then he gave me a sexy half smile. One that would have knocked the breath out of me had I not been staring at his one visible canine. It was extended.

I inhaled. "So, you're like me?"

Caden leaned forward, making me angle back. We were much closer than I remembered us being.

"Yes." His voice was soft, almost a whisper.

My heart was hammering inside my rib cage. I was almost sure Caden could hear it.

"Was it coincidence we met at the lake Friday?"

"Maybe."

I leaned back farther. He was making it hard to concentrate being this close.

"Look, I just want answers. Is this some kind of mutation? Disease? Are we vampires?"

That last question made him laugh.

"No, we aren't vampires. It's just a lot to answer for. I don't think it's my place to tell you when I know someone who would like to tell you himself."

"Who?" I said sternly.

"I can't tell you that, yet, either."

I let out a frustrated huff but before I could get

up and storm off, Caden bent forward and looked at me for a long time, our noses practically touching. I held my breath. I was trying my very best to look anywhere but at him. Suddenly I felt my phone go off in my pocket. Normally I would just ignore it, but it was vibrating consistently. Maybe it was Aunt Claire.

"Do you need to get that?"

I took my phone out of my pocket. It was Aunt Claire. I checked the time on my phone. It was eight o'clock. She must have just woken up.

"It's my aunt. I was sick yesterday and had her a little worried. She's probably calling to check on me."

"You were sick? What kind of sick? Fever? Aches and pains?"

I looked up at him, my brows furrowed. "Yeah, why?"

"Do you still feel sick?"

"I mean a little hot and still a bit achy but not as bad as yesterday."

He looked a little worried. He was about to say something else, but my phone started to vibrate again.

"I have to answer this." I clicked the answer button and stood up, brushing the dirt and grass from the back of my pants. "Hello?"

"Hazel! Are you all right? What's going on? Molly's mother just called. She said that some wild animal attacked Molly and a few others down at Colonial Springs? I thought she was home with you this week?"

Fear and shock rolled through my body. "Molly's been hurt? Where is she?"

"She's at the hospital in Colonial. That's where her mother is now. Hazel, please—"

"I gotta go. I'm sorry, Aunt Claire. I'll call you when

I get there." I knew there would be hell to pay later for hanging up on her like that.

I turned to Caden. "I have to go. My best friend's in the hospital."

Caden stood up. "Which hospital? I can drive you."

I shook my head. The distance to his cabin would probably be the same as the distance to my house where Aunt Claire had left me her car in case of emergencies.

"It's okay. My aunt left me her car. I can drive."

"Hazel, you said you were sick."

"I said I was feeling better. I have to go." I started to walk away, but Caden called to me.

"Wait." He came up to me and held out his hand. "Let me see your phone."

I handed it to him quickly. He typed in his number and gave it back to me.

"Let me know how your friend is, okay? And when you have time, call me. I can take you to him and you'll get your answers."

He gave me an "I'm serious" expression. I nodded and took off running toward home. I didn't have time to ponder on who this person with all the answers could be. All I could think about was Molly. I didn't stop till I reached the house. My sides ached and breathing was difficult. Under normal circumstances I would have been fine to run this far, but I still wasn't feeling well and the worry for my friend had me in a panic.

I unlocked the front door. The house was empty and all the lights were off. *Good.* I raced to the kitchen and grabbed the keys to Aunt Claire's Mazda and made for the garage. I didn't remember getting in the car or driving for an hour and half to Colonial. My brain was on autopilot the whole way there. I was lucky a cop hadn't stopped me, or worse, gotten into a wreck.

Once at the hospital, I made a beeline for the front desk, but before I could ask the nurse if I could see Molly, I heard her mother's voice from the waiting room.

"Hazel, honey, over here."

I turned toward her right as her body collided with mine, hugging me tightly.

She was a mess, which was saying something, because Molly's mom was a nurse and usually worked late nights at the hospital on the far side of Crescent Falls. She always had a tired look about her when she came home after her shifts. Her bun was lopsided, strands of blond falling around her face, and I hardly ever saw her without scrubs or pajamas on. Today was no different, except her eyes were red from crying, her makeup smeared, and her face a blotchy mess.

"Where's Molly? Is she okay?"

She gestured for us to sit. "She's doing okay. The nurses are running some tests on her now, making sure there's no internal problems. She has multiple gashes and teeth marks on her legs, stomach, back, arms, and her face…" She choked back a sob. "There's severe cuts and bruises from the fall too. I guess in her attempt to escape the animal, she took a tumble down the side of a cliff. She's received a lot of stitches and they are saying she dislocated her shoulder. It's a miracle she didn't break anything, but I'm worried the scans will show something wrong internally. It's not exactly easy falling off a cliff."

She burst into tears.

"I shouldn't have let her go. A boy died. They said he tried to protect her and it…it lashed out at him and…" She sobbed harder. "It cut his stomach clean open. What kind of animal could do something like that?"

I shook my head in disbelief. I wanted to say something, but she seemed to be talking to herself.

"The rest of the kids were thrown around like rag dolls. One has four broken ribs, and another has a broken leg and a concussion. There have been several news reports of vicious, wild animal attacks within the past week or so. They're saying it could be a new strain of rabies, but the doctors did blood work on her and they didn't find any signs of the virus. The game warden says it's wolves, big wolves. I should have taken it as a sign. I shouldn't have let her go, but I thought…I thought she would be safe at camp. I shouldn't have let her go!" she yelled.

I took her hand and laid her head on my shoulder as she sobbed for a while. I let her know it wasn't her fault. It was hard to watch a respected adult break down, but I had learned from years of watching my aunt's heart get broken how to comfort someone. And sometimes all it took was a shoulder to cry on. Just another body in the room.

When she finally calmed down, I asked, "Where's your husband?"

She looked at me through blurry eyes. "He went to grab us something to eat from the cafeteria." She rested her elbow on the arm of the chair and sniffled, whipping her eyes with the palms of her hands. It smeared her eye makeup even more, but I couldn't imagine that she cared.

A doctor came and told Molly's mom that we could go see her now. It was family only, but she assured the doctor I was Molly's sister. It warmed my heart to see her stick up for me like that.

Molly had a room all to herself. Her mom rushed to the bed, taking Molly's hand in hers, but I held back, leaning on the edge of the doorway. My stomach clenched at the sight of my best friend. She seemed to be asleep, her once beautiful face cut and bruised beyond recognition. A bandage lay across her left cheek and forehead, and her right eye was swollen. Her arms bandaged, with her left arm in a sling.

None of this felt real. I knew from the way her mom described it that she was in bad shape, but it didn't prepare me for the real thing. The stupid part of me just expected to see her lying in a hospital gown, a few cuts and bruises, maybe a sling, but still looking like Molly. The same girl I'd left Saturday morning—whole and peacefully asleep.

I let out a shaky breath. When I composed myself enough, I walked forward and sat in the chair on the opposite side of the bed and took Molly's other hand, the one in the sling. A nurse came into the room. She checked the machines beside Molly's bed and wrote something down on a chart. She turned to Molly's mother.

"She's still heavily sedated, but she should come out of it in a couple of hours. It's good she'll be getting some undisturbed rest," she said gently, then left the room.

I pulled out my phone to message Aunt Claire. I didn't have the heart to talk to her over the phone, so I decided to send her a text.

```
You: I'm at the hospital. Molly's
doing okay. I'm sorry I lied to you
about staying with her. She was
going to a camp for the week, but I
didn't want you to worry.
```

She replied immediately.

Aunt Claire: `I'm glad she's okay. I'm coming home.`

You: `You don't have to, everything is fine.`

Aunt Claire: `You don't get to tell me what to do, Hazel Bethany Lowell. I'm booking a flight now. I'll message you when my plane lands.`

I didn't say anything more. I knew my aunt. She was like me, stubborn.

Molly's dad came back with two trays full of food. I decided to give Molly's parents a moment alone with their daughter and went to get some food of my own. The lunch rush was already over so there wasn't much selection. I bought two turkey sandwiches and ate them begrudgingly.

When I returned, Molly was awake, sitting up in the bed. She gave me a small smile and winced.

"Hey," I said as I headed to the side of her bed and sat down.

"Hey yourself," she croaked.

I hadn't been on the verge of crying this whole time, but now that Molly was awake and alive, I felt myself getting a little choked up. I glanced at Molly's parents. Their faces mirrored how I felt.

I focused on Molly and asked, "How are you feeling? Do you remember what happened?"

Molly's parents stared at their daughter. Molly was quiet for a long time. Remembering what had happened to her, much less talking about it, had to be hard, and for a moment, I regretted asking her.

Her mother must have sensed Molly's distress, too, because she said, "Honey, you don't have to talk about it right now if you don't want to."

Molly shook her head, her throat bobbing as she swallowed.

"A small group of us decided to sneak out of our rooms and go to the springs for a midnight swim. We thought it was harmless...I didn't...no one thought..." She looked up, panic written on her face. "Are the others okay?"

Molly's mom looked over at me, then at her husband. She paused for a long moment and then told Molly about the boy who had died and the injuries the others had sustained. Molly began to cry. I took her right hand in mine to comfort her.

"What was it?" I asked.

Molly shook her head again and sniffled. "I can't say it. You'd think I'm crazy."

"No we won't," I reassured her.

"Honey, you are a great many things, but crazy isn't one of them," her mom added.

She let out a heavy breath, and the tears stopped for the time being.

"It was huge, maybe the size of a small bear, but it was..." She focused on me, then her mother.

"Go on, sweetie. What was it?" her mother urged.

"It looked like a wolf...and its eyes...they looked almost human, intelligent. It came straight for me. I didn't even have time to run."

She stared at the wall with a far-off look. I could tell she was trying to remember the details of what had happened. When she blinked and came to, she whispered, "I don't remember much after that."

She choked up and cried again.

"I really thought I was going to die. Oh God... Tommy." She put her hand over her eyes. Her mom and dad both came to either side of the bed and wrapped their daughter in their arms, resting their heads in her hair and kissing her bandaged forehead. Her mother repeated over and over again, "Shhh, it's okay."

I wanted the animal to pay for what it had done.

I decided to let Molly spend time with her parents while I went to get some much-needed rest in the waiting room. I grabbed a Coke from the machine and settled into one of the comfier-looking chairs. I propped my left elbow up on the arm of the chair and used my hand to support my head, removing my shoes to curl my legs underneath me. The exhaustion of the day was finally catching up to me and before I knew it, I was asleep.

WHEN I WOKE, MY NECK ACHED FROM BEING AWKWARDLY positioned for too long and my left arm and my legs were asleep. I stood up and stretched them out. Picking up my Coke, I downed whatever was left inside.

I felt like hell. My body was still fighting off the strange sickness, on top of being worried for Molly. I wasn't exactly doing my best to recover. I rubbed my face with both hands, trying to clear my head. I checked my phone to see if Aunt Claire had called. Nothing. She might still be on her way here, assuming she was able to book a flight so soon.

I put my shoes on quickly and went to Molly's room. She was awake, nursing a cup of coffee. Her parents were asleep in the nook of the large hospital windowsill.

She smiled at me, the bandage on her cheek crinkling. "Hey, I was wondering if you were getting any decent rest. Guess not, huh?"

I gave a tired laugh and pointed at the cup. "I could probably use some of that. They let you have coffee?"

"It's decaf. Can't have any caffeine. Doctor's orders. They want me to sleep as much as possible, but I'm having a hard time." She looked down at her cup. "I have nightmares."

I nodded in understanding. I was still a little taken back by how horrible Molly looked. "Does it hurt?"

She stared at her coffee.

"Not so much right now. They give me meds for the pain, but I imagine once I start walking around it will be unbearable."

"And your…" I pointed to her face.

She shook her head. "It's okay. Just sore. The doctor said there would be a scar."

I lowered my gaze to my hands. "I'm so sorry, Molly."

"It's not your fault," she whispered.

I raised my head as we sat in silence for a minute. Molly looked at her parents who were still fast asleep.

"I lied before, about not remembering. I remember everything, right up until I blacked out at the bottom of the cliff." She appeared scared now, shaken. She looked me in the eye.

"I even remember right before. I remember us all standing around, talking by the spring, and then, there was this man. He stood in the shadow of the bush and… one second, he was there and then the next… I sound so crazy saying this. It's why I didn't say anything to my parents before. One minute there was a man and the next there was a wolf. I'm still not really sure it was real."

"What? Like the guy was a werewolf or something?" I gave a small laugh, trying to lighten the mood, but

Molly didn't laugh or smile. She just continued to have that scared, far-off look.

"Molly? You okay?"

She shook her head and gave a small laugh.

"Yeah, that sounds completely crazy. A werewolf attacked me. Hey, maybe I'll turn into one too."

I smiled at her joke. "Wouldn't that be cool. My best friend, a werewolf."

We laughed together, resulting in Molly's parents waking up. We apologized, still giggling, but they didn't seem to mind. I think they were just happy to see Molly smile.

Suddenly my phone pinged, letting me know I had a text. I stared at the name in shock. It was from Molly, or Molly's phone anyway. I got up and opened the message.

Hello.

I looked up at Molly. She was talking quietly with her mom and dad. Maybe someone had found Molly's phone and wished to return it.

But why would they text me?

I decided to reply.

Who is this?

Immediate response.

Someone who knew your father. Meet me at Colonial State Park. 2 p.m.

Molly looked over at me and sighed. "I wish I had my phone. It feels so weird without it. I had so many pictures I wanted to save, but now I guess I'll never get the chance."

I laughed a little at the irony of the situation. Molly

smiled. She thought I was laughing at her dependency of her phone.

"I'm gonna run to the bathroom," I said. "Be right back."

"Okay. Hey, on your way back, could you please bring me something from the cafeteria? Breakfast is another hour away, but I'm starving."

I gave her my most convincing smile. "Sure."

I walked to the nearest bathroom and locked the door. I turned on the sink and splashed my face. The cold water was bracing. Looking up into the mirror at my wet face, I opened my mouth and showed my teeth. I pictured my canines extending. They grew at will now. *Great.* I wasn't sure what that meant. I lowered my lips back over my teeth and stared at myself as realization set in.

Someone who said they knew my father just messaged me off my best friend's phone. No one besides my Aunt Claire had ever claimed to know my father. People only told me about my mother and Aunt Claire growing up. My father had been an outsider to the town.

Could this person really tell me more about him?

I shook my head, hair falling in my face.

I was actually considering meeting some stranger *alone* to get answers about my father…and to possibly retrieve Molly's phone, which should say enough about my sanity. He or she could be a serial killer or some sick pervert. This person probably saw that I was the last one Molly texted and decided to screw with me, but that didn't explain why they said they knew my father.

I shouldn't even consider going. I should just text this person back, tell them I'm not interested, and to keep the phone. Molly thought it was a lost cause anyway.

I sighed and sat on the edge of the toilet, putting my face in my hands.

For a long time, I clung to the idea that if I could just learn more about my parents, maybe learn the details of my father's death, then maybe I wouldn't feel so lost, and maybe I could find some kind of closure. Caden had asked me if I knew who my parents were, as if that was the answer to my question. The answer to what was going on with me.

It wasn't just about my teeth anymore. I was starting to feel different. My thoughts were more aggressive. I was taking more risks, doing things I would have never considered a week ago. Like jumping into lakes in the middle of the woods or climbing out of two-story bedroom windows. This wasn't me at all, and I had a feeling this sickness was connected somehow.

The old Hazel wouldn't meet a stranger for answers about her father, but this Hazel would. Caden might not be the only one with answers. This didn't mean I had to be reckless or stupid, though. I should at least tell someone where I was going, but the only person I felt I could tell that wouldn't be able to stop me was Caden.

I pulled out my phone and sent a quick text.

```
Hey, it's Hazel. My friend is okay.
I'm going to Colonial State Park to
meet someone who has her phone. I
just wanted someone to know just in
case.
```

For some reason I didn't feel like I should tell him the real reason I was going. I worried he would think I was crazy and end up convincing me not to go. I stuck my phone in my back pocket before he could send a reply. I wasn't sure I wanted to see it.

When I returned to Molly's room twenty minutes later, my arms loaded with snacks and drinks, her parents were talking with the doctor as a nurse wheeled Molly's wheelchair back from the bathroom. Molly sucked in her breath as the nurse helped her out of the wheelchair, cradling her as she set her down on the bed. I walked over to hear what the doctor had to say.

"I think she can go home today if the scans come back clear for any internal damage. We should be getting the results in about an hour. She'll be wheelchair bound for about a week, and we'll contact your family doctor and have them set up an appointment with a physical therapist, but for now, it's best to let the stitches do its job. Make sure she gets plenty of rest and time to heal."

Molly's mom was holding on to her dad, nodding.

The doctor turned to Molly and placed a gentle hand on her shoulder. "You're going to be fine."

He winked at her and nodded my way as he walked out. Molly's face was pink. I went and hugged her gently. When I let go, she gestured toward the door.

"I mean he's like forty, but he's really cute, and I didn't see a ring on his finger."

"Molly!" her mom shouted, then smiled. I laughed.

I stayed with her through breakfast and when her results verified that she could go home, I hugged my best friend and told her to text me from her mom's phone later.

"Hey," she said as I headed to the door. Both her parents went to get coffee. "Sorry about Mom calling Aunt Claire."

I gave her a halfhearted smile. "No, it's okay. I

shouldn't have lied to her anyway." I fluttered my fingers at her. "See ya. Text me later."

She gave a small wave bye.

As I walked into the hospital elevator, I tried my best not to think about how stupid I was being. I should stay with Molly and make sure she was okay till my aunt got home, but I knew I'd be in major trouble when she did, and I'd likely not get an opportunity like this again.

Getting Molly's phone would mean the world to her and if this stranger could tell me more about my father in the process, then that was just a bonus.

Yeah...definitely not being stupid.

I rolled my eyes at my own sarcasm.

FIVE

I proceeded to my car in the parking garage. My body started to feel bad again, the aches getting worse. I felt hotter and now there was this piercing ache right behind my eyes. I took some Tylenol Aunt Claire kept in the car, then turned on the radio to distract myself. A song had just ended, and the announcer came back on air.

"A group of teens at a camp in Colonial Springs were attacked last night by what witnesses claim to be a giant wolf. Several kids were hospitalized, one having died on the scene. We have Sara Kenndle here with us today, one of the teens injured during this brutal attack, for details."

A small female voice comes through the speakers.

"It was awful. That poor girl, Molly, right? It went straight for her. It came up from behind us. We heard a growl and turned around to see what it was, shining our lights into the brush, but it just leaped right in the midst of us, throwing us around with its paws and its mouth like we were rag dolls. It was huge! The size of a bear! But I knew it was a wolf. I saw its face and long snout. It was jet black with golden-yellow eyes. It started on Molly and Tommy…he…"

She started sniffling, her throat thick with emotion.

"He stepped in front of the wolf to protect her and it…it swiped at him with its huge paw right across Tommy's stomach. I held him the whole time."

She was full-on crying now. I could tell because, when she spoke again, her voice sounded choked.

"I watched Molly roll herself off the cliff's edge. I screamed and the wolf, it turned toward me. I thought I was going to be next, but then it just ran back the way it came. It was the most terrifying thing I've ever been through. It was, I know I'm going to sound crazy for saying this, but it wasn't normal. It was like it had a purpose, and it was smart. You could see it in its eyes. I just hope Molly is okay…and Tommy… He didn't deserve to die like that." She sobbed again.

The announcer came back on the air soon after.

"Thank you so much, Sara, for sharing your story with us. I know it must have been hard for you to talk about it so soon after it happened. Reports say there were no signs of the wolf or a pack in or around Colonial Springs, and with this being the fourth animal attack this year—the first fatal attack in nearly four years—Crescent Falls and neighboring towns are urged to not go hiking or camping this spring break. We'll keep you updated here on WXCV."

A new song started to play, but I wasn't in the mood to listen anymore. I turned off the radio, driving in silence toward Colonial State Park. I twisted the air on full blast, my body still felt too hot, like I'd been in the sun all day and now I had a sunburn. My head was pounding. I clenched my hands hard on the steering wheel and drove faster. I was almost to Colonial Park.

I paid the fee to enter, the guard warning me that the springs were closed until further notice and of the revised park hours. I knew I would probably have to sneak my way into the springs. There were only a few scattered cars in the parking lot. I imagined people had probably taken the advice I'd heard over the radio and were staying away from the parks and camping grounds.

I followed the trail leading to the springs. As I suspected, two park rangers were standing near the entrance, radios in hand, warding off anyone who wanted to enter. Caution tape lined both fences.

I inhaled a calming breath.

I walked up to the park rangers, giving a polite smile and wave as I went. They only stared at me. I must have been the first person to walk down this way today. I decided to feign ignorance to avoid suspicion.

"Umm, what happened to the spring? Is it under construction or something?"

Both rangers stared at me as if I were the stupidest girl they had ever come across. Clearly, I didn't know that springs were natural occurrences.

"No, ma'am," the one on the left answered. The other snickered.

"There was an animal attack here and its under investigation."

I closed my hand over my mouth, pretending to be shocked.

"Oh wow. I've got to tell my friend about this. She's supposed to meet me here, by the butterfly garden."

I had been here countless times and knew the butterfly garden was in my intended direction, but I also wanted them to think I had no interest in going to the springs.

So, I asked, "Do you know where that is? Sorry, it's

my first time here. I guess I picked a horrible day to come."

I faked a worried look.

"Sure thing. It's just down this way, to your left," said the guard who'd snickered.

"Oh, thank you so much."

I gave him the biggest smile I could muster.

He smiled back and said, "You're most welcome, ma'am. You be careful now and don't forget the park closes at five today."

"I won't, thanks again!" I called as I started walking toward the left. I followed the trail for about ten minutes. When I was far enough away from the rangers, I side-stepped off the trail and started walking toward my right. I continued for a few minutes longer until I hit the chain-link fence, which separated the rest of the park from the springs. I climbed up and over it, stumbling on the way down. My body was hurting worse than ever and sweat now fell freely off my heated skin. I made a silent wish not to pass out again. I doubted anyone would find me out here if I did.

It took me a good twenty minutes to find the trail to the springs and another ten before I reached it, going uphill the whole way. There was now a hollow ache inside my stomach, possibly hunger pangs, but I couldn't be sure. I finally had a direct view of the spring. This was the clearing where Molly was attacked.

The waterfall was a smooth trickle down the side of the cliff, free-flowing into the small spring. It had been known to be a roaring mass during rainy season. The spring itself was on top of another cliff. I walked toward the edge. Molly must have rolled off here. There was blood on the grass nearby. Was it Molly's or Tommy's?

I looked down. The ledge was quite steep. It was

hard to believe she'd survived the roll down. There were plenty of trees she had to have hit along the way. My throat closed and my breath quickened. I hated imagining how much pain she must have endured.

"Hello," a deep voice called behind me.

I jumped in surprise, turning around quickly. A handsome, middle-aged man in a suit stood in front of me. He had short jet-black hair and a closely trimmed mustache with a goatee to match. He stood calmly, his hands behind his back, giving off an air of authority.

Obey, a small part of me whispered.

A wave of nausea rushed through me. It felt like an invasion in my mind. I was repulsed by this thought. It was not my own. I shook my head, trying to compose myself.

"Something the matter?" he asked, but he was still smiling, unconcerned.

I sensed a sinister nature about him. I suddenly regretted coming here.

I tried desperately to take control of the situation.

"Are you the one with my friend's phone?" I asked.

He brought his hand around, Molly's phone between his fingers.

A pulse ran through me, like a heartbeat. I gasped, clutching my chest. I was growing nervous with each passing minute. My body was hitting another breaking point. Standing had become difficult. My breathing was labored as I spoke quickly. I didn't want to show any signs of weakness.

"You said you knew my father?"

He placed the phone in the front pocket of his jacket and put his hands behind his back again.

"I knew both of your parents, but your father and I, we were close. I know what happened to him and I know what's happening to you right now." He paced as he pointed toward me.

"It's hard to deal with the change, isn't it? It feels like a sickness, but it's just your body's way of killing off the weak parts. Your skin feels like fire, your muscles ache. Your teeth grow at will. You can see better, hear better, smell better."

"I don't…I don't know what you mean."

But of course I did.

"Look, I just want my friend's phone back. You can keep your answers."

I sounded much braver than I felt.

He stopped pacing and turned toward me. Was that anger I saw on his face? He wiggled his finger at me in a come-hither motion.

"Come here," he said aloud, and I suddenly had no control over my body. My back straightened and I walked toward him.

I tried to fight the urge. A horrible growl ripped through my lungs, my teeth bared, but still, I obeyed. Fighting it was like trying not to breathe. I could hold my breath but eventually my body would force me to inhale air. His word was law, and it would have been against my nature to disobey.

I was now face-to-face with him. He smelled of expensive cologne and copper, like blood. I was still growling. He was still smiling. He gripped my cheeks between his thumb and forefinger. I had no choice but to look him in the eye as my lips puckered between his fingers.

"You poor girl. Your parents left you with no answers. You had to go your whole life believing you were just a worthless human. I will admit, I do take some pleasure from this. Seeing you so confused. Your father wouldn't have wanted this for you."

His smile was menacing, vicious. There was hate in his eyes.

"You look so much like him. Those eyes, especially. Is that why they named you Hazel?"

Tears began to prick my eyes, but I did not want this horrible man to see me cry. How could someone I didn't even know have such hatred directed toward me? He spun me around. My back was now to his chest as he gripped my shoulders. He leaned into my ear.

"I can only imagine the shock you will receive soon, but I can make the process easier for you."

There was a rumble of growls, and a pack of wolves appeared from the brush. They were huge, much larger than the average wolf. I could now see what Sara had meant. They stood at least five and a half feet tall and were as broad as bears. And their eyes, they had the kind of intelligence no animal possessed.

I began to sob. This couldn't be real. None of this was real.

They circled us, their teeth bared and snapping, hackles raised. He pushed me in the middle of them. I cried out as I landed on all fours. Dirt caked my hands and knees. I breathed in dust and coughed. He came up to me, taking my hair in his hand, yanking my head so I was looking up at him. I let out a cry, baring my teeth at him.

"Listen to your body, Hazel. Don't let them tear you apart. Fight."

He let go of my hair and backed away from me. I watched in horror as the man before me changed into a wolf. He was the biggest of the pack with fur as black as night. I tried to stand, but I couldn't. The wolves were closing in on me, their teeth snapping. A few lunged, ripping at my clothes with their teeth, toying with me.

I sobbed and screamed in fear, swiping at them with my hands like it would make a difference. My body began to ache so badly I could hardly move. My blood boiled inside my skin. I cried out, looking down at my hands digging in the dirt. My nails were now claws. I let out a frustrated sob. I had never been in so much pain in my life. It was like a war was waging within my body.

The bodies of the wolves hit me, but I felt nothing but the pain within.

A flash of white hit my eyelids and lightning pain shot through my head. My scream turned into a long, beautifully rich howl. I sensed the wolves back away. When I opened my eyes, everything was black and white, but the world was now far more beautiful than I could have imagined. My senses picked up every detail and I was aware of everything around me. It was like half my senses had been asleep my whole life and were now fully awake.

Shaking my head, I looked down. Paws now held me upright and I was no longer in pain. In fact, I'd never felt this good in my life. I almost forgot I was in danger. The wolves still circled me, their teeth snapping. I knew I should be scared, confused at best, but I wasn't. This felt right, natural. All my doubts and weaknesses had burned away until all that remained of me was strength and anger.

The black wolf stood tall. Growls from the others quieted. I now understood why he had such a presence I found hard to resist. I remember watching a documentary about wolves with my aunt one night. They had a hierarchy, an alpha. A wolf's nature is to be accepted, to be a part of the pack, and to obey their alpha.

But he was not my alpha, and he never would be. I realized that he was the one who'd attacked Molly. He was the one who hurt my best friend, the one who'd killed Tommy. I felt nothing but rage. I wanted him dead.

He walked toward me, hackles raised, but he didn't growl. I felt his voice, faint but recognizable, inside my head.

"Obey me, Hazel. Join me and I will teach you everything I know. I will give you the answers you've been searching for so long."

I let out a growl. He showed his teeth.

"Obey," he said again.

I pinned my ears back. It was taking everything I had not to roll over and submit. I growled again, showing my defiance. The wolves around him snapped and growled, angry. I stood tall and spoke with my own mind.

"I will not."

I watched the rage roll through his body.

"Then you will die!"

He lunged toward me, but I met him halfway, our bodies colliding. The others joined in, and I felt myself being crushed by them. Teeth and claws scraped and pierced my thick fur, but I continued to fight, anger alone kept me going. Pain was everywhere, but I would not give them the pleasure of seeing me submit. I would die first.

Suddenly, wolves were pushed off me. Another had joined the mix. He was broad-chested with a dusty, dark coat. He easily threw off several of the wolves at once.

I lay there shocked.

It couldn't be.

If I were in human form, I never would have recognized him, but as a wolf, his smell was familiar.

It was David.

He looked me in the eye.

The other wolves pounced on him.

"*Go!*" he yelled and lashed out at the others.

I hesitated, wanting to help him. He growled and jumped in front of me, separating me from the wolves. I scrambled to my feet and ran, hoping David would follow. I didn't know what possessed me to jump from the cliff instead of running into the brush, but I knew it was my best option. My new body landed with the grace I never had as a human. I slid down the side, avoiding all the trees, and rolled to a stop at the bottom. I looked up. The wolves stood at the ledge and glared down at me. I worried about David. *Had they killed him?* I didn't have time to contemplate it further because three of the wolves had already made their descent toward me.

I ran as fast as my four legs could take me. I was out of their sight in minutes, but I knew they would track my scent. I finally reached the fence that cut off the spring from the rest of the park.

Panic took over. I realized I couldn't jump the fence as a wolf, and I didn't know how to change back into a human—or if I'd ever be able to again. I would have to find another way around or risk the park rangers seeing me and calling animal control.

I decided to go right, the opposite direction from the entrance where the rangers were standing guard. My nose guided me away from any humans who might see me across the fence. I caught the scent of the others. They were gaining on me.

The rushing water thundered in the background.

I noticed a break in the fence and for a split second I was relieved. I could slip past to the other side and make my way back to the parking lot without being spotted.

But the feeling was short-lived as I realized why there was a break.

Just past was a wide river that fell into a massive waterfall. It cascaded at least two hundred feet down. I knew this river. I had always found it ironic that a river with a waterfall this massive would have a name like Trickledown.

Three wolves finally caught up with me. They growled as they circled, pushing me closer to the river. I turned to them and growled back, my hackles raised, chest high.

"Stop," I commanded. *"Don't come any closer."*

But they continued. I was not their alpha and I had no control over them. I smelled the pleasure of the hunt roll off their bodies and felt their anticipation for the kill, but I would not give them that satisfaction. The alpha and the rest of his pack finally showed. They parted for him as he walked toward me, his calm demeanor so unwolflike.

He let out a low growl.

"You will die here, Hazel. Is that what you want? To end up like your father?"

I looked at the river and then back to the wolves.

I'd made my decision. Turning my back on the alpha, I leaped into the river.

Icy water seeped through my undercoat. I broke through to the surface, snorting water out my nose as I started to dog-paddle, hoping maybe I could reach the other side of the river before I hit the waterfall. I listened to the howls of the wolves as they mourned the loss of a kill.

My efforts were useless. The current was too strong and the waterfall too close. I braced myself for the fall as best I could. I let out a yelp, my gut giving a jolt as I tumbled over the side. For a few seconds, I was in a free fall and when I hit the bottom, I was unprepared.

Water filled my lungs and my field of vision. My throat and nose burned, begging for air. I tried to paddle my way to the surface, but the waterfall's current continued to push me down toward the bottom of the river. I saw the sun glistening off the surface of the water. Growing tired and weak, I was pushed downward. My eyelids grew heavy and I started to black out. On my last attempt at opening them, I saw someone dive into the river. A hand touched my paw, then everything went dark.

SIX

I was tired, falling in and out of sleep, but I was warm, comfortable. I could smell campfire and freshly cut wood, and I sensed Caden close by. This was a much nicer dream, nothing like the one before with the wolves and the waterfall.

After a while, I started to come to and fully opened my eyes. I was lying by a fireplace, wrapped in several blankets. Everything was still in black and white. When I went to stretch, I noticed I still had paws. *It wasn't a dream then.* Alarmed, I stood up a little too quickly and had to lie back down. My head was spinning. I surveyed my surroundings.

I seemed to be in a log cabin, only bigger. Maybe a lodge? Lying in the middle of what I assumed to be the living room. It was so big that the two dark leather couches, matching recliner, and end tables appeared out of place, like they should be closer together. The coffee table had been pushed to the side. Probably moved to make room for me by the fire. Past the couches was a large dining room table, which could easily seat ten people.

Behind the open dining room was a doorway where I spotted a fridge and figured that was the kitchen. On the left of the kitchen door was a beautiful spiral staircase, which led up to an open balcony on the second floor. I looked up at all the doors. There were so many upstairs. I wondered what was behind them all.

Beautiful paintings of tribal Indians and wolves, so many wolves, covered the walls. The paintings seemed to show a coexistence between the two: human and wolf. Even without color, they were mesmerizing. Native American-style rugs lined the rails of the second-story balcony. I wished I could see the extravagant rainbow of colors I knew to be there. My body gave me my request, and my eyes began showing pigments of color. It was even more beautiful than I realized.

The paintings and rugs gave the cabin a vibrant array of hues that clashed well with the dark brown of the cabin's wood and furniture. I inhaled deeply. Every-thing smelled like a combination of wood, paint, camp-fire, and men's deodorant. It smelled like Caden.

A door opened. I stood up and let out a low growl. Caden entered the hallway by the stairs. As soon as he noticed me, a surprised expression crossed his face.

"Hey, you're awake. How are you feeling?"

He came down the stairs slowly, perhaps sensing my caution. I relaxed and sat down on the blankets. He approached gingerly and sat on the rug in front of me.

"I'm so sorry you had to find out this way, Hazel. I had no idea he would…attack like that." He paused. "I should have just told you. It would have been better than this. When you texted me, I tried to get to you before he did, but I was ambushed."

I became very aware of the smell of blood. Caden's

arm had a large bandage on it. He also had a small bruise on his cheek and a gash on his upper lip. I sniffed toward his bandaged arm.

"I'll be fine," he said earnestly.

We were silent for a while, on my end mainly because I couldn't speak.

Finally, Caden asked, "Do you want to see what you look like? I can't imagine you've gotten a good look yet."

I stood to answer yes. I was somehow a lot calmer than I should have been. Maybe it was the exhaustion. He got up and waved toward the stairs. We climbed up to the second floor and headed down the hallway hidden by a wall on the right of the stairs. I counted at least five doors. He opened the last door to a bedroom.

Like the rest of the lodge, everything was in warm colors. There was a queen-size bed against the far wall. It had a beautiful burgundy head- and footboard. A matching desk and chair sat in the corner next to the window. Caden pulled out a round, full-length mirror from the closet behind him.

I hesitated. I knew what I was, or at least I had a general idea, but truly seeing it was a different story. I was afraid I wouldn't recognize my own reflection.

I inched toward the mirror, took a deep breath, then looked up.

A wolf stared back at me. A timber wolf with hazel-colored eyes, my eyes. My fur had several colors. My muzzle was white underneath and the apex of my nose was a caramel brown. The top half of my coat was a multicolored coalition of black at the tips and a light brown as it reached my undercoat. My lower half was a combination of white and caramel brown, the same brown that matched my nose.

I swished my bushy tail. Its top half was the colors of

my upper body, the underside the colors of my belly. I never knew a wolf could have so many colors. My fur was thicker in the chest, tail, and upper body.

The wolf before me was beautiful, but more than that, I recognized myself in her. This body felt like my body, the face felt like my face. It was still me staring back through the mirror.

Caden sat on the bed behind me.

"The eyes are what give us away. It's eerie to see human eyes peering back through a wolf's body."

I turned to look at him. He seemed tired. I knew I was. I jumped up on the bed and lay next to him, he moved so we were eye level. He laughed as he stared at me. I let out a long whistling breath through my nose. He reached out and stroked my fur. It felt nice. I closed my eyes and let him pet me for a moment. I had so many questions, but they could wait, I supposed.

A stream of light hit my face. It took me several minutes to remember where I was. I opened my eyes and gazed around the bedroom groggily. Caden was gone.

My senses felt dull, like a veil had been pulled over them. I held up my hands and found that I was human again and in the bed. I peeked under the sheets to find I was completely naked. Sucking in a breath, I bolted upright, tucking the sheet around me so nothing was showing. I had never slept naked before, especially not while Rob had been in the house.

Feeling exposed, I panicked and called out for Caden. Quick footsteps sounded from down the hall, and I watched him burst through the door, a worried look on his face.

It almost made me want to laugh, but I kept my

expression controlled, and asked, "Where are my clothes?"

He smiled. "*Your* clothes, I imagine, were ripped to shreds when you shifted."

He pointed to the desk chair. It had a pair of blue basketball shorts and a green T-shirt.

"I left you some spare clothes. They're mine. I hope they'll do for now. They might be a little big."

My face heated. I hadn't realized Caden had left me any clothes. I should have paid more attention.

"Did you…?" I paused, my cheeks getting hotter still. "Did you put me to bed?"

He placed his hands behind his head, looking sheepish.

"Yeah, I fell asleep beside you. When I woke up, you'd shifted back, so I put you under the covers and went to find you some clothes."

He shrugged, as if trying to play it off as no big deal.

I was horrified. Not only had another guy seen me naked while I was unconscious, but it was Caden!

"Could you please leave so I can get dressed," I said icily.

He held both his hands up in surrender as he stepped out and closed the door. I stood and wrapped the sheet completely around me, hurrying to lock the door. I tried to think of what to do next. In truth, I desperately wanted a shower. I spotted a door on the left and opened it, hoping it was a bathroom. To my relief it was.

When I entered, I noticed two doors. One led to my room and the other, I realized upon opening, led to another bedroom. I locked them both. There was a walk-in shower, toilet, and sink. I didn't see much to wash with except a bar of soap sitting on the sink. It looked like it had been there for a while, but it would have to do. There was a towel hanging by the shower.

I turned the water on and waited for it to heat up. I gave myself a moment to think about everything that had happened to me in the past few days. My teeth hurting during seventh period on Friday felt like a million years ago. Would anyone else be able to cope with the things I'd been through? How was I coping? In truth, I wasn't even sure how I was feeling. Mostly just dazed and still a little overwhelmed, but strangely at peace. Staring at my hazel eyes in the mirror, I felt more in tune with myself than I ever had. I hadn't realized how uncomfortable I'd been in my own skin until I wasn't anymore. I felt whole.

After watching the glass fog, I hopped in the shower. I washed my body and hair quickly with the bar of soap. As I washed, I remembered the fight with the wolves. How their claws and teeth had dug into my fur and skin. I examined my body but found no scratches or bite marks.

Strange.

I turned off the shower, dried off, then returned to the bedroom to get dressed. Caden's clothes were a little too big, but they would have to do for now. I unwrapped the towel around my head. I couldn't find a brush or comb, so I just used my fingers as I headed down the hall. I realized I had no idea where Caden was. I called out his name.

"I'm in here!" he answered from down the hall.

I went to the closest door to the stairs and knocked.

"You can come in," he said.

I opened the door and was immediately hit with the strong scent of paint. The room was littered with art supplies, from tubes of different colored paints to a range of various paintbrushes, pencils, markers, and even charcoal. The ground was covered with a clear plastic to protect the hardwood floor.

There were canvases everywhere: pushed up against the walls, sitting on easels, hung on the wall. All the paintings were of nature and animals. Trees, forests, mountains, streams, rivers, deer, rabbits, leaves, rocks, mountains, and wolves, so many wolves.

Caden sat on a tall wooden stool, his back to the only window in the room. He was working on another canvas. His shirt and ripped jeans were covered in splotches of paint. *Was he this messy when he checked on me earlier?* I couldn't remember.

I was in awe of the room. I had always been jealous of people who could draw or paint. Like Molly. She was amazing with just a pencil and paper. The detail in anything she drew was breathtaking, just like Caden's artwork.

"I didn't know you could paint," I said. "Did you do all of these yourself?"

He looked up from what he was doing.

"No, not all of them. The ones hanging up on the walls are my dad's."

I walked over and sat on the stool nearest him.

"How did the paintings make it…through the fire?"

He kept his focus on his work.

"They weren't in the house when it burned down," he said simply. "They were on display in the main hall at Crescent Peak. I decided to take them back when I rebuilt this place."

I looked at him in shock.

"You had this entire place rebuilt?"

He nodded soberly.

"So, you're a painter, sculptor, *and* a carpenter? Is there anything you can't do?"

He laughed. "I actually had a little help building this place. Sculpting isn't a permanent thing. The inspiration for the wolf and human came from the boulder's natural beauty. I just decided to help it along. I doubt I'll ever do it again, though I'll admit, it was a nice challenge."

"What about painting?"

"I've been painting a long time. Since I was about six or seven. My dad taught me."

I smiled. I was once again taken back by how handsome Caden was. I found it hard to look at him for too long. The tension in the room grew with our silence. He set his paintbrush down and looked me in the face. His eyes trailed me, making me feel a little self-conscience. It made me a little embarrassed. No one had ever looked at me so closely before. I raised a hand to my head. My hair was still wet and I knew how horrible it must look— I hadn't even combed it. Not to mention my outfit wasn't exactly flattering. I shifted my gaze and pretended to look closely at a painting nearest to me on the wall.

"I'll make a deal with you," he said finally. "If you let me paint you, I'll let you ask whatever questions you want, and in return, I promise to answer them, as best as I can."

I was a bit thrown off by his request. Why on earth would he want to paint a girl with wet hair in a large T-shirt and basketball shorts?

"Umm…" I glanced down at my outfit. "I'm not exactly painting worthy."

He smiled and wrinkled his eyebrows as if confused.

"Are you kidding? You're perfect."

I looked at him wide-eyed. He cleared his throat and sat up straight.

"Anyway, those are my terms. Do we have a deal?"

All I could do was nod. If that was what it took to get answers, then who was I to judge his taste in inspiration?

He grabbed a blank canvas from the closet and asked me to sit facing the window. I moved my stool over as Caden sat to the right of me.

"Okay, face me a little."

I turned toward him. He smiled. It was infectious. I couldn't help but smile back.

"Perfect," he said on a breath as he began to work.

I wasn't sure where to begin, so I started with what I knew. "I can change into a wolf."

Saying that out loud sounded ridiculous.

"Yes, but that's not a question for me," he answered.

"No," I said. "But it's just hard to wrap my head around."

He gave a small nod.

"Can you do it?"

"Yes."

"And your family?"

"Yes."

"What exactly are we?"

"We just call ourselves shifters."

"How did we get this way? Are there a lot of them—I mean—us?" The questions were coming rapid fire.

"We don't really know how we got this way. There's lots of stories of people who could shift into animals, lots of history behind it. My father thought that a long time ago all humans could do it, but when we started creating things to make life easier, we turned our backs on nature and chose to rely on the things we built instead, so most of us lost our abilities. It makes sense. Think of all the technology we rely on now."

I had never thought about it that way. It was true,

though. Nature wasn't a place we lived in anymore, it was a place we visited.

"Can shifters only change into wolves?"

He shrugged. "Supposedly, our ancestors could change into any mammal, big or small. I just know there aren't many of us today. Wolf shifters still rank as the largest group of shifters, but there are other kinds."

"Have you ever met one?"

He looked down a moment longer, cleared his throat, and continued working. "No, but I know someone who met a bear shifter once, and there were rumors of a few fox shifters seen passing through here. We don't usually mingle, though."

I sat silently and processed everything he'd said so far.

"How could humans just forget? Why doesn't anyone know about shifters now? Hasn't a hunter ever mistaken a shifter for an average animal?"

"Well"—he shrugged, not taking his eyes from the canvas—"when a shifter dies, whatever form they are in is the form they stay. I imagine there might be a few shifters hanging on someone's wall somewhere."

I shuttered. "That's so horrible."

He shrugged again, unfazed. "That's our way of life. It's why we like to stick together, a few packs living in the same area, usually away from people. Most of us live in Canada. There's supposedly a haven for shifters there. The cabins up at Crescent Peak is also a shifter community."

My head jerked back. "The people who live in those cabins are *shifters*? All of them?"

He nodded. "I'll take you there soon," Caden said, mumbling past the paintbrush between his teeth as he used another to paint with.

"Okay." I smiled. I was looking forward to it.

My stomach suddenly rumbled.

He gave a crooked smile "Let's take a break and go get some food."

Caden set his paintbrushes down, then pointed at the canvas. "No peeking."

I let out a snort.

We walked downstairs to a large-size kitchen. There was a huge island in the middle with several stools pushed underneath. The countertops and island were made of a beautiful pearl-blue marble. The first things I'd noticed *not* made of wood in the lodge.

Caden opened the fridge and pulled out a very large slab of steak. My mouth watered instantly and my canines extended. He turned and smiled. "How would you like it?"

I hesitated before answering. I had always taken my steaks medium or medium well, but for some reason rare sounded very appealing.

"Umm…maybe medium rare?" Compromise. I couldn't quite let go of all my human habits just yet.

Caden seemed to understand my conflict. "My sister was the same way. She hated when my mom and dad would sit there and eat their steaks nearly raw. It really grossed her out. But after her first shift, her taste buds changed."

"What about you?"

"Me?" He paused for a moment. "I never minded."

I walked over to him. "Can I help?"

He smirked. "Sure."

I found a pan and then some eggs in the fridge.

"Steak and eggs. Breakfast of champions," he said.

I looked out the tiny kitchen window. "Is it even morning still?"

"It's about twelve thirty, close enough." He stuck his tongue out at me.

We both laughed.

"Was this your family's lodge?" I asked.

He nodded.

"It's a bit big for just your parents, your sister, and you. Was the original structure this big?"

He gave a small smile. "The original was slightly bigger. It's a few rooms short now. My family intended to move our pack out here. My father had recently been made their alpha. The building was already here and could have been a lodge set away from the rest of the grounds back when it was still a camp. Maybe to give people privacy. He wanted our pack to have their own place but still be close to the rest of the community. My family moved in early to get it fixed up for the rest of them, but before they could move in, it burned down."

Sorrow crossed his face again. It was hard for him to talk about it. I shouldn't have asked.

"Where's the pack now?"

"Most went to Canada, but a few stayed and joined another pack at Crescent Peak."

I nodded. "So do shifters have a similar hierarchy as wolves?"

Caden nodded. "Somewhat, yes. We have packs, alphas, and betas. The alpha is the leader, so he or she must do whatever is best for their pack. If you're part of a pack, you can't go against any command the alpha makes. But a good alpha knows never to abuse that power. They should only use it to keep the pack safe and protected."

I thought about the man in the clearing. How hard it had been to go against his order. It felt like going against my instinct.

"That guy, at the springs, he was an alpha, wasn't he? He commanded me to go to him and it had felt like I didn't have a choice."

Caden's face darkened. He gathered up the steak and eggs, then walked to the kitchen island. He said nothing for a while as he grabbed a bottle of orange juice from the fridge and poured a couple glasses. I could tell he was trying to rein in his anger.

I didn't blame him. I was still angry too.

Caden sat down and after a moment he spoke. "It's hard not to listen to an alpha when you don't belong to a pack. When you're alone, you are vulnerable. It's how alphas keep packs safe from outsiders, but it can also be used to persuade them to join a pack. Sometimes an alpha can force a person to join against their will, if the alpha is strong enough. It's wrong, though, and against the law in the Crescent Peak community. An alpha can be stripped of his pack if found out. He shouldn't have done that to you."

We were silent as we began eating. I hadn't realized how hungry I was until the first piece of steak hit my tongue. I barely chewed my entire meal. It felt like I hadn't eaten in days. Caden picked at his plate, seemingly not as interested in his food as I was.

Between mouthfuls of steak and eggs I asked, "Who was he? The alpha at the springs. Do you know him?"

He still didn't look up from his food.

"His name is Ross. He is, well, he's the worst kind of alpha. Ruthless and corrupt. He breaks a lot of our laws. He's not shunned from the community, though, because he's the strongest."

We were silent, lost in our own thoughts.

"He said he knew my father," I finally said. I looked

down at my half-eaten plate. "He was a shifter, too, wasn't he?"

Caden said nothing, as if contemplating how to answer.

He got up from his stool and made his way around the island to me. He crouched down so he could look me in the eye. He was quiet for a moment, just staring at me. Finally, he spoke.

"Can I show you something?"

I nodded slowly as he took my hand and led me out of the kitchen and back up the stairs. We walked in the opposite direction of the guest bedroom I stayed in and headed for the last door at the end of the hall. Caden opened the door to a room full of boxes, furniture, and filing cabinets.

As I remained in the hall, Caden jumped and hopped over items and began rummaging. After a few minutes, he returned and handed me a well-worn, wallet-size picture of a group of people.

I recognized my father immediately. He was tall and broad, his face handsome and kind. He stood next to a man leaning close to a pregnant woman. They held the hand of a toddler with two-colored eyes. This must have been Caden's parents. The rest of them I didn't recognize. There were about ten of them, all ranging in different ages. They seemed like one big happy family.

"I didn't really know your father, but my parents did. He was their alpha for a time. A natural-born leader, but when word got out that he'd bonded with a human, well, it was unheard of. It didn't sit well with a lot of shifters."

"Why? What does bonding mean?"

"For shifters, bonding is like finding your soulmate. It mostly happens between shifters. You become connected in a way no normal couple experiences. You share memories, feelings, sometimes thoughts. It's different with every bond, but as far as I know, the stronger the bond, the stronger the connection."

"That is…strange. How does it even work? Is it as soon as you meet?"

Caden shook his head. "I think it's gradual, a small connection that builds the longer you are with that person. Just like falling in love, but the bond isn't sealed until…" He paused and smiled sheepishly.

My eyes widened as the realization dawned on me. "*Sex?*"

He laughed. "Yeah."

"Okay, okay. I get it." My face had to be five shades of red by then.

Caden laughed.

"Were your parents bonded?" I asked.

"No, no they weren't, but they loved each other very much. A bond is a rare thing. That's why when your father bonded with a human, it was so unheard of. It made shifters uneasy seeing a human and shifter not only together, but also bonded. So your dad left his pack and the shifter community behind and started a new life with your mom."

I looked at the picture closely again and realized I did recognize someone. I almost didn't because of the lack of facial hair. He stood behind my father. "Is that Ross?"

Caden never looked at the picture. He seemed to know exactly who I meant.

"Yes. He was your father's beta. When your father left the pack, he didn't make Ross alpha. He named my father instead, and that pissed Ross off, so he left and started his own pack. I don't think he's ever been able to let what your father did go. He loved him, looked up to him, and he felt betrayed. I think that's why he wants you."

We sat against the wall in the hallway.

"I'm sorry I wasn't up-front with you. There's someone else who wanted to do this himself. I think it would be best if he answers the rest of your questions, he'll be able to explain it better. I know he'll be happy to finally meet you."

"Who is he?"

"Someone who was close to your father. His best friend, in fact."

I let out a long sigh as I leaned my head back against the wall. I still had a million questions. So many secrets, so many things kept from me. I had known so little about my parents, my father especially. My aunt had a hard time talking about them. She claimed to hardly know my dad and that it was too painful to talk about my mom. I didn't think my aunt knew any of this, though, that she knew any of the world her sister had fallen into. The world I was now a part of.

"I didn't even know my father had a best friend, a pack, people who relied on him…anything."

Caden nodded. "If you are free soon, we can go meet him."

Perhaps this friend of my father's held the answers to all of my questions. Questions I'd had my whole life.

I knew I needed to go home. My aunt had probably landed and was home worried sick, but there was still a question in the back of my mind. One I didn't want to wait to be answered.

"Do you think Ross had something to do with our families' deaths?"

Caden suddenly went rigid. For a split second he was no longer the carefree Caden I was getting to know. His expression took on a look of carnal rage. He clenched his jaw and narrowed his eyes. His pupils were dilated, and I noticed a quiver in his lip, like he was holding back a snarl. The next words he spoke were with cold certainty.

"I don't think, Hazel. I know."

SEVEN

Caden handed me the key to my aunt's car and apologized for the lingering wet-dog smell. I realized the odor inside the car was probably because of me.

Weird.

When he'd fished me out of the river, he'd somehow found my aunt's car and the spare key underneath the tire, then drove us back to his cabin. When I asked him how he knew what car I had been driving, he tapped his nose in response and gave me a wink. It made me laugh. Right. Heightened sense of smell.

I promised to text him when I was free to go with him to Crescent Peak. We stood there in awkward silence. I knew there were a lot of things left unsaid, but they would have to wait.

"Thank you, for saving my me."

He just stood there and smiled.

And then he brought me in for a hug. I felt a jolt of excitement at his sudden closeness. I could feel the contour of his muscles through his T-shirt, and man, did he smell good.

I was still thinking about how good he smelled on my drive home.

I hadn't realized Caden lived so far. It was a good ten minutes before I even reached the highway that led me back to town and another twenty-minute drive before I even reached the town itself. The longer I drove the more I felt like I was coming back to the real world, the one I'd spent nearly eighteen years living in. So many things had changed within me, while the rest of the world had stayed the same. It was almost like reliving a childhood memory in real time.

It wasn't until I entered my neighborhood that I started to worry about what I would tell Aunt Claire. I still hadn't come up with a reasonable explanation when I pulled into the driveway. I thought I would have had time to think of something, but Aunt Claire must have been watching for me, because she came storming out of the house.

I got out of the car and prepared myself for the rage my aunt would bestow upon me. She came toward me, fury in her eyes. When she was close enough, she took a long look at me and my outfit…then slapped me.

I inhaled sharply. Aunt Claire had never hit me before, granted I had never given her a reason to, but still. I looked up at her, the wolf inside me stirred, but I quieted it immediately.

"Is *this* why you wouldn't answer your damn phone? Off screwing around with some boy? What in the *hell* has gotten into you, Hazel?"

She was practically screaming.

"I was terrified when you wouldn't answer my calls! I had to involve Rob! He came and got me from the airport and when you still weren't home when I got here, I had half a mind to call the police."

"Why didn't you?" I asked evenly.

She looked away from me, but not before I saw the bruise forming on her cheek.

"He hit you?" I asked.

She was quiet at first.

"This isn't about me, Hazel," she said, a bit subdued.

Rob had never left a mark on my aunt before. He'd pushed her and slapped her countless times, but this time it looked like he'd gotten a good punch in. I never hated Rob as much as I did at that moment. The wolf in me was now begging to be released. It took everything inside me to keep it at bay. The fury and anger left me irrational. I pushed past my aunt and stormed into the house, thoughts of murder running through my head. I never thought about killing anyone before, but the wolf inside had heightened my need for blood. Aunt Claire was yelling my name, trying to stop me from doing something stupid.

When I walked inside, the sight before me was enough to send me over the edge. There was a small amount of blood on the floor leading to the kitchen. Rob was leaning against the counter, an ice pack over his right knuckles.

An ice pack over the knuckles that had struck my aunt.

He looked up at me. There was anger in his eyes, but it would never match the fury inside of me.

"There you are, you little shit. I—" But before he could say more, I had him by the throat, pushing him hard against the fridge. He stared wild-eyed, scared and choking, unable to unhook my hands from his throat. My teeth extended and my nails became claws. I let out a vicious growl.

I realized now how stupid I had been to ever fear this man. He was nothing but a weak, feeble human. His threats to take away everything were like air. I now understood that nothing was worth my aunt getting hurt. Nothing was worth the emotional abuse I'd received. I'd rather be homeless and starving than spend another second in the same house with this man.

Besides, how could he make threats if he was dead?

My aunt had now reached the kitchen, screaming. "Hazel! Don't!"

Don't what? Rip his stupid throat out? Break every bone in his body? Stop his beating heart? Every fiber of my being wanted to do all these things, but I stopped myself. I glanced toward my aunt and saw fear.

That fear was because of me, and I didn't want someone I loved to fear me.

But I knew Rob's game was over. I would make sure of it. I loosened my grip on him so he could breathe, but I kept him pinned against the fridge. Tears were streaming down his face and judging from the smell and the wet spot on his pants, I was pretty sure he'd pissed himself.

"I'm sick of you. You will never lay your hands on my aunt or me ever again. You do not own us. We are not yours to control or to do with as you please. I want you out of this house and all your things gone by tomorrow or so help me." I began choking him again. His eyes bulged with terror, his face red as a tomato.

"You will tell no one what happened here, and once you are gone, you will do nothing to hurt or take away from us. Do I make myself clear, *Uncle Rob*?"

He choked out a yes.

I let go of him and turned to Aunt Claire. Her hands were over her mouth. She let out a scream. "Rob! No!"

I spun around just in time to see Rob lunge at me with a knife. I dodged quickly with an agility I hadn't possessed before the change. He went to grab my aunt, but I pulled her behind me. She clutched my arms tightly. Rob backed away down the hall with the knife still in hand, pointing it at us.

"You're a freak! This isn't the end," he said shakily.

He looked at Aunt Claire and then at me. "I'll find a way to steer her away from you. You monster."

My aunt finally spoke, anger overruling her shock. She stepped out from behind me and pointed at her face. "The only monster in this house is *you*, Robert. If somewhere in that twisted head of yours you think you are protecting me, then do me a favor and go. You have tortured my family long enough. I don't ever want to see you again. Do you hear me?"

Rob looked shell-shocked and dazed. He seemed to finally realize he was losing everything and fast.

"Claire, you know I didn't mean to. I would never—"

I let out a snarl, showing my fangs. Rob flinched and opened the door. There was anger on his face. He wouldn't be able to talk his way out of this one.

He released a frustrated hiss. "I'll be back for my things tomorrow," he spat, putting on his shoes. "But this isn't over, do you hear me, Claire?"

I made advances toward him, growling, making it very clear that it was in fact over. He stumbled, dropping the knife. He quickly grabbed his jacket and car keys, then bolted out the front door.

As soon as he was gone, I started to calm down. The wolf inside me settled, my teeth and claws disappeared. I slowly went to the door, gently closing it, then returned to the kitchen. Aunt Claire sat at the table, her face white except for the now growing bruise.

I grabbed an ice pack from the freezer and handed it to her. She took it, not looking at me, and placed it against her cheek. I sat down in the chair across from her, staring out the sliding glass door to the backyard. *I can't tell her everything.* So what could I say to her?

"I wasn't having sex with some guy," I said, because it felt important she knew. I cared deeply what my aunt thought of me.

Her gaze flickered to me, as if she was in a daze and had just realized I was there. She cleared her throat and looked down at her left hand, limply resting in her lap. Her silence made me nervous.

Finally, she spoke. "You look very much like your father right now."

I was confused by her statement, but relieved she was talking to me at all.

"Really? How so?" I asked.

"He always had an air about him. Something that demanded respect, but he was kind...and I...I always knew there was something different about him. There were things about his life that just didn't make sense, secrets he kept, but your mother trusted him with all her heart, and I trusted your mother."

I was silent for a moment, choosing my next words carefully.

"I think I might have inherited those secrets."

She shook her head. I spoke faster, knowing she would cut me off soon.

"I'm different, like he was, and these secrets have to be kept. I'm okay, though, Aunt Claire, really..."

She stood abruptly. "No. No. No. No. NO!" she yelled, throwing the ice pack on the table as she paced the room. "It was different with your father, Hazel. He was his own man, but you..." She paused, choking back tears. "You are like a daughter to me. I need to know everything. I need to know exactly what it is you inherited. I need to know so I can protect you."

Aunt Claire wasn't stupid, but I also believed she would die for me, and that was something I couldn't live with either. I couldn't drag her into this world. I didn't have a choice, though. I was a part of this whether I wanted to be or not.

"I can't, Aunt Claire. It's *you* I have to protect."

She was crying hard now. She reached out and grabbed both my hands.

"No, I'm the adult. I'm the parent. I'm supposed to protect you. You are my only family, Hazel. When your grandparents died in that car crash, it had just been your mother and I, and then she met Clark and she lost him to the same fate as our parents, and it was like watching her die twice. I have watched everyone I love suffer and die. I couldn't—*I can't*—bear to lose you too."

I shuttered. I felt sorry for her. We'd both lost people important to us but the difference was I never had the chance to know any of them. I didn't have to carry around the same loss of them being in my life one minute and gone the next. I had no memories of the parents who had loved me so dearly, or the grandparents who had loved my mother and my aunt. I only had the ache of never knowing them. Aunt Claire had been in the dark far longer than I had been. She watched my father's world destroy my parents, and she never really knew why. She deserved to know the truth, just as much as I did.

I sighed. I'd changed my mind. I knew how hard it would be to tell her the truth, but I decided it would be harder to keep her in the dark. A part of me knew that after tonight, I would know if Aunt Claire really did love me like a daughter and if she was strong enough to handle the same world her sister had been brought into.

"Okay, sit down." I lead her back to the chair, facing her toward me. I stood in the middle of the kitchen. I knew Aunt Claire would never believe me if I simply told her. It would be easier just to show her and go from there.

"You deserve to know the truth, so I'm going to be completely open and honest with you, but in return, you are going to have to keep an open mind, okay? Don't be scared."

I could see "don't be scared" was the wrong choice of words, because just by saying them, I had made my aunt nervous. She was gripping the table hard.

"Hazel, what—" I held up my hand. I wasn't sure how to shift at will. I'd never done it before, and I needed all the concentration I could get. I imagined how it had felt the first time I'd shifted. The ache in my muscles and joints, the fire on my skin. I pictured my wolf form and willed myself to become her.

I began to feel it, first in my hands and feet and then as it spread through the rest of my body. The experience was not as painful as before but still uncomfortable. I let out a small groan. Aunt Claire, seeing me in pain, went to get up, a worried look on her face.

"Hazel? What's wrong?"

I held up my hand, stopping her.

My vision turned white and I felt that familiar explosive pop in my head. My aunt let out a scream. When I opened my eyes, I was seeing everything in black-and-white detail, taking in the kitchen as if for the first time. I shook out my fur.

My aunt wore a look of pure terror. Her now trembling hands were over her mouth, tears streaking her face. She let out a small sob. I wanted to show her it was okay and that I was still me. I sat down, almost doglike, and wagged my tail, panting. I let out a small whistle through my nose. *See, Aunt Claire. I'm like a big puppy. Nothing to be afraid of,* I thought.

I was patient. I waited for her to calm down and collect her thoughts. She stood up, shaking all over, and got down on her knees. She very slowly scooted closer to me.

"Hazel?" she whispered through a shaky voice. I knew she was still unsure. I gave a small nod. *It's me, Aunt Claire. I promise it's still me.* I wished I could talk to her in this form.

She reached a hand toward my head. I lowered it so she could touch me. Her fingers brushed the fur behind my ears.

"Oh my God," she whispered.

I glanced at my reflection through the surface of the oven on my right. It was almost comical. The clothes Caden had given me were large enough to stretch around my wolf form. So I was literally a wolf in a pair of basketball shorts and a T-shirt in a kitchen. I snorted through my nose, as if to say *pfft, how ridiculous.*

Aunt Claire laughed, as if she, too, realized how ridiculous this was. I never loved her more than in that moment. I wanted to be human again, to hug her and take comfort in her, but I'd never changed back on my own before, not while conscious anyway. I pictured being human just like I had pictured being a wolf. My body temperature lowered, and I began to feel like static, like that pins-and-needles feeling you get when you lose blood circulation in a limb, only I felt it through my whole body. There was a familiar white flash behind my eyes and there I was, human and hugging my aunt. She was sobbing into my shoulder, stroking my hair. I held her tight, letting her comfort me while I did the same for her.

We stayed like this for a long time, until her tears had ceased and my anxiety settled. She looked in my eyes—hers so much like my mom's, and mine so much like my father's. She placed her hands on the sides of my head and stroked my cheeks with her thumbs, like she used to do when I was little and upset.

"I love you, Hazel. Nothing you say or do will ever change that. This however..." She paused. "Will take some adjusting." She let out a tear-filled laugh.

"There's more I have to tell you," I said in a whisper.

We sat at the kitchen table again. Aunt Claire made us coffee. I knew I couldn't tell her everything. I didn't want her to know how serious the situation was just yet. I did, however, tell her about meeting Caden and getting sick. I told her all the things I learned about shifters from Caden—how my father had been one—and about the community at Crescent Peak.

I didn't tell her about Ross or that I suspected he had a hand in my father's death or that he'd attacked Molly. I would tell her eventually, but right now I think she just needed to adjust to the situation at hand.

"What do we do now, Hazel?" she asked. "Is there a way you could...stop?"

I shook my head. I knew I couldn't. It was a part of me now. I would be incomplete. It had already been two days and I couldn't imagine how I'd lived this long without it.

Aunt Claire looked over at the microwave clock. It was nearly three in the morning and she decided to head to bed. "We can discuss this more tomorrow," she said. She kissed my forehead and held my gaze a moment before smiling faintly and going upstairs. I took pleasure in knowing she'd be sleeping alone tonight, without Rob, and I hoped she felt the same way.

I headed upstairs rummaging through my dresser drawers. I came across my old phone and plugged it in the charger by my bed. I wouldn't be able to use it without Wi-Fi, but something was better than nothing. I wanted to be able to touch base with Molly and Caden tomorrow.

I lay on my bed. I could still smell him on me. Campfire, men's deodorant, and a hint of the cabin's old wood smell. In a way, I wished I were there now with him, talking more about the life and world I never knew I belonged to. I held up the old stuffed wolf sitting on my pillow.

I felt that familiar ache I always got when I thought of my mom. The ache of never really knowing her, never having the chance to meet her. I hugged the wolf tightly and heard the crinkle it made. I looked at the tag. I realized there was something written there, right behind the how-to-wash instructions. I would have never noticed had it not been for my newly heightened senses.

There, in the smallest letters I'd ever seen, was written:

Open me.

I bolted upright in my bed.

What?

I squeezed him, hearing the noise again. I always thought it was just the crinkle sound some kids' toys made to stimulate them. Now it sounded more like paper being scrunched. What if there was a note inside? How had I never noticed before? He had been in my life for so long, so familiar. The stuffed animal came from a mother who possibly sought to comfort her child when she couldn't be there. I realized now why she'd chosen a wolf.

I got up and sat in my desk chair, pulling out a pair of scissors from my pencil holder. I hesitated. I felt a little uneasy at the thought of cutting Wolfy open. He meant so much to me, he'd always been there, sitting on my bed and waiting for me. He was the symbol of love from a mom I would never meet.

But what if she had left me something inside? Something she knew I would eventually realize was there as I got older?

I resolved myself. If there was nothing inside, I'd simply just sew him back up and be done with it, because I knew if I didn't do it, the question would plague me like all the other questions I'd had for so long.

I decided to make a cut down his back. I did my best to make the hole as small as possible, but still big enough to be able to stick two fingers inside and feel around the stuffing. I felt nothing but cotton at first, but as I reached the bottom, toward the tail's end, I felt it: a triangular piece of paper. I pinched it between my two fingers and pulled it out. I had been right. My mother must have known I might become a shifter someday. She knew that when the time came, I would be able to see the tag and find the note inside.

I stared down at the piece of paper, suddenly hesitant. I could see the handwriting through the lined paper. I unfolded it slowly, realizing it wasn't just one piece of paper, but two. Once it was spread out before me, I closed my eyes and took a deep breath, preparing myself before I opened them again and began to read.

My dearest Hazel,

Sweet girl, if you've found this letter, then that can

only mean you have inherited your father's gift. You are a shifter, a human who can change between forms.

Your father and I were unsure if you would shift at all. It was a question we asked ourselves often during the pregnancy. We had never met anyone in our situation. We had no idea if your shifter genes would even kick in or if you would remain human, like me.

So, we decided long before he died that when you were born, we would keep your heritage a secret from you until you started to show signs. I knew that it wouldn't be fair to you and that you might someday come to resent us for it, but your father and I didn't want you to have to deal with the burden of his world for as long as possible. I wanted you to have a normal, carefree, HUMAN life.

I do not regret this decision, even now, even if you never shift and you never find this note. But if you do, I hope that you will take my advice and seek out the community at Crescent Peak. They, too, are shifters. This will give you a chance to be around others like you. It's what your father would have wanted. When you get there, look for a man named Lucas. He will guide and teach you everything you need to know.

And please, whatever you do, do not tell your aunt Claire. I left her out of this to protect her. This life I was brought into isn't easy for a human, and the shifter community doesn't take kindly to people knowing about them. I do not blame or resent them. It's how they've survived this long without anyone knowing, and besides, Claire deserves a normal life.

I know my days are numbered. I can feel myself getting weaker as you grow stronger inside me. I'm sick. I haven't told Claire. I know I'm being selfish, but

I don't want my last moments with her to be filled with sadness. I want her to only be excited to meet you.

My heart breaks, like it still does when I think of your father. It breaks for all the time we won't get to spend with one another, all the moments stolen from us. I wish more than anything that we could all be together, but I am so happy to know that you will live on when I'm gone.

My sweet baby, please remember that you are so loved, and even though your father and I aren't there, our love is still unconditional, even in death, and it can always be carried in your heart.

I know you are exactly the kind of woman I knew you'd turn out to be, and I am so proud of you. I love you, Hazel, never ever forget that.

Love always, Mom.

My breath was ragged as tears streamed freely down my face. My heart ached, heavy with longing. I sewed Wolfy back together. I did a terrible job, honestly. I couldn't really sew, and it was an even harder task to accomplish with watery, tear-filled eyes, but I managed, and in the end, it served as a reminder when I looked at the small, uneven stitching. I stuck my mother's note inside a small red envelope I was saving for something special. I'm not sure what that special was going to be, but this seemed as good as any. I wanted to protect and preserve this note for as long as possible.

I placed the note inside my desk and wiped my eyes. I thought of Aunt Claire. I felt bad for telling her the truth now. I had gone against my mother's wishes. But even if I had known, I might have told her the truth anyway. I think my mother hadn't given her sister enough credit. I don't think it was the right decision to keep this a secret from either of us.

What if I had never met Caden—or never went to meet Ross—and I ended up shifting for the first time in a public place? I realized now that I had probably come close that day with David at the coffee shop. What if I never found Mom's note in my stuffed animal? Or found it too late? I could have exposed the other shifters. I could have accidentally hurt someone. I'd just been lucky. Mom took a big risk in not telling me.

I leaned back in my chair and scrubbed my face with my hands, letting out my breath. My heart still ached for my parents and the time we would never have, but at least now I had a bit of closure. I knew my parents had loved me, my aunt knew, too, but reading it from my mother's own handwriting, it made me realize just how much. It suddenly made it feel real, tangible, like an invisible line was tethered to me and my parents wherever they were now, and I felt a little bit closer to them. Mom was right, this was the kind of love I could carry with me.

I must have fallen asleep at some point, because the next thing I knew, I was awoken by the smell of bacon and eggs. I checked the clock on my phone. It was about nine in the morning. I had slept in Caden's clothes, the scent of him now faded. I grabbed a change of my own clothes and headed for the shower. I went to lock the door and stopped myself.

Despite everything that was happening and all the information I still needed time to process, I felt good. It was a relief to finally have some answers, to finally have Rob out of the house, and to know my mom had found a way to reach out to me. I wanted to enjoy these small victories, this temporary peace.

I fished out Caden's number and sent him a quick text before hopping in the shower. I hummed a tune as I washed my hair and decided I would go see Molly. I would put aside my other worries for the moment. I dressed, brushed my hair and teeth, and checked my phone. Nothing from Caden yet. I sent a text to Molly. I assumed she was using her old phone like me, but just to be sure I sent a text to her mom's phone too.

```
Hey, it's Hazel. Looks like I lost
my phone too. Currently using my old
phone on Wi-Fi. How is everything?
```

I headed downstairs. Aunt Claire sat at the kitchen table, eating breakfast and looking at her laptop. She wore the glasses she needed for reading and computer use.

"Morning," I announced cheerfully.

She grunted, still staring at her computer. She took a sip of coffee.

"Morning," she said finally.

I fixed myself a plate and sat down. I would have liked the bacon a little less cooked, but meat was meat, and my wolf was content either way.

"What do you think of this place?" she said and turned her laptop to show me a house. Aunt Claire was always showing me places she'd love to move to or open her floral shop in someday. I leaned in to get a closer look. It was a cute little house, one story and bright yellow. It looked very homey. I glanced at where it was located, expecting to see a familiar zip code.

"*Florida?*"

She nodded eagerly, smiling.

"It's just the right price, with the money we were

saving for my business someday, and Florals has a branch there. I know we can have that savings back up in no time and then I can start my business. It's so tropical and the winters are so mild that plants and flowers grow year-round."

"You want to move all the way to Florida?"

She took both my hands in hers.

"No silly, I want *us* to move to Florida, together. We can start fresh, away from Rob and from…" She paused.

I took my hands away from hers and sat back in my chair.

"Away from what, Aunt Claire? From what I am? Because I can promise you, I will still be able to shift in Florida too. It just might be a bit harder to explain a wolf on a sandy beach, wouldn't you think?"

She frowned at me. She didn't think my joke was any funnier than I did. Clearly this had not gone the way she had planned. My good mood was going south.

"I just thought that maybe you didn't have to change. Maybe you could just—"

"Keep it hidden? Keep a part of me locked away?"

I could almost feel the wolf inside me howl in fear and rage at the idea of never being able to come out now that she was free. My wolf would never be caged. "I already told you I can't."

"I'm sorry, Hazel. I just thought that after everything that's happened to us here, you'd maybe want a fresh start, somewhere new."

"Well, you thought wrong!" I shouted.

I could see she was trying to understand, but it was hard for her. She would never know, because she wasn't a shifter. Mom was right, maybe I had made a mistake all along. Aunt Claire couldn't handle this. I shouldn't have expected her to understand.

She had a lot of bad memories here, same as me, so of course she would have thought I wanted a fresh start, but now that I knew what I was, who I was, I knew I couldn't leave this place, not yet anyway. It still held so many answers. This was home. There were people here just like me who had been right under my nose the whole time. I could finally fit in here, and there was Molly and Caden to think about too. There was still so much I wanted to know about him.

I sighed. My anger was gone as quickly as it had come. I got up and started to head out of the kitchen. Aunt Claire had turned her computer back around and was staring at it in anger. I knew now what mom would say. She'd tell Aunt Claire to go to Florida. She'd tell her she deserved a fresh start.

"You should go to Florida, Aunt Claire. I'm almost eighteen. I can take care of myself."

She shook her head, not looking at me.

"I'm sorry, but I can't leave. There's a lot of questions I need answers to here and a whole community of people just like me who I need to go see. I hope you understand that at least."

When she didn't look up, I left the room and headed upstairs. I knew deep down she wouldn't go to Florida without me, and in a small, selfish way, I was a little relieved, but there was that larger part of me that wished she would go. I imagined what had happened to Molly happening to Aunt Claire and I shuttered at the thought.

I checked my phone. Nothing from Caden, but Molly had texted me back on her mom's phone.

```
Hey! Come over? And can you run to
the  bookstore  and  grab  me  a  new
sketchbook? :D Love you!!!
```

I smiled. A trip to the bookstore sounded like a good idea. I'd grab us both a frappe too. I know that would make her day. Rob wouldn't be back for his things until after work, later in the evening. I wanted to be here to make sure he didn't do anything stupid. I texted Molly that I'd get her sketchbook and be by in a bit, then headed downstairs, put on my shoes, and walked outside. It was a beautiful day. Sunny without a cloud in the sky. Aunt Claire was outside watering her plants. She still had her reading glasses on. She sometimes forgot to take them off.

"I'm going to run to the bookstore to pick up a sketchbook for Molly and then I'm going to her house. Is that okay?"

She nodded and continued watering her plants. I was getting the silent treatment. I hated when she did that. It was almost better to have her yell at me, because then at least I'd know she was just angry with me. When she gave me the silent treatment it usually meant I'd hurt her feelings. I hated hurting her feelings. I sighed and continued down the stairs. I'd find some way to make it up to her.

When I got to the bookstore, I felt a bit of relief, breathing in the smell of coffee and books. I loved this place. It made me think that maybe I could own a bookstore someday, or maybe just a coffee shop. Either way I would be content. I thought about Aunt Claire and moving to Florida. Did Florida even have coffee shops like this?

I waved at John behind the counter and ordered two frappes to go, then went to find a sketchbook for Molly. I grabbed the one I thought she'd like the most.

While John worked on the frappes, I browsed the books. I picked up two with wolves on the cover and smiled. One was a horror and the other was a romance. *Go figure.* I shrugged and decided to purchase both. I paid for my items and the coffees. John made a joke about how all the money I made here just went right back into the store. I laughed and said it was probably true as I waved goodbye.

Heading for the door, I nearly bumped into someone coming in and turned to apologize.

It was David, a huge grin on his face. I stood there shocked and nearly dropped my frappes as I hugged him.

"Oh my God, David! You're okay."

I wasn't usually that affectionate with people, but I was just so happy to know he'd made it out alive. How had he escaped? Why was he here, smiling and unscathed?

"Hey, I've been trying to text you."

I pulled away from him and we both stepped outside.

"I lost my phone when...well, you were there."

He nodded.

So, he wasn't hiding it. He really had saved me from Ross and his pack. For a brief moment I thought I'd imagined it was him who'd saved me, but I knew I'd recognized his scent. He smelled like cologne, pine needles, and an earthy scent, like loose soil and freshly cut grass.

"Why didn't they hurt you?" I asked as we started to walk.

He shrugged. "I escaped while they were distracted. You were their main priority after all. While they weren't looking, I ran the other way, back toward the entrance. I shifted, hopped the fence, and headed toward my car. I wanted to find you after, but I knew the others would be looking for you and I couldn't risk running into them."

I side-eyed him skeptically. His golden eyes stared back. They were a bit unnerving. I looked away quickly.

"What were you even doing there?"

He rubbed the back of his neck, looking down. "Don't get mad, but I've kinda been following you."

My initial reaction was in fact anger. "What! Why? Are you some kind of stalker now?"

He made a calm-down motion with his hand.

"No nothing like that. I just knew your first shift was soon and I wanted to be close by in case you needed help. First shifts aren't easy."

I narrowed my eyes at him, still a little unnerved. "You knew I was a shifter? Why didn't you say something?"

"I wasn't quite sure, and we'd just met again after all these years. I didn't know what you did and didn't know. I had a hunch you had no idea, especially when you didn't lock yourself in the nearest room and just force yourself to shift. It's what we're taught to do. If you let the sickness drag on, it could kill you."

He positioned himself so we were eye level. He said nothing for a moment, just scanned my face, up and down, left to right.

I gazed at him for a long moment, trying to piece together my thoughts and feelings before staring down at the coffees in my hand. I wasn't sure if I could trust David, but I wanted to. It would be nice to have an old friend in my corner. He seemed to genuinely care.

"You were right. I didn't know what I was till recently," I said hesitantly.

David didn't seem surprised. He just nodded. "You and I are more alike than you think."

"Because we're shifters?" I asked.

"Because we're both half shifters. The only difference is, I grew up with a shifter for a father and you just happened to grow up with a human."

I looked at him a little surprised. "I was told half shifters are rare."

"Not necessarily. The ones that shift are rare, but humans and shifters reproduce all the time. It's just the shifter half usually remains dormant. Shifters, after all, are already half human. So that would technically make us a quarter human. That amount of human gene usually cancels out the wolf."

I was silent for a moment, taking in this information. "What happened to your mom?"

He shrugged. "As far as I know she's dead. I never met her, and my father never talks about her."

"I'm sorry," I said, and meant it.

"It's fine. You know what it's like. You lost both your parents."

I gave him a sympathetic smile and put my free hand on his shoulder. "At least you still have your dad."

He shrugged, looking somber. "If you knew my dad, I don't think you'd be saying that."

I wanted to ask what he meant but we were almost to Molly's. I did have one more question before I went, though.

"Is there anything special about half shifters? I mean besides how rare it is to be able to shift at all."

He looked a little thrown off by the question. He stretched his lips to one side, eyes looking up in concentration.

"I guess the most important part is the wolf in us can never take over, no matter how long you stay in that form. Maybe because we have more human in us. For shifters, it's a constant struggle between animal instinct and higher intelligence. That part of the brain that makes us human."

"Wait, you mean it's not easy to keep control for shifters?"

He shook his head. "No. It takes a lot of discipline and years of training—from a young age—to keep the balance between wolf and human."

I had no idea. I thought it was as easy for everyone as it was for me. The first shift had been uncomfortable, but I never felt out of control. *It must be painful to constantly keep the wolf at bay, to have to always be in check to make sure you don't forget you're human.* I was very aware of the wolf within me. She spoke to me on an instinctual level ever since my first shift, but she was tame. She patiently waited to be set free. She only ever tried to claw her way out when I was angry, and even then, it never felt like it wouldn't be my choice. I couldn't imagine her trying to take that choice away from me.

This is heavy information. But I can process it later.

I turned toward David. "This is my stop," I said and pointed at the house behind me.

He half smiled, kicking a loose rock on the road.

Did he seem sad? I wondered why.

"Thank you, for saving me, again." I rolled my eyes and gave a crooked smile.

He peered up at me. There was a glimmer in those unnerving eyes. How had I never noticed how strange they were when we were kids?

The innocence of youth, I suppose.

"You're something special, Hazel. I knew it the moment we met in that park all those years ago. Now look at us, meeting again just to find out we are both shifters, not only that, but half shifters. I think—I don't know—maybe it's fate."

I furrowed my brow.

"Maybe it is," I said casually.

"We don't know each other well anymore, but I'd like for us to be friends again. Do you think we could do that?"

My smile widened. "Of course. I'd like that."

And I meant it. In a weird way I'd missed our friendship, and now that I knew he was like me, I could talk to someone other than Caden about what I was going through. Perhaps even more so, considering David was a half shifter too.

David smiled and we stood there a moment before I cleared my throat.

"I gotta go. These frappes are melting. I'll see you around?" I asked and started to walk away.

"Hazel, wait, one more thing."

I turned around.

"I know it's none of my business, but be careful around Caden. He hides it well, but he's more wolf than human."

David turned to walk in the opposite direction. "If you need me, I'll be around," he said as he threw a casual wave goodbye.

I watched him walk away for a moment, wondering what exactly I was getting myself into these days.

EIGHT

When I reached Molly's, I knocked with my foot. I'd have walked right in, but my hands were full. Her dad answered. We mumbled casual hellos, then he told me Molly was upstairs in bed. I thanked him and took the stairs two at a time.

"Hey," I announced when I arrived at her bedroom. "How are you feeling?"

Molly looked up, a sketchbook in hand as she drew.

Most of the small scratches on her face had already started to scab over, but she still had gauze down her forehead to the bottom of her cheek. The bruises on her face and body had turned a nasty yellow. She still wore a sling on her left arm.

She gave me a half smile as if she were afraid to hurt her face.

"I've had better spring breaks, I'll tell you that."

I sat down next to her on the bed. "Here's your new sketchbook." I pulled it out of the plastic bag. "And I brought us Conner's famous frappes."

"Oh yay! Thanks, Haze." She beamed.

She took a sip as she stared at her sketch, no doubt looking for ways to improve it.

"Can I see?" I asked.

She handed me the sketchbook. It was a very detailed outline of a monster hiding in the brush. Its black fur faded in with the shadows. It had a large snout with a wide, snarling mouth and huge fangs, its claws reaching out to devour. The only color she had added was to its eyes. They were a golden yellow, almost glowing. I flipped the sketchbook back to the first page and leafed through it. They were all different sketches of the same monster, all equally unnerving. I handed it back to her.

"Still having nightmares?" I asked.

She nodded and continued working on her sketch. "Is Aunt Claire home?"

"Yeah," I answered.

She glanced up at me, eyebrows raised, her gauze crinkling. "And? Are you in trouble?"

I shrugged. "Yeah at first, but then she and Rob got into a huge fight and Rob left."

"*What?* Rob left? Like, for good?"

I nodded. "He's coming to get his stuff this evening."

She smiled, even though I knew it hurt her. "Hazel, that's great. You and your aunt are free of that monster."

I smiled back, remembering how good it felt to no longer feel the tension in the house, but the guilt of lying to Molly dampened the feeling. I wanted to tell her about staying at Caden's and why Rob had really left, but I couldn't. I knew now that Ross had attacked Molly to get to me. He'd wanted me alone and scared.

It was my fault Molly had gotten hurt and worse still, how could I tell her I was now like the thing that had attacked her? The same monster that plagued her dreams at night. I didn't want her to look at me with that same fear. It would crush me. I didn't want to become the monster she feared. Molly had always accepted me for who I was, but this was something I just couldn't share with her. This was a part of me I didn't think she would accept.

I spent some time reading beside Molly while she sketched. This was what I loved most about our friendship. We could be comfortably silent, doing separate things while still enjoying each other's company. After she finished her last sketch, we spent the rest of the afternoon watching movies on her laptop.

I knew Molly was in a lot of pain. Her dad had come up twice to give her pain meds. She tried her best to hide the fact, but I knew my best friend too well. When it started getting dark, I told her I had to go. I wanted to be home when Rob stopped by to get his things, and I could tell that she was a little out of it from all the meds. As I left, she gave me a lopsided wave goodbye, giggling to herself.

When I neared home, I saw Rob's car in the driveway in the fading dusk light. He must have gotten off early. As I jogged up to the house, I got the feeling that something was wrong. My instincts hit me with a wave of dread. I imagined the worst as I bounded up the steps, the porch light flickering on

Rob had done something to Aunt Claire. I just knew it. I twisted the door handle in panic. It was locked. I grabbed the hidden key underneath the plant and unlocked the door quickly. When I stepped inside, I was hit with the smell of blood. Lots of blood. The wolf in me stirred, her instincts were telling me to be on guard. Panic now gripped me.

"Aunt Claire?" I called.

A noise came from down the hall. My eyes adjusted quickly. I didn't bother trying to turn the lights on. I followed the trail of blood leading into the kitchen. I was slow and hesitant, fear gripped me tight, threatening to choke me. I heard my heartbeat and felt the throb of my pulse in my neck.

A small sob escaped my throat. Nothing could have prepared me for the scene in my kitchen. It was like something right out of a horror movie. The sliding glass window was busted open, the blinds blowing softly in the wind, making small fluttering noises. The floor was covered in glass. Rob's body lay face-first in a pool of his own blood, his eyes staring distantly, cold and vacant. His throat was ripped so deeply, he was nearly decapitated. Claw marks racked down his back and legs.

I wanted to scream but instinct told me to be quiet. Where was Aunt Claire? I prayed I didn't find her this way. I nearly collapsed into a fit of sobs on the floor at the idea, but my worry for her safety kept me from falling apart. There was a bang upstairs and Aunt Claire's scream. I ran quickly down the hallway, slipping in blood. The trail led upstairs toward the master bedroom. The door was closed. I heard Aunt Claire's muffled sobs. Someone was in there with her, hurting her. Anger replaced all fear. I tried the doorknob, but it was locked. I kicked in the door with my newfound strength. Pieces of wood flew as I stepped inside. My eyes adjusted to the thickness of the dark.

Aunt Claire lay unconscious on the bed, her head a bloody mess, her shirt ripped, revealing shallow claw marks. Someone turned on the lights. I sucked in a breath, closing my eyes to the sudden brightness. I was kicked in the side. I grunted as I hit the wall to my right, sliding down to the floor. I let out a hiss, gripping my side in pain. Ross hovered over me as he smiled.

"Hazel. So happy you could join us." His voice was like honey.

I glared at him with hatred and snarled. His smile faded and he bared his teeth, his face suddenly contorting with rage.

"Why do you look at me like that? I just did you a favor. Word has it that your aunt's husband was not good to you and your aunt. Was I wrong?"

My face gave nothing.

"I didn't think so." He stretched his arms and looked around dramatically. "Well, problem solved. He'll never bother you again."

I inhaled and exhaled heavily. My side hurt horribly.

"You hurt her," I said on a growl, nodding toward my aunt.

He sighed. "She'll live"—he gestured with his head toward the bed—"she's a fighter, that one. She came at me with a knife, you know. I was only defending myself, not to mention the screaming. We don't want to alert the whole neighborhood, do we?"

"What do you want from me!" I half screamed, half growled.

He crouched so he was eye level with me. He let out another sigh as he brushed a hand against my cheek. I flinched away from his touch.

"Sweet girl, you don't realize how long I've been looking for you. You were so human before, blending in so well with the rest of them. I feared you would never change. I thought perhaps if you did, you'd have moved far from here, and of course there was a possibility that you were dead, but I was patient, you see, so very patient."

He took my chin and squeezed my cheeks between his forefinger and thumb. I tried to jerk away but couldn't. His grip was too tight.

"You've become a bit of an obsession for me. If I had found you sooner, I could have raised you as my own. Your father was everything to me. My leader, my alpha. I did whatever he asked. I looked up to him, bled for him, killed for him."

He glanced at Aunt Claire.

"And what does he do? He runs off with some human. Not only that, but he leaves his pack for her and makes someone else the alpha. Not me! His beta!" He paused. "I realized then that my affections for him were misplaced. He was weak."

He looked back at me.

"But not you, Hazel. You are not weak. You could be the strongest of us all. A shifter not chained to her wolf. You have total control. I could teach you about our world. I could show you how to hunt, to kill, and to be a part of a pack."

He finally let go of my face and took both my hands in his. I inhaled sharply at the sudden change of movement. I tried to jerk my hands away, but he held tight.

"You could be my beta, maybe even my mate."

I scoffed, disgusted.

"It is not so strange in our world. Age has no meaning. The only thing that matters is strength." He shrugged. "But if you are so opposed by the idea, it is of little consequence. I also have a son. You would make fine offspring someday. Join me and you will want for nothing, Hazel. I will give you a family, a place to belong. Just leave these humans behind, kill them if you must. You will learn soon enough how weak they are. They are holding you back. Your father couldn't see it, but I know you can."

He was crazy. That was all I could think. Even if I was insane enough to join, Caden seemed certain Ross had a hand in our parents' deaths. That was something I could never let go. I looked him in the eye, steeling myself.

"Did you kill him? My father?"

Ross stood, glaring down at me. For just a second there was a flash of sadness on his face, but it was gone before I could make anything of it. He replaced it with a look of detachment.

"Clark's weakness killed him, Hazel."

The way he said it sealed the truth. Ross had somehow had a hand in my father's death. He walked over to the side of the bed and glanced down at Aunt Claire. I got up slowly, my side still hurting. I let out a hiss of pain.

"She's a beautiful thing, this human, just like your mother was." He stroked her cheek. "I could see the appeal this family has had on shifters."

He shot forward, taking her throat in his hands and squeezing. Aunt Claire let out a choked scream, pain bringing her out of unconsciousness.

"But they are weak." He growled. "Pathetic."

I was quick, lunging forward and removing his hand from her throat. I let out a half yell, half growl as I pushed him sideways. He crashed into the nightstand, breaking it to pieces.

"Don't you ever touch her again!" I screamed.

My canines were sharp, my nails now claws. I crouched over my aunt in a protective stance. I watched him lose his composure. With a look of pure rage on his face, he gave me a menacing growl as he began to shift. I didn't have time to think. I shifted, too, letting all the anger and hate I felt drive me. There was the familiar flash of white, the sound of ripping fabric and then a wolf stood over Aunt Claire, shielding her from the massive black wolf growling on the floor.

I lunged for him, all teeth and claws. We rolled around on the floor, scratching and biting. His mind reached out.

"Obey me, Hazel! Obey!"

I fought the alpha's pull. All I could think about was protecting Aunt Claire. I thought about all the lives he took from us—from Caden—all so he could gain power. I thought of my father. I would never allow this man to have any power over me. I would die first.

He was gaining the upper hand. He pinned me down, my throat exposed. I looked up at the window behind us. His mouth closed around my throat. I let out a growl and with one swift movement I used my back legs to push his body over me. He crashed through the glass window. I got up and ran to the window just in time to see him roll off the roof. I wondered if I'd injured or possibly killed him when the rough outline of his black form hopped over the fence. He glanced toward my direction, his voice ever so faintly.

"I'll let you think on it, but my patience runs thin, Hazel, and the longer you wait, the more danger you put these humans in. I will not hesitate next time. I will take them from you." He glared at me a moment, letting his words set in. I snarled back. A group of figures materialized from the shadows, coming from down the quiet street. His pack. Together they disappeared into the night.

Aunt Claire groaned behind me. I shifted back and grabbed an oversize T-shirt from off the floor. It was possibly Rob's, but I didn't care. I threw it on and went to Aunt Claire. She blinked a couple of times, focusing on me.

"Hazel," she whispered.

She sat up slowly, wincing, looked at me for a long moment and then embraced me. She began to sob.

"Thank God, thank God, thank God," she repeated. "I watched him. I watched him rip Rob's throat out, Hazel."

I was numb. I should have felt scared, angry, relieved, but I felt nothing. I stared off, hugging Aunt Claire back. Then suddenly, sharp and familiar, the feeling of guilt hit me like a brick. I blinked back tears. How could I have been so stupid? How could I have possibly thought that after learning the truth I could still live a normal life? How could I, when the man who'd killed my father was still out there, was still trying to destroy the only family I had left?

I couldn't pretend anymore. I couldn't put Aunt Claire or Molly at risk anymore. Ross said he could smell me the moment my change started. He had waited for me to show myself and expose the people closest to me. Because of me, a man lost his life tonight.

Rob wasn't a good man, but that didn't mean he deserved to die. I had thought of killing him numerous times, I almost did the night before, but now I realized that thinking it and doing it were far from the same thing.

I felt sick. I got up and told Aunt Claire to call the police, then I went to my room and pulled out a duffel bag from under the bed. I began packing my things. Mostly clothes, a few books, Wolfy, and my mother's letter. I walked across the hall to throw in my toiletries. Aunt Claire came out of the bedroom in a daze. She looked awful. I couldn't make myself look her in the eye.

"The police are on their way."

"Good," I said. "When they get here tell them there was another animal attack. It attacked you and killed Rob. It then chased you upstairs. You trapped it in the master bedroom, and it made an escape out the window."

I went back to my bedroom, Aunt Claire following.

"Hazel, what are you doing?"

I changed into my own clothes. I made a mental note to buy extras soon, because I had a feeling, I'd probably find myself ripping them apart every other day.

"I'm packing, and you should too."

I moved past her and toward her bedroom, grabbing her suitcase.

"Where are we going?"

I started throwing her clothes inside. She seemed to have come out of her daze and started pairing jeans with tops and shoes.

"You," I said, "are going to get in your car and drive as far away from here as possible. Move to Florida like you wanted. I don't care. Just as long as you aren't here anymore."

"I'm not leaving without you, Hazel."

She was using her motherly voice, but I didn't care, not right now. I needed to protect her, and this felt like the only way.

"You have to."

"Like hell I do. That man—that monster—is a sick, twisted killer, Hazel. He killed Rob and made me watch. He tortured me. He was going to torture you."

I turned on her, angry.

"Well that's nothing new for us is it, Aunt Claire? Abuse. So why all of a sudden do you care?"

I threw her suitcase across the room. I knew this was

a low blow, but I was angry and part of me hoped that would make it easier for her to leave me behind.

"Did you know he touched me?" I said evenly. "Did you ever realize just how scared I was? To come home and to check he wasn't nearby. To constantly be on guard. To make sure, *repeatedly*, that my door was locked every time I walked into my bedroom or bathroom. To never feel safe in my own home. *DID YOU?*" I screamed the last part.

Aunt Claire jerked like I'd physically hit her. She began to sob, both her hands over her mouth, staring at me in shock.

"Hazel," she whispered through her hands. "I didn't know. I swear I didn't know."

I left her standing in the room. She didn't follow. I went to my room and started throwing things. I screamed in anger, heaving books from their shelves, knocking things off my desk. A growl ripped through my throat as I tore open my pillows and shredded my sheets. Hot angry tears streamed down my face.

A part of me broke just then. I hated myself for ever speaking to Aunt Claire that way. I hated myself for the way I blamed her, but I was tired of the crappy hand I'd been dealt.

I was like a magnet for the twisted and damaged. Maybe because I, too, was damaged. I had tried to hide it, to bury it in the books I read and the distance I put between myself and everyone else, but it was always there. My aunt had been too afraid to leave a man who abused us both, and it had left me bitter.

But I'd changed so dramatically in such a small amount of time since then. The wolf inside had changed me. I could no longer understand how I'd ever let a man like Rob control my life. So what if we lost the house?

Our money? The car? What was being homeless to a wolf? A wolf had no home. I realized now, thanks to Ross, that there were worse people out there than Rob, and there were worse things to worry about than being homeless.

It wasn't just Aunt Claire's fault for staying. We'd both let Rob control our lives. We'd both let him make us believe that our own worth was less than our house, our money, and our possessions. He'd threatened us with things, that in the end, didn't really matter. Why? Maybe because a small part of us felt like we deserved this. That maybe we didn't deserve something better. Maybe we were just too afraid to leave and start over. Maybe we didn't think we could make it on our own with nothing. It was our insecurities that had let Rob control us.

Now what was I? Just a girl who realized her worth a little too late. I hoped that someday my aunt would realize hers too. I wish now, more than anything, that we had figured it out sooner. That we had packed up a couple of suitcases, looked Rob in the face, and said, "Take it all, we don't need it, because we have everything we could ever need in each other, and that's something you will never have," and just walked out. Not caring where we were going or what we would do when we got there. Maybe Rob would still be alive. Maybe Ross would have never found me. Maybe we'd have moved to Florida before I even realized what I'd become and just went on believing that my father had died in an accident. But that was all too late now, and the most important thing was protecting the ones I loved, even if they hated me for it.

I wiped the tears from my face and stood, walking to the full-length mirror behind my door. When I looked at myself, I no longer recognized the person staring back. I no longer looked like the tainted, broken girl who'd been touched by a man she'd feared for years. I no longer looked like the girl who hid behind locked doors, opened books, and a wall she'd built between herself and everyone else. I no longer looked like the weak, pathetic girl I once was. I no longer looked like a girl, at all in fact, but a wolf in sheep's clothing.

My anger had brought on clarity. Everything that had ever gone wrong in my life had started with one man. My eyes reflected off the light in the room, a wolfish glow. I knew what needed to be done. I didn't care how long it took, or what I would need to do, but I knew one thing was clear, Ross had to die. I gave myself one last look in the mirror, clenching my fists and hardening my heart.

"Enjoy what little time you have left, Ross, because I'm coming for you," I whispered aloud.

The ambulance wheeled Rob away, a black sheet covering his lifeless body. I stared as Aunt Claire gave her statement to the police. When she finished talking, they turned to me.

"And you were where?" they asked me.

I sniffed, pretending to be shaken up. "I was at my friend's, three houses down." I pointed in the direction of Molly's house. "I came home to find…all this. Aunt Claire was a mess, crying over Rob's body. When I finally got her to calm down and tell me what happened, I told her to call you."

"What did this animal look like?" he asked, addressing Aunt Claire again.

"I can't be sure. It was dark. I was too afraid to turn the lights on. All I know is it was big, like the size of a small bear."

The officer nodded, writing our statements down on a small notepad. He looked up at Aunt Claire again. "I'm assuming the animal did that to you, ma'am?" He pointed at her bruised face.

She'd already had the medics check her out. She'd had a few scratches on her stomach and a gash on the back of her head, but nothing too severe to need stitches. Everyone seemed to assume the bruises came from the animal, but I suspected the cop knew otherwise.

Aunt Claire gave him a reserved look. "Yes," she said firmly.

He looked at her for a moment, then nodded and closed his notepad. "All right, thank you both. We'll let you know when we've caught the animal. We've had similar reports like this recently. This has been the second kill it's made. We think it might have to do with a pack of wolves living in the strip of mountains between us and Creekwood. It could possibly be a rabies epidemic. Nevertheless, I'm very sorry for your loss."

We both nodded sullenly.

I now feared for the community living up at Crescent Peak. I wondered if they knew what was going on. Did they know that Ross was behind it? I had a feeling I would find out. I made up my mind that after I got ahold of Caden that would be my next stop.

As the police left, we took our packed bags and locked up. Caution tape now looped around the porch and across the door. I took a good, long look at the house. I wasn't sure I would be coming back.

The keys to Rob's car were nowhere to be found, so that left us with only one vehicle. I was tempted to drive Aunt Claire to the airport and buy her the first ticket to Florida, but it was late and we were both exhausted. I decided to take her with me to Caden's. I had a feeling he would understand.

"Where are we going?" she asked.

"A friend's house. The one who told me about being a shifter." It was the only information I would give her. I couldn't help but feel like we'd hit some weird twilight zone where I was the adult now and my aunt was the teenager. She was in way over her head.

"We should grab a hotel. You barely know this boy."

"He saved my life, Aunt Claire. I trust him well enough."

She looked frustrated, but she didn't comment, seemingly distracted by something else. There was silent tension for a while, neither of us knowing what to say to the other.

"He was a good man at first...until he wasn't." Aunt Claire stared down at her hands. "I was hoping we'd have enough hidden away soon to finally get away from him. I fought him for so long."

She sighed as if the weight of that fight still tired her. None of it was news to me and I think she knew that and just wanted to say it out loud.

"I know, Aunt Claire. I know how hard you were trying to leave him."

She continued as if she hadn't heard me. "I knew it wasn't a healthy relationship, but I thought you were...I thought you were left out of it. I didn't know that he...I didn't know he touched you. I was so stupid. I worried about you every time I left for those godforsaken conferences, but I was naive. The worst I thought that man could do was lose his temper."

She started to cry.

"But that's no excuse, Hazel. I should never have left you alone with him. I should never have married him. I...I should have had the strength to leave him. If I had known...Hazel, you should have told me. We never would have stayed. I could have dealt with his abuse if it meant we could start over with enough money, but if I had known he was abusing you, we never would've stayed, money be damned."

She hit the dashboard in anger.

I knew she was probably right. She might have really left Rob if I had been up-front and told her the truth, but we were both fools, and sometimes when we tried to protect the ones we loved, we ended up hurting them more.

I touched her knee lightly, keeping my eyes on the road. "What's done is done," I said softly. It wasn't a reassuring answer, but it wasn't cruel either. It was just a statement made by a girl who had hardened her heart already and was hoping her aunt would do the same.

We sat in silence until I turned down the dirt road leading to Caden's. I hoped he was home. He hadn't returned my texts today, but then again, I hadn't checked them after what happened to Rob.

We said nothing else as we pulled up and parked in the circular driveway. As soon as the lights hit the cabin, Caden stepped outside. He had a worried expression on his face. My heart gave a sudden lurch seeing him again. I hadn't really thought of what it would mean being here, asking for his help.

He walked up to the car as I rolled the window down. His worried look increased upon seeing me. "What happened?"

"I'll explain inside," I replied. "But we need a place to stay tonight, is that okay?"

He gave me a reassuring half smile. "Are you kidding? Of course, there's plenty of room here."

I nodded. "Thank you."

I turned the car off while Aunt Claire grabbed our bags. As we got out and started walking toward the lodge, Caden took the bags from Aunt Claire and raised his hand to shake hers.

"Hi, I'm Caden Ulrika."

She shook his hand. "Claire Morris, Hazel's aunt."

He gave her his most dazzling smile as he looked from me to her.

"Aunt? You sure you two aren't sisters?"

I rolled my eyes at the cheesy remark. It was one we'd heard often. My aunt smiled at him as I gave his arm a light smack, smiling too. I adored him for trying to lighten the mood, if only for a moment.

Caden put me in the bedroom I'd stayed in last time, with Aunt Claire residing in the one next door. I could never imagine living in a place this big all by myself. I wasn't sure how Caden did it. How did he keep everything clean? I caught Caden in the hallway and asked if we could talk while Aunt Claire was in the shower.

"Ross found my house. He killed my aunt's husband and he would have killed her, too, if I hadn't stopped him. He was waiting for me to get home." I explained the whole story in detail, including what Ross wanted with me.

Caden had that look on his face again. It was nothing but rage, more animal than human. His eyes were glazed over and his pupils dilated. It was terrifying to see on his handsome face. I wondered if this was what David had meant about keeping control of the wolf inside. Was Caden fighting it now? He let out a long breath and his pupils returned to normal. He looked at me, his face kind once again. He touched my arm. I felt a jolt run through me.

"Hazel, I'm so sorry about your uncle."

I shook my head, almost wanting to laugh. I looked down, halfway between smiling and grimacing.

"It's all right. He—Rob—wasn't a good man." I realized there were a lot of things Caden didn't know about me, and a lot of things I didn't know about him; yet, I trusted him enough to come to him for help. His expression was sober, eyes drawn together in confusion. I could tell he wanted to ask me more, but he was kind enough not to pry. I turned away from him, staring at my aunt's bedroom door.

"I told her the truth, about what I am. I thought she had a right to know."

He nodded.

"My mom didn't think so, though," I said, pulling the note from my pocket and handing it to him. He narrowed his eyes as he unfolded it and began to read. When he finished, he handed it back.

"Your mom wasn't sure you'd change. She wanted to keep this life hidden from you just in case. I don't blame her. Our way of life is tough. Only the strong survive. We may be human, but we are also wolf, and our laws and hierarchy can sometimes seem cruel. She wanted to give you the best chance at a normal life."

I shook my head. "I never had a normal life."

Aunt Claire came out of the shower shortly after. Caden asked if we were hungry. I said yes, but Aunt Claire wanted to call it night. She seemed far away, like she was in a daze. I didn't blame her. She probably had a lot on her mind. If she were in her right mind, I imagined she wouldn't be leaving me alone with some strange boy she just met. I hated leaving her alone too. I knew she was hurting and would probably spend the night crying. She had loved Rob at one point, and although she had wanted to leave him for a long time, she never wanted him dead. I knew it was best to leave her be.

I was, at least, happy for the chance to talk with

Caden more. We made our way to the kitchen. Caden began making dinner, mostly involving various meats. It didn't take long since the meat didn't need to be cooked all the way, anyway. He set our plates down and paused. He shot a finger in the air and went rummaging through some cabinets.

"I know what will go perfectly with this meal." He pulled out a bottle of wine and two wineglasses.

I furrowed my brow. "I'm not even eighteen, much less twenty-one."

He shrugged. "I also live out in the middle of nowhere, where the rules hardly apply. I'm sure no one would blame you for having one glass of wine. You've had a really rough day."

I laughed. "I've had a rough life."

He popped open the cork and set the glasses down.

"All the more reason!" he exclaimed. He poured the dark-red content into the glasses.

"Besides, a glass of red wine a day has been proven to have excellent health benefits."

I smiled, raising my glass. "Well, then, here's to good health."

He grinned back, taking his glass and clinking it with mine. "To good health," he replied, and we took a sip.

I nearly spat the dark liquid out of my mouth. I realized very quickly that I hated the taste of wine, but the effects were quite enjoyable. I'd never had alcohol before, much less been drunk, but I could see the appeal. I started to feel light and bubbly. Everything would be okay if I just kept laughing and having a good time. By my third glass, I was feeling great.

After dinner, Caden insisted that crepes were the best dessert for the occasion. I'd never seen anyone make a crepe. I couldn't stop laughing at him trying to flip the batter with just the pan. He burned nearly half of them.

He watched me with amusement while he cooked.

"Wow, Haze, you're kind of a lightweight." He chuckled as I laughed myself to tears.

I put my hands over my mouth, trying to suppress my laughter. "Is it that noticeable?"

"Oh yeah." He laughed.

My cheeks flamed. "I've never been drunk before."

He looked over his shoulder at me. "Never?"

I shook my head. "Nope."

"Well, then, it is an honor to be the first person you ever get drunk with, Hazel Lowell." He gave a small bow. I laughed again.

As it turned out, Caden was right, the crepes were amazing. They paired nicely with vanilla ice cream and caramel syrup. I was in sugar heaven.

After we finished, we sprawled out on the floor of the living room. Caden was pretty drunk by that point too. We laughed at each other's jokes and asked questions about our normal everyday life. It was something I hadn't realized I'd been craving until now. Just an easygoing conversation. I rarely had them with anyone but Molly.

I stared up at the ceiling, beams crisscrossing through one another.

"I meant to ask, why'd you rebuild this place so big? Why not build a small cottage for yourself?"

He looked around, as if just realizing this place was too big for just himself. He released a drawn-out sigh.

"I was still heavy with grief over the death of my family when I started rebuilding and at the time, I couldn't imagine building it any differently than the way my father had wanted it." He paused. "And over time, I think a small part of me hoped I'd heal enough someday to be a part of a pack again. Not as their alpha, the way my father had wanted, I'm too broken for that, but maybe as a member…someday."

I watched him for a long moment. A sad expression lined his face. He didn't look back at me, just continued to stare at the ceiling.

"Hey," I said, trying to get his attention.

He finally looked at me. His eyes were red.

"I think you'd make a great alpha," I said softly, and I meant it.

He gave me a sad smile. "So would you."

I doubt that, I thought. *I just found out about this world. I'd make a terrible alpha.*

I tried to find a lighter subject to talk about. I couldn't stand seeing Caden sad.

"So what's with the lip piercings? What made you get them?"

Caden puckered his lips and gazed down, trying to look at his piercings. It made his eyes cross. We both laughed.

"In all honesty, I can't really explain why I got them. I saw someone else who had them and thought they looked cool, and for some reason…they make me feel more human."

I was about to ask him what he meant, but he changed the subject quickly.

"So, you love to read, yeah? What's your favorite book?"

I scrunched my nose, giving him a sideways push. "Everyone always asks that, but for me, it's too hard to have just one favorite book. I love so many."

He laughed. "Okay, then what's your favorite genre?"

I thought for a moment. It was getting hard to

concentrate. "I like fiction the most, I think. I like knowing there are infinite possibilities for stories. It's fun to imagine and immerse yourself in different worlds so unlike your own."

Caden nodded. "I know what you mean," he said. "It's kind of like seeing other people's paintings. I like trying to imagine the world they were trying to create. The feelings they were trying to make you feel. I wanted to make paintings like that."

I beamed. "That's a great idea. Maybe I'll try and be a writer someday. Create my own worlds too."

He held up both hands, gazing at them, fingers spread wide. I did the same, laughing at our silliness.

"I have a confession to make." He was still smiling.

"Yeah?"

He nodded. "The first time I ever saw you wasn't in the clearing by the lake."

I glanced over at him, but he was still staring at our hands held up in the air. I felt Caden's left hand grasp my right and we both stared at our hands intertwined together for a moment. That electric pulse I felt every time we touched pounded through my hand. The tension grew between us as we rested our hands down, still intertwined.

Caden spoke casually, as if he hadn't even noticed.

"The first time I ever saw you was in town. I didn't know who you were at the time, not until much later, but you were about ten or eleven and I was about fifteen or sixteen. It was the Christmas holiday and everyone was out and about shopping for presents. I remember glancing at you from across the street and you had your nose stuck in a book. It was the strangest thing I had ever seen."

I giggled, because that sounded exactly like something I would do. I learned at a very early age that I had a love for reading and it was my preferred method of distraction and entertainment.

"And you just kept walking with your aunt, slipping and sliding in the snow, but you never took your eyes off that book. I just kept thinking, 'What a really weird little girl. While other kids were hopping, skipping, and pulling around their parents, pointing and begging for things they wanted for Christmas, she's just reading, in her own little world.' Then you stopped, right in front of this antique jewelry store, like you'd done it a hundred times, and you looked up and stared at something in the display window.

"When you finally walked away, I was so curious to see what made you look up from that book when nothing else would. I ran across the street and peeked in the window and saw a necklace with a little gold wolf charm. It stood tall, head back, howling at the moon. I couldn't believe it. I thought it had to be a sign. You were only human then. I didn't know you'd someday be a shifter.

"I thought of you often after that. I hoped someday, when you were older of course, that I'd see you again and maybe capture your attention the same way that necklace had." He winked at me playfully.

I was surprised. The fact that Caden had been thinking of me long before I knew him sent a warmth of excitement and satisfaction through me. No one ever really noticed me, let alone thought of me for as long as Caden had.

I remembered that day too. The snow was thick that year and I found Christmas shopping with Aunt Claire to be dull, so I brought a book to help ease the boredom.

"I wanted that necklace for a long time. My mom

had given me a stuffed wolf before she died, and it reminded me so much of her. Every time I walked by, I pictured myself wearing it. I even asked the store owner how much it was, but he just told me it was much too expensive for a little girl like me. I was so upset. I told Aunt Claire how much I wanted it and when Christmas came, she admitted she'd wanted to get it for me. It was the first time I had ever asked for anything other than books. But when she went to buy it, the store owner said he'd already sold it to someone else."

I looked at Caden. He was staring at me, as if he were longing. It made my heart beat faster and my cheeks heat. I hadn't realized how close we were till now…and his eyes. How had I ever thought that his eyes were only two different colors? Up close, I realized they each had flecks of the other colors inside one another, a ring of gold set around the irises. They were the most beautiful eyes I had ever seen.

He glanced down at my lips and I found myself drawn to his. I wondered what the cold metal of those rings would feel like, the softness of his lips. I wanted to find out. We were leaning in, our breaths ragged. I could hear my heartbeat in my ears and feel my pulse in my throat. His breath smelled like wine. His body next to mine was comforting, natural. I closed my eyes. We were so close, our lips nearly touching. I was anticipating the kiss when suddenly I felt Caden pull back.

I opened my eyes. Doubt began to creep in my mind as I realized what had happened. The tension between us was immediately broken.

I stood up, embarrassed.

He sat up. "I'm sorry. It's not that I didn't want to, it's just…you probably don't even…and you aren't even eighteen yet. I just, I didn't want to…"

He wasn't making any sense. Was he saying I was too young for him?

The need to flee the room was growing within me. He shook his head, as if trying to clear his thoughts. When he looked up at me, our eyes locked. I must have looked like a deer in headlights, my face spelling fear and embarrassment, because Caden's face showed what looked like regret.

"Let's call it a night, yeah? I think we've had a bit too much to drink." he said, letting out a breathless, embarrassed laugh as he looked down at the floor.

I only nodded, then we headed up the stairs. I was still tense when we reached our separate doors. I realized his bedroom was right across from mine.

He turned to me and gave me a shy smile. I looked down, not smiling back.

He suddenly lifted my chin to meet his gaze. There was something in his eyes now, something wild and unchained. Feral. It was so unlike the shy smile I'd witnessed two seconds ago. It made me feel like a trapped animal about to be devoured by a predator. It should have scared me, but instead, it was exciting. My thighs clenched as I let my breath out through my nose. I was still feeling the sting of his rejection and yet I still wanted him, badly.

"I'm sorry, Hazel," he whispered. "I didn't mean to hurt your feelings. I wanted to, God, I wanted to, but I don't want to rush anything. I think it's important that we don't. You still have a lot to learn about my world, and right now, it would feel like I'm taking advantage."

I wanted to whimper like a puppy. This want I had inside me was something I couldn't explain, but it made the wolf in me furious. She wanted him, too, and she was pissed that she couldn't have him.

He pulled away, the primal look in his eyes was gone.

"Good night, Hazel. See you tomorrow." He went to open his bedroom door.

I was about to tell him good night when I suddenly remembered something. Despite my hurt and confusion, I felt it was important that I asked him.

"Caden, wait."

He paused, glancing over his shoulder.

"Why didn't you tell me it was hard for shifters to keep control of their wolf half?"

He turned toward me and looked me in the eye. "I thought you knew. Is it not hard for you?"

I shook my head. Was that a hint of jealousy in Caden's eyes? I realized then just how hard it must be to keep control.

"Is it only when a shifter is a wolf or is it all the time?"

His expression looked pained. "It's…only as a wolf."

"Does it hurt?"

"Not in a physical sense, no. It's just tiring, draining. You have to constantly be in check with your thoughts and emotions. The need to let instincts take over is hard. It's enticing, like a drug. We as humans have complex minds and emotions, but as a wolf, there is none of that. You just simply are. You don't care why something is, just that it is."

His gaze became distant.

"We have to be careful, or we can suddenly find ourselves unable to remember the things that made us human. Over time, we won't recall how to shift back and then soon after, we'll forget we were ever human at all. The amount of time someone has before they lose themselves to their instincts is different for every shifter."

"That's…really sad," I said. I imagined it was kind of like dying.

Caden's stare was intense, his expression one of raw pain.

"Is it?" he asked calmly. "That simplicity might be freeing to some. Ignorance is bliss, Hazel. You can't miss something you can't remember."

I thought of the death of his family. How much he must miss them. How lonely he must feel. I felt something similar with my parents, but I missed my parents in a detached sort of way. I lost them before I had any memory of them. The pain I felt in their absence was the pain of never knowing them, not the pain of knowing them and then losing them. That kind of pain, I imagined, was far worse.

I could see how he might want to lose himself to his wolf.

I wondered if our human halves were ever fully gone or just dormant. The wolf was still us, just a different part, so did that mean our souls were still there, even if our humanity wasn't?

I hadn't realized I was crying till Caden brushed a tear from my cheek. He let his hand linger there, his thumb brushing my cheek, back and forth.

"You have no idea how badly I want to kiss you right now."

And just like that, the hunger was back. He leaned in and I felt myself grip the front of his shirt, to pull him forward or push him back, I wasn't sure. For the second time that night, I thought I would finally feel his lips on mine, but instead, he kissed my cheek. His lips lingered, the rings cold on my skin. I had to hold back a growl of frustration.

He brought his lips to my ear and whispered good night.

When he pulled back, he gave me a sexy, heart-breaking smile.

He stepped into his room, closing the door.

"Good night, Caden," I whispered back. I touched the tips of my fingers to my cheek. The sensation of his lips still there. I felt defeated and a little sad, for me and for Caden. What kind of complicated mess had I gotten myself into?

Aunt Claire's voice drifted from downstairs, along with the smell of breakfast, and for a split second I thought I was at home, in my room, in my own bed. I opened my eyes and the memories of yesterday caught up to me. Surprisingly, I didn't have a hangover after being drunk for the first time, but I guessed that was just luck because I'd had enough to warrant one. Though still groggy, I had a lot on my mind. I got up to take a shower.

As I stepped into the bathroom, I noticed it had more amenities than last time. There was a toothbrush and toothpaste in the holder by the sink, and the shower now had shampoo, conditioner, and body wash. *Caden.* I smiled.

After washing my hair and body, I took a moment to just stand under the showerhead and enjoy the warmth. I let myself think about Caden and the embarrassments of last night. I had been stupid and drunk, drooling over him like some lovesick teenager. I'd never let myself act like that with anyone.

But Caden was different.

We'd both lost people we loved and we'd both had to learn to deal with it in our own ways. He was sweet, artistic, funny, and a genuinely good person at heart. He fascinated me, not just with his unique appearance but because there was also something underneath it all. A sadness, sure, but something else too. Something dark and untamed. Like an animal in a cage. It should have scared me, but in truth, I was drawn to it. It spurred me. The wolf in me hungered for it.

And there was that instinctive part of me that felt like I'd always known him. That he had always just been there. It was there the moment I'd met him, and I just couldn't explain it. I'd never felt such familiarity with anyone so quickly.

There was an answer buried deep within me, but I wasn't sure if I was ready to ask the question.

All I knew was in the short time I'd known Caden, I'd developed feelings for him, and it scared me. I'd never been in a real relationship before, never kissed a guy, never had sex. I wanted all these things of course, but I'd watched my aunt have enough heartbreaks to know it was better to have a guarded heart than to open up and watch it be broken.

I'd almost let my guard down last night. No, not almost, my walls had been completely obliterated. I should have been the one who pulled back. I should have been the one to suggest we take it slow, but it was Caden who'd done those things. Caden had all the control and I couldn't let that happen again.

I steeled myself. It was stupid to be thinking about relationships and vulnerability. Stopping Ross was the most important thing right now. Nothing else mattered. I wouldn't let Caden distract me from the real goal here.

I stepped out of the shower, dried off, and got dressed. I brushed my hair and teeth quickly, then headed downstairs. I heard Aunt Claire laughing. As I entered the kitchen, she and Caden were dancing to some pop song I'd never heard before. I took in the scene before me with surprise. My aunt looked younger and happier than I'd seen her in a long time. She was wearing shorts and a tank top, something I rarely saw her wear.

Watching them laugh and dance together, I was suddenly reminded of one of my aunt's ex-husbands. The one who had been ten years younger than her. I felt a bite of jealousy looking at them, but I quickly pushed it away. That was years ago, and Aunt Claire was nearly twice Caden's age. Not to mention my aunt was a different person now. She was wiser, older, and hardened by the mistakes she'd made.

If there was any trace of jealousy left, it was blown away when the two of them turned and saw me, both smiling, both with looks of adoration and affection toward me in their eyes. I smiled back, feeling nothing but the same. Caden motioned for me to join them, then the three of us danced around the kitchen and cooked breakfast. I couldn't remember a time we had ever been this carefree and happy back home.

We sat and laughed and talked. I figured there would be some awkwardness between us after last night but there wasn't. Caden told us stories of growing up as a shifter and Crescent Peak. I asked him if he stayed in touch with some of his father's former pack. He claimed to still keep in contact with the younger kids living there. Normally when a shifter had their first shift, they were able to choose whether to stay with their parents' pack or join another.

"At what age does a shifter have their first shift?" Aunt Claire asked. She was taking all this information in stride.

She was different today, like she'd woken up and decided not to take life for granted. She was accepting things for what they were and moving forward. I liked this Aunt Claire. I hoped wherever she went after this, she stayed this way. I knew she had a long road of healing ahead of her, but seeing her like this gave me hope that she could make it through.

"Usually around puberty, thirteen or fourteen, but there are rare cases where kids have shifted later or earlier."

They both glanced in my direction. I had a hot cup of coffee perched on my lips, mid-sip.

He nodded in my direction "You probably shifted later because you're half shifter."

"When did you first shift?" I asked over my mug. I pictured Caden as a little pup and it amused me greatly.

Caden was clearing our plates and putting them in the sink, his back to us.

"I'm a rare case."

I raised my eyebrows. "Early or late?"

"Early," he said curtly. That was apparently a sore subject. I wasn't sure why, but I also didn't want to pry, so I changed the topic.

"Didn't Crescent Peak use to be a camp?" I directed my question to Aunt Claire.

"It was. Your mother and I visited one summer. That's actually where your parents met. They were so young." She looked up at me. "Not much older than you are now." She smiled, reminiscing.

"He and his friend were such troublemakers, with their leather jackets, slicked back hair, and those silly earrings." She laughed. "But they were both so handsome. The four of us spent that whole summer together. We were inseparable, even after camp."

She seemed to become lost in her memories. When she came to, she just shrugged. "But summers always end, I guess." She stared down at her coffee, still half smiling to herself.

I had a sneaky suspicion my dad's friend meant something to her.

"What happened to him? Dad's friend from camp, I mean?"

She shrugged. "I don't really know, your father said he moved back to Canada. He had only been down for the summer."

I looked at Caden. We were both thinking the same thing. Of course his friend had been a shifter too. It made sense. I wondered where he was now. At the same moment the thought popped into my head, my aunt whispered it into her coffee.

I CALLED MOLLY AFTER BREAKFAST. SHE ANSWERED ON the first ring. "Heeelllooo?"

"Hey, Molly, it's me."

She sounded off, probably from all the medicine she was still on.

"Helloooo, me. Whatttt's uuup?" She yawned.

"Listen I have something important to tell you, are you listening?" I heard sheets rustle.

"Oookay. You have my *undivived*_attention."

She tried several more times to say "undivided."

I sighed. I needed Molly to take me seriously. I couldn't have her laughing this off in her drug-induced state. So I did something I'd never done before. I yelled at her.

"MOLLY! Please. Something has happened and I need you to listen, *okay*?"

That got her attention.

"What's wrong? What happened?"

I told her about last night, giving her the same story we'd told the cops. It still pained me to lie to her, but I needed to protect her, and this was the only way, or so I told myself. As I recounted the events, I heard her gasps and continuous repeats of "oh my God." I knew she was scared, and I needed to use that to my advantage, in order to protect her.

"Rob's dead? Like, really dead?"

"Yes," I replied.

My story seemed to have sobered her up.

"My God, Hazel. I know he was a horrible person, but dead? That's not something I'd ever wish on anyone."

I could think of one person.

"I know. It's a rough time for us right now—"

"Where are you guys staying? Is Aunt Claire okay?"

I glanced over at her sitting at the kitchen island, looking at something on her laptop.

"We're fine. We're staying with a friend. Listen, I know this is going to sound crazy, but whatever attacked Aunt Claire is dangerous. It might be the same thing that attacked you. It's big and smart. It might try to break into your house the same way it did mine, so you need to board up all the windows and sliding glass doors, and don't answer the front door for anyone unless you know them, okay?"

She said nothing for a while.

"Molly?"

"Hazel, what is going on? You're really freaking me out. If this is a joke, it isn't funny."

My heart ached for my friend. "I'm not being funny, Molly. Please just trust me."

There was another long pause.

Finally she said, "Okay, okay. I'll talk to my parents. I can't promise they'll listen, though."

I breathed a sigh of relief. "Thank you, Molly. I have to go now, but I'll call you again soon, okay? Stay safe, you and your family both."

We said our goodbyes and hung up. Just as I put my phone down, Caden called from the top of the stairs.

"Hey, you busy? I want to show you something."

I followed him into his art room. He walked over to the easel by the window, its back to me. He gestured to me. I went to see what it was and gasped. It was the painting of me that Caden had been working on. I had forgotten all about it.

The girl in the painting was me, but a version of myself I had never seen before. For one, she was far more beautiful than I could ever be. Her hazel eyes stared back at me with an intensity and air of confidence I never possessed. The face of my wolf form was faded into the background behind me, so eerily alike. We blended together, meeting in the middle so we shared the same eyes.

I was blown away, truly speechless. My cheeks flamed. No one had ever made me feel as beautiful as Caden did in that moment. I was reminded of his words about looking into the minds of painters, and I realized that this was how Caden saw me. He probably had no clue the effect his painting had on me. To him this piece was just a truth brought to life through his eyes.

"Caden," I said on a breath. "This is amazing. There are no words."

His smile was so big, you'd have thought nothing else in the world brought him as much pleasure as hearing me praise his work.

He shrugged, still smiling. "I think you are far prettier than this painting, but I suppose it's a rather close resemblance."

"Shut up!" I scoffed, punching him on the arm playfully. He peered up at me, his gaze softening. We stared at each other for a moment.

"It's true," he whispered. "You're beautiful, Hazel."

If my cheeks were pink before, they were blazing red now. I'd never been able to handle compliments well and a guy had never called me beautiful before, especially not one as handsome as Caden. I quickly bent down and kissed his cheek to show him just how much I appreciated it. When I pulled away, we both stood there, seemingly shocked.

"Thank you, Caden. This is the nicest thing anyone has ever done for me," I finally said.

He smiled. "The pleasure was all mine."

I headed back down to the living room, my face still heated from Caden's flattering painting. His feelings for me had never been so clear. My heart felt a little lighter. When Aunt Claire saw me, she raised her eyebrows at me and smirked. I chose to ignore her knowing look, and she chose not to ask yet.

CADEN HAD AGREED TO TAKE US TO CRESCENT PEAK. I'D tried to convince Aunt Claire to go to Florida like she'd wanted to, but she wouldn't have it. I was at a loss. She was still my aunt and still an authority figure in my eyes, and I knew she'd never leave without me. I would have to lie to her or hurt her somehow. If it would make her leave me behind, if it would make her safe, I could do it. I closed my eyes for a moment, leaning my head against the car window and breathing deeply. I wasn't quite ready to do that to her just yet, though. She'd already endured so much. So for now, she stayed, at least till I got the answers I needed at Crescent Peak.

I sat in the passenger seat, with Aunt Claire in the back. I was keenly aware of how close Caden's hand was to my leg while it rested on the gear shift. At one point, I felt it brush against me as he pretended to fiddle with an air vent. When he moved it back, he'd positioned his hand so that his pinkie rested on top of my leg. I gave him a side-glance. He did the same, smiling. I turned my head to look out the window so he wouldn't see me smirk. I glanced behind at Aunt Claire to see if she'd noticed anything. Luckily, she was too busy staring out the window.

After a forty-minute drive, we finally reached a sign reading WELCOME TO CRESCENT PEAK. I stared in awe as we drove past the gate. It was odd seeing these cabins turned into homes. Like seeing a hotel turned into an apartment complex. It still had that coming-and-going air about it, even though people lived here permanently.

They were their own self-sustaining community. There were about forty or so cabins, some with small picket fences, gardens, and cars parked in front. Each had a unique touch, an extension of the person or people living inside. Some of the larger ones looked like they'd been turned into stores and shops. As Caden drove, he pointed things out to us.

"Over there is the mess hall. It's usually where the alphas have their meetings. That's Tim's Bait Shop.

We're fairly close to Colonial River, and that building next to it is the cafeteria. There are several packs living here, so sometimes they need a large space to eat on big holidays or events."

I took note of the way he said "they" and not "us" or "we." A small pang of pity for Caden and his solitude settled within me. I realized it must be hard not having a pack when it was in your very nature to be a part of a group, a family. I wondered why he hadn't tried to make a home here and become part of a new pack, but I had a feeling that was a sore subject and best left alone for now.

Caden pointed over to a large building with a white tarp for a roof. Next to it was a small field with a tiny red barn.

"Over there is the greenhouse. Crescent Peak grows all their own vegetables and even some fruit."

I glanced at Aunt Claire. She'd perked up at the word "greenhouse." Growing flowers was her passion, but I knew she'd always wanted to try growing vegetables and fruits.

Caden continued. "And next to that is the barn. They pretty much raise everything. Cows, chickens, pigs, a few horses, and goats. Everything here is to make things easier for shifters, so they don't have to rely so much on humans and to have more time to just be themselves. For the few things they can't grow or make themselves, there are a handful of volunteers who go into town every so often to get the rest. I usually make a lot of those trips. I also help keep up with the greenhouse and farm. In exchange, they give me food and supplies I need."

We finally arrived at what appeared to be a lodge similar to the one that Caden had, if not slightly larger.

"We call this the 'Orphanage,'" he said, pulling up and parking the car.

I looked at him, confused. He laughed.

"It's not actually an orphanage. They call it that because the entire pack is made up of the youngest shifters to date. Most packs living here are housed with individual families. Young shifters who choose another pack usually get put with an adult or another family until they are old enough, but since these kids and teens had neither, Lucas stepped up and became not only their alpha, but also their sole guardian. He's kind of like their father figure. He was a father figure to me, too, at one point."

"What happened?"

He shook his head. "A story for another time."

We got out of the car and walked up the front steps. Caden knocked. We could hear a lot of commotion inside and someone yelling to get the door. A few minutes later a little girl answered. She wore pink leggings, a flowery skirt, a purple top, and a glittery jean jacket. Obviously this girl had dressed herself. She had beautiful porcelain skin, wide violet eyes, and exceedingly long platinum-blond hair, french braided into two separate pigtails. She was quite possibly the cutest little girl I had ever seen. She seemed to be maybe twelve or thirteen but sounded much younger when she squealed "Caden!" excitedly and ran, jumping into his arms.

He grunted but smiled widely.

"Hello, Sophie." He put her down gently. "Is Lue home?"

She smiled brightly. "Yes! He's upstairs in his study. He's gonna be so happy to see you."

She grabbed his hand, and we followed her inside as she led us into a spacious living room where two shirtless boys in basketball shorts were sitting on a large couch playing a video game together. They were identical: tan, chocolate-brown eyes, and brown hair. Except one had long, shoulder-length hair while the other had a buzz cut. They were arguing about the game they were playing, not paying any attention to us.

"I'll go up ahead and then you come up on my left," said the long-haired twin.

"NO! There's a whole horde of them up on our left, we should go right!"

The short-haired twin shot up from the couch and they both started screaming dramatically as the game suddenly got harder. The long-haired boy was bouncing up and down on the couch. Both were fervently mashing buttons on their controllers. I stifled a laugh. Sophie rolled her eyes at them. They looked to be about the same age as Sophie. She finally looked at me and then Aunt Claire. She pointed at her.

"She smells human."

A boy, roughly sixteen or so came up behind Sophie and gave her a light smack behind her head.

"Ow, Jake! What was that for?" she cried out.

He popped open a soda in his hand and smirked. "You aren't supposed to say things like that, Sophie."

She pointed at the can, glaring at him.

"And you aren't supposed to have soda. Lue says it's bad for you."

Jake only shrugged, taking a sip of his drink.

I took a good look at him. I thought Caden was a bit exotic with his lip piercings, but he had nothing on Jake. His face was covered in piercings. He had a lip ring, a nose ring, an eyebrow ring, and at least three ear piercings on each ear. He was pale, with electric-blue eyes that were a little intimidating to stare at for too long. His outfit was a cross between punk rock and skater kid: all black, ripped everything. He was like those teens I'd see at school who smoked pot behind the lunchroom building and hissed at anyone who came near them, but Jake smiled at each of us.

"Hey, Caden, long time no see, buddy." Caden did not smile back.

Jake glanced at each of us, lingering a little too long on me. He held out his hand. "I'm Jacob."

I took it firmly. "Hazel."

He nodded, still holding on to my hand, and stared intently with a smirk. Aunt Claire cut in.

"Hi, I'm Claire."

She held her hand out, leaving Jacob no choice but to let go of mine and take hers. I breathed a sigh of relief and looked at her knowingly. She winked at me. I turned to Caden. He was giving warning glares at Jake, who seemed to completely ignore him.

As Sophie ran upstairs to get Lucas, a dark-skinned guy with dreads came out of the kitchen, smiling broadly. He looked to be about Caden's age. Caden smiled back. They walked up to each other and embraced, patting each other on the back and then holding the other at arm's length.

"Good to see you, man."

Caden nodded in agreement. "You, too, Izzy."

They whispered to each other for a moment, the stranger looking concerned. I guessed them to be old friends. Caden looked at me and they both smiled. I heated, realizing they were talking about me. I wondered what he was saying. They walked over and Caden introduced us. "Hazel, Claire, this is Isaac."

Isaac had a warm smile and light-brown eyes.

"It's a pleasure to meet you," he said, in a deep voice.

He gave me a kiss on the hand, not breaking eye contact, and did the same to Aunt Claire. She laughed.

I liked Isaac. There was a mature, respectful nature about him. I wanted to know more about Caden and Isaac's relationship. I was about to ask when Aunt Claire suddenly let out a small gasp. I looked at her worryingly. She had her hand over her mouth and was staring at the upstairs balcony. I glanced up to see what had made her gasp and found that it was not a what, but a who.

A handsome middle-aged man stood at the top of the stairs. He was broad-shouldered and burly looking with a muscular build and thick, hairy arms. His face was covered with a short salt-and-pepper beard. His flannel T-shirt and jeans made him look like a hiker or a lumberjack. His moss green eyes stared back at Aunt Claire, equally surprised.

"Lucas?" she whispered.

He walked down the stairs still staring at my aunt as if she were a dream or a figment of his imagination.

"Claire? Wow. It's…it's been a long time." He smiled with a look of tender affection aimed at her.

I stood confused. "You know him?"

Her eyes darted to me with an almost panicked expression on her face. "I…yes…" she stammered.

"This is Lucas, your father's friend from the camp that used to be here." She paused, breathless, never taking her eyes off him. "That was so long ago."

He smiled at her. "You look amazing as ever, Claire, simply breathtaking."

Aunt Claire stood speechless, her cheeks turning a bright pink. Everyone in the room, including the twins on the couch, were silent and staring. I half expected Aunt Claire and Lucas to embrace, but instead, she walked right up to him and slapped him across the face.

Everyone gasped. She glanced around, embarrassment bringing her back to her senses. She turned and walked right out of the house.

The twins seemed ready to burst into a fit of laughter, Sofia looked embarrassed, and everyone else just stood shocked and confused. I was about to follow Aunt Claire outside, but Caden gently grabbed my wrist and shook his head.

"Maybe it's best to leave her alone." He was addressing both me and Lucas.

We both nodded. Lucas looked at me for the first time and gestured for me to follow him upstairs. My eyes met Caden's and he nodded. "I'll wait down here, keep an eye on your aunt."

I agreed, even though I wished he'd come with me. I was nervous as I walked up the stairs. When we entered his study, I took in the room. It smelled like old books and wood stain. There was an old oak desk surrounded by several overflowing bookshelves. So much so that some books had been stacked on the floor and desk. The only thing electrical in the room was a small laptop sitting on top of the large desk.

I turned to face Lucas and stiffened in shock as he walked over and gave me a big hug. There was nothing sexual about it, only affection, almost fatherly. He smelled like tree sap and spearmint gum. I was taken aback. I'd never been hugged by a stranger before and the PTSD from years of living with Rob left me nearly paralyzed with fear. He finally held me at arm's length and looked me up and down, a proud smile on his face.

"Look at you. You look so much like your father."

I gave him an awkward smile.

He hugged me again, but this time I was prepared and the choking feeling subsided.

"I'm sorry," he said. "You don't know me, but I feel like I know you. I never thought I'd ever get to meet my goddaughter."

I pulled back, speaking to him for the first time. "Goddaughter?"

He nodded, eyes watering. "Your father was my best friend, practically my brother. When he had his first shift, he joined our pack and lived with my family."

I was shocked. Here was a man who truly knew my father. No one else had been able to tell me much about him. Everyone in town only knew my mother, who had grown up there. My father, to them, was a stranger. Even Aunt Claire couldn't give me much. She told me he'd been a carpenter and that he was a good man who loved my mother more than anything, but I didn't know who he was as a person. What were his hobbies? His favorite food? What did he like? What did he hate? Was he funny or serious? These were a few of the millions of questions that had plagued me my whole life…and here was a man who could give me those answers.

I was so happy over this realization that I did something I'd probably never do in any other situation, I hugged him back. He released a throaty laugh at my enthusiastic hug and ruffled my hair. It was such a fatherly gesture I almost cried.

We talked for a while, mostly about my father. I could finally start to paint a picture of the man he was. He was confident, smart, and a natural-born leader destined to be an alpha from the start. He loved the outdoors and building things with his own hands. He was funny, kind, and sometimes even gentle, despite his burly nature. He could be bigheaded, stubborn, and overconfident, but he never cared what people thought of him.

Lucas also told me about how my parents had met

and how he, like my aunt, hadn't approved of their relationship.

"Your mother and father hit it off immediately. They were like magnets being pulled together, but your aunt and I, we fought like cats and dogs. We argued over everything, the main argument being your mom and dad's relationship. Claire didn't think your father was good enough for her, and I just didn't want to see your father get hung up on a human, but it became clear the longer the summer went on that your aunt and I were getting left behind. I guess we bonded over that. Before I knew it, we even became friends, and then I realized I was falling in love with her. It was like getting hit by a car, this love, it was so sudden and...painful."

He looked down at his desk and sighed. "I knew I'd have to go back to Canada. My father expected me to take over as alpha someday. I feared him, but that wasn't the only thing I was afraid of. I wasn't brave enough to face my feelings for your aunt. Not in the way your father was with your mom. I feared what Claire would think of me if she found out what I was, and even worse, I was scared of the disdain and hatred I would receive from other shifters if they, too, found out about our relationship. I thought it would just be easier to leave and let her forget me...but I never forgot her. I thought of her every day. I envied your mother and father's relationship and when he died..." He released a shaky breath. "I should have been here."

He paused a moment, then continued. "I came back for the funeral, but I didn't tell Claire. I was too ashamed of what I had done to her. When I left, she was convinced it was the distance that was keeping us apart. She called, she wrote, she emailed, but I never responded. I didn't have the heart to break it off with her the right way. Your mother sought me out, though. We comforted each other and she told me something she hadn't told anyone, not even her own sister. She told me she was dying."

I felt my heart constrict. I knew this. In her letter she told me she knew she was dying, but it still pained me to hear it.

"She made me promise to look out for you, but from a distance. She wanted you to have a normal human childhood, but she also wanted someone you could come to if you ever took after your father. I promised her I would stay. I owed her that much."

He let out a long sigh.

"So, I came here, to Crescent Peak. By now it had long since been abandoned, so I decided to turn it into a community for the shifters nearby. A haven like the one I grew up in."

That shocked me. "You made all of this?"

"Well, yes, but don't get it twisted. I may be the founder, but it took an entire community to make this place a home. They are the ones who deserve the credit."

"That's still pretty amazing."

He smiled but it quickly faded. "Caden told me what happened to you, Hazel, why you're here. I'm so sorry about your friend and your uncle."

My whole demeanor changed with the mention of Rob.

"My friend is recovering, and as for my uncle, well, he wasn't exactly someone to be missed," I said coolly.

Lucas narrowed his eyes at my sudden change in attitude, but he didn't press further. I was glad. I felt Aunt Claire should be the one to tell him. They were the ones with the history, after all.

I was silent for a moment. "I'm so happy I got to meet you, Lucas—"

"You can call me Lue, everyone else here does." He smiled.

I gave a small nod. "Lue. There were so many things about my father I'd always wished to know, answers no one could give me, but there is another reason I came here today."

He nodded, waiting for me to continue.

"This past week has been, well, insane."

"I know this all must be strange for you, but I can help you adjust—"

I held up my hand, asking him to let me finish. "I appreciate that, Lucas, and I graciously accept, but where were you before now? Why didn't you seek me out? I'm sure Caden must have told you about me. I know he's told me about you. When he realized I would shift soon, he said that I should seek you out if I wanted answers. If the circumstances were different, it would have been *you* helping me with my first shift, helping me through that near-death sickness, but you weren't. I have to know, did you send Caden to that lake the day we met? Has Caden been watching me because you asked him to?"

Lucas began to laugh. Small chuckles at first, but then they gradually grew to big booming laughs. I crossed my arms over my chest, scowling. When he finally calmed down, he spoke.

"I'm sorry for laughing. I just find it funny that you'd think Caden would do anything I tell him to. Caden doesn't take orders, he accepts the advice given and then does whatever the hell he wants. In fact, I told him countless times to stay away from you and that it was your mother's wish that you grow up a normal human girl, but I guess when he sensed the change in you, he didn't see the need to stay away. I've known Caden a long time and that boy has been infatuated with you since the first time he ever saw you."

I felt my heart flutter. So it wasn't a coincidence that Caden and I ran into each other that day at the lake. He'd been waiting for me. I should be mad at him for lying but instead I found it all a bit endearing. If it had been any other guy, I may have been angry, or even slightly creeped out by such a stalkeresque gesture, but this was Caden, and if I noticed anything about my judgment and morals toward him, it was that they were dipped in rose-colored paint.

There was still this constant struggle going on in my head when it came to him. The struggle between the instincts I'd always lived by—to keep everyone at a distance and to never trust—and this new instinct that, if I wasn't paying attention, automatically relaxed when he was around. Caden was as familiar to me as someone I'd grown up with my whole life and it sometimes scared me. I should not feel this way about someone I'd only known for about a week.

Lucas was smirking at me, like he knew something I didn't, but then he continued. "Anyway, as for not coming to you sooner, Caden also doesn't speak to me much these days. By the time he thought to tell me anything, you'd already had your first shift. I asked Caden if he could bring you to me discreetly, so as not to involve your aunt, but then, everything happened and your aunt is now aware, so I guess it was a moot point. I wish things hadn't gone down the way they did, though, Hazel. I'm sorry. It seems I failed your parents again in this regard."

His story made sense and his apology sincere.

I wanted to ask him more about Caden, but it could wait.

"You said there was another reason for coming here?" he asked.

I nodded. "I want Ross to pay for what he's done. I was hoping you could help me. Caden has reason to believe that Ross is responsible for his family's death and my father's. On top of that, he's killed two people that I know of and hurt someone close to me. He has to be stopped."

Lucas was leaning forward, running both hands through his hair.

"Caden has suspected Ross for a long time, but there isn't enough proof to make him guilty."

He got up and walked over to a bookshelf, then pulled out an old photo album. He opened it and after turning a few pages, set the open book in front of me.

"At Crescent Peak we have a select group of alphas we call the 'Alpha Council.' They keep the peace here and the packs united. They make the rules, and everyone must follow them. They are also judge, jury, and executioner when these rules are broken. Caden went to the council once, to plead his case, but they denied him. Ross is the strongest alpha among us, only second to the council…and to your father. Strength in the shifter world is highly respected and coveted. Without proof, Ross will never stand trial."

I looked down at the group in the picture. Six men, all roughly in their late forties and early fifties, stood smiling, each holding a pint of beer. I noticed that not one of them was younger than forty and not one of them was a woman. I already knew I would get nothing from them.

"I'm not looking for judgment, Lucas. I'm looking for revenge. I want Ross dead."

"If Ross were to be found guilty, the penalty would be death. It is dishonorable to kill another shifter in such a shady manner. Shifters die at the hands of other shifters all the time, but only while engaged in combat and always while they are both aware. If Ross did kill your father and Caden's family in this way, it would show that he is weak, and weakness is unacceptable here."

"Could we reopen the trial now that he's killed again? Could this be brought to the council?"

"Perhaps. It's against our laws to kill humans, too, unless, of course, in self-defense."

"And if they find him not guilty again?"

"Hazel…"

I stood up.

"What if they find him not guilty again, Lucas? Will you still help me? Don't you have a say here? You founded this place. Why are you not their leader?"

"I have my own pack, Hazel. I cannot lead this community too. I could have, once, but I had a choice to make between these kids and being a leader to this community, and I chose these kids."

"So, there's nothing you can do?"

"I can teach you, Hazel. I can make you even better than your father. I can show you our customs, teach you to shift with ease, to fight, to grow stronger and faster. I can give you a home here, a place to belong. I can offer protection from Ross, for you and those you love. I can be there for you, the way I should have been for your father."

"But how can you just stand by while my father's killer, your best friend's killer, runs free and without consequence? Free to continue to hurt and murder others? Do you think he'll stop with me? Because I don't. This man—no, this monster—wants nothing but power, and he is never going to stop, Lucas. Trust me, I know, I've seen his kind."

Lucas said nothing and his silence cut deep. I'd had enough. I walked out the office door, slamming it behind me. Everyone was silent as I went down the stairs. Caden came out of the kitchen with Isaac and Jake. He touched my shoulder, but I shrugged it off. His lips parted like he was about to say something, his eyebrows drawn together in concern. I turned around and snapped at him.

"This was a waste of time! What made you think I'd receive any help here?"

"Hazel."

I ignored Caden and spun around to leave. Lucas walked out of his office.

"Hazel, wait!" he called.

He ran down the stairs and gripped my arm before I could walk outside to find Aunt Claire.

"Please stay, at least for dinner, all three of you. I just met my goddaughter and I feel like I'm already losing her."

He looked from me to Caden, whose eyes were only on me. I suddenly felt guilty. I had just met my godfather and already we were fighting. I still wanted to be angry, but I didn't want to ruin this small thing we had either. I sighed and let go of the door handle, just as Aunt Claire opened it. Her eyes found Lucas immediately.

"Can we talk?" she asked him.

He looked at me, and I gave a small nod. He glanced back at Aunt Claire. "I think that's a good idea."

They both walked outside. I looked around the room at everyone. I felt a little foolish for not only being angry in front of them, but for also losing that anger so quickly.

The twins looked at each other and jumped up off the couch at the same time. They ran to me and each grabbed one of my hands in theirs.

"We haven't introduced ourselves," they spoke at the same time. They shook my hands vigorously till I couldn't help but laugh.

"I'm Brandon," said the long-haired twin.

"And I'm Brian," said the buzz cut.

"It's nice to meet you both. How old are you?"

"Eleven!" they said.

They pointed at everybody and spoke their ages as if it was the most important thing about them.

"Sophie's twelve."

She stuck her tongue out at them. Brandon lunged at her, making her flinch and squeal. They pointed at Jake lounging on the recliner sideways. "Jake's sixteen."

Jake winked and added, "Turning seventeen this year."

I tried not to notice how close Caden was suddenly standing next to me.

"And Isaac is—" They twisted around to find him.

He stood behind the bar window, looking into the kitchen. "I'm twenty-two, a year younger than Caden. I'm Lucas's beta."

He gave me a warm smile. The twins crossed their arms, clearly not happy with being interrupted.

I smiled at everyone. They were all so different and yet they'd chosen to stick together. I found myself feeling the same affection for them that I had for Lucas.

"Nice to meet you all," I said, and I meant it.

"Wait!" yelled Sophie. "You haven't met Eva yet."

She ran upstairs and into one of the bedrooms. I stood a little confused. I had no idea there was someone else. Jake let out a groan and Isaac coughed awkwardly.

When Sophie returned, she was holding hands with a girl a little older than me. She was gorgeous in every way. Curvy in all the right places, flat stomach, long eyelashes, and full lips. A natural beauty who needed no makeup. She had long, sleek jet-black hair, beautiful olive-colored skin, and bright-green, catlike eyes. She looked like a modern Egyptian goddess.

She wore short jean cutoffs and a tight revealing white halter top that showed off a rather large chest size. It was obvious the girl knew she was beautiful and loved to flaunt it. Her expression was one of mild annoyance and disinterest. I couldn't tell if it was naturally her face or if she just disliked everyone and everything.

Sophie was the opposite of this girl, all smiles and excitement.

"This is Evangeline," Sophie announced with delight. "Eva for short."

"She's twenty!" Brandon added.

Sophie showed her annoyance. "Shut up, Brandon!"

Evangeline crossed her arms over her chest, eyeing me. "Hello."

Even her voice conveyed disinterest.

"This is Hazel," Sophie said to Eva. "She's Lue's goddaughter."

There was a flash of jealousy in her eyes. "Good to know," she said unimpressed.

She turned to go back upstairs when she spotted Caden and paused.

"Caden," she said in a surprised tone. The first tone that didn't sound disinterested or bored.

"Hello, Eva," he said politely.

I knew instantly there had been something between them. It was now my turn to feel jealousy creep up. I wasn't sure what exactly was going on, whether it was in the past or still happening, but it was clear by Eva's face that she was in love with Caden.

The door suddenly opened. Aunt Claire and Lucas stepped in, laughing. Lucas looked over at all of us and noticed Evangeline.

"Ah, Eva, you've left your room, I see."

Lucas then gave proper introductions and once everyone was introduced, he started dinner. I wanted to ask Aunt Claire what they'd talked about, but she never left his side as she volunteered to help make dinner.

The boys decided to play a game of football in the field behind the house, leaving me, Sophie, and Evangeline to watch from the sidelines. I took note of the fact that Evangeline chose not to hide in her room any longer once she realized Caden was here. She'd changed into a bikini and was lying down on a towel, tanning.

I looked at her and rolled my eyes. She wore sunglasses, as she chewed gum and played on her phone. She saw me looking at her and inched her glasses down, popping her gum.

"What?" she said acidly.

I was tempted to shy away from asking, but I wasn't about to let her intimidate me. "Is there history between you and Caden?"

She smiled, which in her case looked like a sneer. "I don't know, is there something between *you* and Caden?"

I looked down at my Converse, pretending to tie the shoelaces. I wasn't sure how to answer that question. I wanted so badly to say yes, to stake my claim. The wolf in me would have loved that, but I wasn't sure what we were right now. I realized by looking at Eva and Caden that there was still so much I didn't know about him. I looked up and watched him running, tossing the football, laughing, and smiling. My heart gave that familiar, excited lurch every time I looked at him.

Eva looked down at her phone again. "I'm gonna take that as a no."

Sophie let out a yell of excitement next to me. "He caught it!"

I looked over at the field. Isaac now held the football, jumping up and dancing the funniest dance I had ever seen. I laughed when Jake and Caden tackled him. Brandon and Brian were jumping up and down, hollering and cheering as the three older boys wrestled on the ground.

Suddenly their yells of excitement turned into yells of concern. Isaac was standing and two balls of massive fur were rolling on the ground. I got up, but before I could do anything more, Sophie tugged on my arm.

"They do this a lot," she said plainly.

I looked back. Isaac was yelling at them to cut it out. Jake and Caden were nothing but fur, teeth, and claws. I couldn't just stand there and watch, but I wasn't sure what I should do. I was about to start running over to them, hoping to break it off, when I heard a groan of frustration come from Eva.

"Ugh, fine. I'll go."

I watched in horror and embarrassment as Evangeline took off her top and bottoms. She was now completely naked as she ran. She shifted quickly into a sleek black wolf with a white diamond-shaped star on her chest. She was beautiful even in wolf form.

"Does she always do that?" I asked Sophie.

She laughed. "Yeah. She says she doesn't like ruining her clothes."

I tried to forget the image of Eva's naked body. "Let's head over."

Sophie nodded and we jogged over to the massive mound of fur, which now included Eva. Isaac stood back from the brawl, a look of anger and disappointment on his face. The twins were still yelling at them to cut it out.

"What happened?" I asked Isaac.

"I have no idea. One minute we were wrestling and joking around, then the next..." He pointed toward them. "Jake most likely said something he shouldn't have. He tends to rub Caden the wrong way."

My anxiety increased as they continued to fight, Evangeline doing her best to pull them apart.

"Shouldn't we help?"

He shook his head. "I don't even know why Eva bothers. I think she just likes to be in the center of it all. They'll either quit or Lue will pull them apart."

The back door opened. I turned around to see Lucas running toward us, Aunt Claire stood on the porch steps, a worried look on her face. Lucas was yelling for them to stop, but they weren't listening. I couldn't tell who was who. They were just one giant mass of fur. Eva had stopped trying to break them up and now sat on her hind legs, panting like a dog.

Once Lucas reached us, there was fury in his eyes and his face was red.

"ENOUGH!" he commanded.

The power behind his command shot through me to the center where my wolf dwelled. I suddenly found myself bowing my head and averting my eyes from Lucas. Isaac, Brandon, and Brian were all kneeling. Evangeline lay on her stomach, whimpering. Jake and Caden had finally stopped fighting.

I'd once again experienced the power of an alpha's command. It wasn't something I think I'd ever get used to. If the urge to obey was this strong while not being in a pack, I could only imagine how the others felt kneeling and lying on the ground. I felt the dominance radiating off Lucas.

The two wolves now stood facing each other, panting, their breathing so heavy you could see their ribs through their fur. Leaves and dirt smeared their coats. I took a moment to admire Caden in wolf form. He was a handsome, regal creature. His coat was a dark gray and though it was now covered in dirt and leaves, it looked shiny and soft. He was skinny, but broad in the chest, and his eyes were still two colored.

Jake was much skinnier and far less broad in the chest than Caden. His fur was light gray around the eyes, mouth, and underbelly. It slowly transitioned into his top coat, which was a long, thick black. It complemented his electric-blue eyes.

Lucas stood before them with his arms crossed. His gaze landed on Jake, who immediately lay down and rolled over, exposing his stomach. When he looked at Caden, though, Caden just stared back. Lucas had no hold on him. He looked back at Jake as he spoke.

"What did I tell you, Jake? You can't keep doing this, especially not with Caden."

Jake sat up and looked away, his ears pinned behind his head.

Caden, who'd been sitting calmly—or so it had seemed to me—while Lucas was scolding Jake, now looked to be in distress. He stood and began to whimper, shaking his head as his eyes closed.

Lucas had a look of panic. "Caden, are you still with us?"

I was in a panic now too. "What's happening?"

Lucas ignored my question. Caden began to growl, his fur bristling. He opened his eyes, and when he looked at us, there was no sign of recognition. I no longer saw Caden in those two-colored eyes. All I saw was a wolf.

Lucas went toward Caden, slowly.

"Caden, come back to us, okay? Look at me. LOOK AT ME, CADEN!"

Caden looked at him and released another growl. When Lucas was in front of Caden and sure that he wasn't going to run, he knelt so their faces were eye level. Caden's hackles were raised and I feared he'd bite Lucas. My hand covered my mouth in silent horror.

Then Lucas did something only an insane person would do. He grabbed Caden's face in both his hands. Caden released a vicious growl, his mouth opened, exposing his teeth. I inhaled.

"Caden, I'm here. You remember me? It's Lucas. Come back to us, Caden, it's okay. Remember your name? Caden Ulrika. Your mother's name was Melissa Ulrika, your father's name was Jason Ulrika. You remember them? You remember your sister, Caden? You remember Kara?"

Caden struggled for a moment and released a whine. I saw a wet streak run down his fur-lined cheeks. It nearly broke me. I could feel myself falling to my knees. The sudden movement made him look at me and I saw the recognition there. I could hear a whisper in my mind, so faint I almost believed I'd imagined it. It sounded like Caden's voice.

"Hazel."

"That's right, Caden, you know me. I'm right here," I said aloud. I wasn't sure if he could understand me, but I hoped he could. I hoped my eyes said it all.

He then looked back at Lucas, and Lucas smiled.

"There you are. Welcome back."

Lucas stood up, brushed the dirt from his pants, and

looked at all of us, lingering a little longer on Jake in a stern scowl. He then nodded and said, "Dinner is ready. Come inside and wash up. Brandon, Brian, I better see you washing those hands."

He turned and walked back toward the lodge. I turned around to find not one, but two naked people in front of me. Jake and Evangeline.

"Ah!" I turned back around quickly.

Jake laughed. "Like what you see?"

I heard Caden growling behind me. I kept my back to the naked pair as they walked back to the house. Isaac gave me the okay to look. Eva had put her bathing suit back on and had given Jake her towel.

"You guys really don't mind being nude out in the open, do you?"

Isaac laughed. "As shifters, we find ourselves naked in front of one another a lot. You get used to it."

He looked at Caden. "Though some of us are a bit more discreet, even if they shouldn't be."

Caden gave a snort. I smiled down at him, relieved to see he was okay. I wasn't exactly sure what happened, but if I had to guess, I'd say he lost himself for a second to his wolf. David had made it sound like an uncomfortable struggle, but with Caden, it looked like a full-on battle, and one he was losing fast.

"Are you okay?" I asked. He gave me a small nod. I kneeled down and let Caden approach me. I looked into his familiar multicolored eyes and touched the fur on his head, giving him a scratch behind the ear. I heard that faint voice again inside my head.

"That feels good."

I stared at him a little perplexed. I didn't know we could communicate through our minds outside of our wolf forms.

"I'm not sure everyone can." His voice was a little louder this time.

"Come on, man, you can borrow some of my clothes. Let's get you back on two legs."

Caden nodded toward Isaac and then gave my face a lick.

"Ugh, Caden!" I yelled but found myself laughing.

I picked up Caden's and Jake's shoes and began walking back toward the lodge.

When we entered the house, it smelled of garlic and the mouthwatering scent of steak. Isaac led the large gray wolf up the stairs to, what I imagined, was his room. I found myself staring, so at odds with seeing a wolf inside a house. Having something that clearly belonged outside, wild and free, now inside such a tame domestic home was strange, like finding a bear in your swimming pool or a tiger in your car. The two just didn't mix.

All ten of us sat around a giant oval-shaped wooden table in the kitchen. The food was set family style, everyone grabbing what they wanted. Every meat imaginable sat before me, but the course wasn't without its vegetables either. Instead, it was mixed in with the meats like a stir-fry. My first bite set my eyes wide, making Lucas laugh. It tasted heavenly.

"You like it?" he asked.

I only nodded, unable to answer with my mouth stuffed with food.

I sat next to Aunt Claire, who sat next to Lucas, sitting at the head of the table. She couldn't take her eyes off him while he spoke. She'd never looked at any man that way. I suddenly felt guilty for ever thinking she was a hopeless romantic with terrible taste in men. I realized now that she was just looking for Lucas—and only Lucas

—in every man she'd been with. She *was* a romantic, but maybe not so hopeless after all.

I found myself glancing at Caden, who sat across from me, next to Isaac. He immediately locked eyes with me and smiled. I smiled back. The invisible connection between us crackled with electricity. There was no denying my feelings for him. It left me excited and a little uneasy at the same time. I'd never had a crush on anyone before, anyone real that is. I'd had plenty of book boyfriends I would swoon over and wish for existence but no one that actually existed.

Suddenly Evangeline, who sat on Caden's other side, leaned in next to his ear, cupping her perfectly manicured hand over her perfect mouth as she whispered something in his ear. When she finished, he gave her a sidelong glance, looking her up and down with a questioning expression. My ears burned with anger. I looked at Eva. She gave me a sinister smile, picking up her fork full of meat and biting, yanking the fork from her mouth to chew.

I looked at anyone but Caden and Evangeline for the rest of dinner, which was cut short when the twins and Sophie thought it would be fun to start a food fight with one another. Their anger, not yet resolved, turned into a brawl on the living room floor. They went from three children wrestling to three pups biting and scratching. Lucas only sighed. Apparently, this was also a thing that happened often.

The boys in wolf form were as identical as they were in human form, save for the fact that the one who must have been Brandon had a shaggier coat. Sophie was as white as snow, her violet eyes a perfect contrast with her coat. They were so small and cute, scuffling on the floor,

I almost had to fight the urge to hold and cuddle them like real puppies.

Finally, Lucas thought enough was enough and pulled them apart, sending them to separate corners of the room. He snapped at the twins when they tried to go to the same corner together. This made me smile.

I helped Aunt Claire with the cleanup, which she'd insisted that we do. Of course, there was much protest from Lucas, but she wouldn't hear about it and shooed him and the rest of the bunch out of the kitchen. She said it was our way of saying thank you for dinner.

I dried the dishes while she washed them. There was a dishwasher, but Aunt Claire hated them. She said they never cleaned the dishes properly. We didn't say much as we worked. Caden offered to help, but Aunt Claire had shooed him off too. I had a feeling she wanted to speak to me, alone, but so far, she hadn't said anything. Finally, after the last dish was washed, dried, and put away safely in the cabinet, she looked at me and spoke.

"Lucas has invited us to stay here for a while. He has a spare room for each of us, with a joined bathroom and everything." She gave me a half smile.

I looked away from her for a moment, staring at the empty sink. I was still a little angry at Lucas for not doing something about Ross, for acting like he didn't want to do anything about him, but Lucas had promised he'd help train me to be a better shifter and learn how to fight. I could use that to my advantage. There was nothing to be done until he set up a meeting with the council anyway. I didn't have much hope for the outcome, but maybe I'd be able to change Lucas's mind. I looked back at Aunt Claire. She had a worried, yet hopeful expression on her face.

"I think that's a good idea," I said.

She smiled like she'd won the lottery.

"Are you and Lucas…a thing again?"

She looked down at her hand resting on the counter as she grinned, blushing. "We have a lot to work on, he and I. He feels bad for the way things went down between us, but we were just kids then and of course now, well, things are different. We've both been through a lot. He wants to take it slow, give me time to heal. He told me everything, about how he was afraid of what I'd think of him, and I told him everything too."

"Even about Rob?"

She nodded.

"That's good. I think he deserves to know."

She was silent for a long moment, neither of us looking at each other. Then she placed her hand over mine. I took notice that it was her left hand and there was no longer a wedding band on her ring finger.

"I love you so much, Hazel. The circumstances that brought us together were the worst kind, but you have never been just my niece, you are my daughter too. I never…" She paused. "Look at me."

I looked her in the eye.

"I NEVER would have stayed with Rob had I known. No money, house, or car is worth more than you, Hazel. I wish you would have told me."

I started to speak, but she held up her hand, stopping me.

"I know why you didn't. I should have been a better role model. The first time Rob hit me, I should have packed our things and left that god-awful house. The moment I knew Rob wasn't who I thought he was, we should have left, but instead I let myself believe that you were safe, and that it was only me he wanted to abuse and toy with. I should have set a better example. I made you think that it was okay to let someone abuse you, if it meant protecting someone you love, and I'm here to tell you that is not true, Hazel. Do you understand me? We have to be honest with each other from now on. It is never okay for someone to put their hands on you without permission."

Aunt Claire choked up, tears falling from her face. I was holding them back too.

"I have been the worst mother to you, Hazel, and I'm so sorry. I promise to never put you in that kind of situation again."

I hugged her tight as she sobbed on my shoulder. I let the tears fall freely.

"It's okay, Aunt Claire. We both made mistakes, but that's over now. Rob's gone, and we can start over."

We stayed like that for a bit, just hugging each other while we cried, my face buried in her neck like I used to do when I was little.

When we finally pulled away from each other, my chest felt a little lighter. I hoped hers did too. She smiled at me and we both gave an awkward laugh as we wiped our tears.

She cleared her throat and said, "So, on another, lighter note, tell me. How much do you like this Caden boy?"

I scoffed but she only raised her eyebrows, waiting for a real answer.

I gave a small laugh. "I haven't quite figured that out yet."

It was her turn to laugh. Tears still lingered on her lashes. They sparkled when she moved. "You do like him, though."

It was a statement, not a question. I looked down at our shoes.

"I think it's a bit more complicated than that, but… yeah. I think I do."

I looked up at her again and smiled. She was watching me the way a proud mom would.

"You are far smarter than I was at your age. You've always had a good head on your shoulders, and you never let your emotions get the best of you, just like your mother. I'm so proud of you, Hazel, and I know your mother would be proud of you too."

She put her hands on both my cheeks. "And if you're wondering if I approve, I do. Although, I'm not sure how I feel about those lip piercings."

She kissed my forehead and we both laughed.

Someone coughed. We looked over and saw Caden in the entryway of the kitchen, a sheepish expression on his face.

"Sorry to interrupt," he said.

We laughed again, separating and composing ourselves.

"It's fine, we just finished cleaning up," Aunt Claire said. She winked at me and left the kitchen.

I smiled at Caden. "We had a much-needed heart-to-heart," I said.

He smiled back. "Well, it's good to know she approves of me."

I let out a choked cough, my cheeks heating up.

He tapped one of his ears with his finger. "Shifter hearing. You got to be careful around here, the whole house could have heard you." He winked.

I felt the need to explain myself but before I could, he asked, "Have you and your aunt decided to stay then?"

I cleared my throat. I realized staying here would mean no longer staying with Caden, but I couldn't deny my aunt's chance at happiness, and I could learn a lot by being here. "Yes. I think my aunt and I should stay here awhile. Lucas has offered to train me. Teach me how to fight and practice shifting."

"I completely understand," he said. Did he seem a little sad? Was this a goodbye? 'Cause this felt a lot like a goodbye.

"You should stay too."

The words were out of my mouth before I'd even fully formed them in my head. I was incredibly embarrassed to have even offered. Caden had his own life, why would he want to stay here? Because I wanted him to? This wasn't even my house. What if Lucas didn't want him to stay here?

Caden said nothing as he stepped into the kitchen and walked toward me, a mischievous look on his face. I backed myself into the counter. He leaned in and placed his hands on either side of me, resting them on the countertop.

"You want me to stay?" he asked, giving me a sexy smile.

I swallowed rather loudly.

I was terrified he'd do something stupid like kiss me. I was desperately hoping he'd do something stupid like kiss me. I'd never seen this side of Caden. It was playful, sexy. It sent my skin ablaze and my heart hammering. I realized with both horror and shock that there was also a pleasurable tightness between my legs.

I cleared my throat nervously.

"I mean if you want, and if Lucas is okay with it. I feel like you're the only one on my side and I could use your help."

I was making stupid excuses and Caden knew it. He still had that sexy smirk on his face. *God those lip rings.* I'd never found piercings on men to be attractive till now. I wanted so badly to feel those cool metal rings on my lips. Caden leaned in, and for a second, I thought he'd oblige and kiss me right there in the kitchen, but instead he whispered, "Good thing I already asked Lucas for a room."

He backed away, giving me a knowing smile, and walked out of the kitchen. It took me several minutes of heavy breathing before I could compose myself.

ELEVEN

Lucas had more space in his lodge than he let on. The second floor, past his office, was nothing but rooms. At one point, the place had been a hotel of sorts. There were six rooms on the second floor, not including Lucas's office, which I imagine had been a receptionist's office, and six more on the third floor.

The staircase leading to the third floor was all the way down the hall. At the end of the third-floor hallway, Aunt Claire and I each had our own room with an adjoining bathroom. We were the last two rooms on the right. There were two more empty rooms beside us, mostly filled with boxes and old furniture. The first room on the left was Lucas's room, choosing to stay separate from the hustle and bustle of the kids on the second floor. Caden had chosen the room next to Lucas, opposite mine.

He'd driven back to his cabin to retrieve our things, along with some of his own. I hadn't had the chance to ask him what exactly happened earlier in the backyard. I hoped to ask him when he got back. David had made it seem like an uncomfortable nuisance to have your instincts always wanting to take over, one that over time could be dangerous, but Caden had seemed like he was battling with his instincts, fighting to stay himself, and it had happened so fast. One moment he was Caden and the next, there was nothing there but a wolf. It was terrifying.

My own wolf stirred within. She wished to be released. It was only a request, a small craving within me. I was so grateful to be in sync with her that I couldn't help but feel I should oblige. She wanted to run, I wanted to run. So I did. I went out to the backyard, passed the line of trees that marked the start of the woods, and when I thought I was a safe distance, I removed my clothes and shifted. I glanced down at my paws, still fascinated by the way they looked. I peeked behind me at my shaggy coat and bushy tail. I wagged it, laughing in my head.

Then I started to run. I had always had a love for running, but this was unlike anything I had ever felt before. I never knew how limited I was on two legs. On four I was incredibly fast, agile, and able to jump over rocks and crawl underneath fallen trees with ease. My stamina was unbelievable. I ran at least three miles nonstop before I started breathing heavily and I ran four more before I was too tired to go any farther. I felt a high I hadn't felt from running in a long time. I felt strong, happy, free, but most importantly, at peace with myself. That part I felt was missing had finally been filled.

But as quickly as this feeling came, it also went. I realized that while this new life of mine felt good, I could never go back to my old life. I wouldn't graduate high school this year, wouldn't go to college, wouldn't be able to work at the bookstore. I wasn't even sure I could continue being friends with Molly anymore. That stopped me in my tracks. Suddenly I was human again, sitting naked in the woods, my knees pulled against my chest.

I hadn't given any thought to this situation long term. My only focus was stopping Ross, but what would I do after this was all over? Would I stay here? Become a part of Lucas's pack? If I did, would I be able to stay friends with Molly? I would have to keep so many secrets from her. I wasn't sure I could handle that. The best thing would be to let her go. My heart broke and it began to open wounds I'd left closed.

I sobbed into my knees, my arms wrapped tightly around them. I cried over everything that had happened these past few days, all the changes that had occurred in such a short period of time, and the horrible things I had to endure. I cried for the old me and the comforts of my old life, despite the bad things in it too. I cried for Molly, I cried for Aunt Claire, and I even cried for Rob. And finally, I let myself cry for my parents, because this was how all my cries ended, with the pain of their absence.

When I had finished crying, I wiped the tears from my face and forced myself to shift and make my way back toward the lodge. Once I was dressed again, I went inside.

Jake and Isaac were sitting on the couch, game controllers in hand. Eva was sitting on a beanbag chair across from them, playing on her phone. The twins and Sophie, seemingly over their earlier fight, were now playing peacefully on the floor with a combination of Legos and Barbie dolls.

I was deciding whether to just head upstairs when Isaac glanced away from the TV and saw me. He motioned for me to go over and sit. I decided it best to sit next to him, remembering Jake's awkward lingering handshake and the way he was always winking at me. As soon as I sat down, Eva looked up from her phone and scoffed. She actually scoffed. Then she stood up, grabbed her beanbag chair, and stormed out the door, slamming it behind her. Why she didn't just go up to her room was beyond me, but if I had to guess, I would say Eva was trying to be dramatic.

Jake and Isaac had paused for a moment to watch her go. As soon as the door had closed, Jake went back to the game, but Isaac continued looking at the door, almost longingly, then glanced over at me.

"She's a bit rough around the edges, but she's actually really sweet once you get to know her. She just doesn't like change."

I let out a snort. "I think she just doesn't like me."

Jake laughed. "Take it as a compliment. If she hates you, then that means she thinks you're competition."

I shook my head in disbelief, but Jake was too busy looking at the TV to notice. Isaac went back to playing but continued to speak.

"She's had it rougher than the rest of us. She didn't choose to be here. She didn't even choose to be a shifter. She was made one. She had to leave behind everyone she knew and loved."

I looked at him, shocked. "I thought you had to be born a shifter?"

He nodded. "You do, usually. There are very, *very* few who can be made. I only know of two, maybe three. It takes a lot to make a human a shifter."

"What does it take?" I asked.

"Usually, death." Jake said bluntly.

Isaac nodded. "But a shifter has to give his or her blood to a human before they die. If they survive, they wake up and go through the changes, just like the rest of us."

"How'd she end up that way?" I asked.

"It's not a pretty story," Isaac replied.

Jake shook his head in disgust.

Isaac continued. "Some sick, lone shifter was going around the country kidnapping teenage girls and feeding off them. Guess he had a taste for human flesh. He snatched up Evangeline on her way home from a party. She was nineteen. He kept her in the trunk of his car until he was ready to feed, but Eva wasn't going down without a fight. When he opened the trunk, she'd untied her hands and leaped at him, bit his ear clean off."

Isaac and Jake both looked a little proud, but it quickly disappeared as Isaac finished. "The shifter was so angry he snapped her neck, didn't even bother feeding on her. He just left her there on the side of the road to die."

I cringed internally and suddenly had a whole new respect for Evangeline.

"Luckily," Isaac continued, "Caden found her not long after. It was on one of the roads near his cabin. She lived, but only because she'd tasted the guy's blood when she bit his ear."

I looked at the spot where Eva had been sitting. It explained why she had such a crush on Caden. He'd saved her life. Despite my deep dislike for her, I did feel sorry for her. I would never wish for that to happen to anyone.

Isaac cleared his throat. "Anyway, she's a bit possessive of the things and people she loves. She won't admit it, but it's true. She'll come around, though, you'll see. You'll be a part of this pack in no time."

He gave me a sideways wink and continued his game

with Jake. I sat on the couch comfortably, watching them play. After a while, I looked over at Isaac and Jake and then to the twins and Sophie, who were playing on the floor, and it hit me that maybe I could make this work. I'd only known this group a day and they were giving me their full acceptance. They did not question me or make me feel unwelcome, except for Eva. But even she and I had something in common, we both had a rough past. They even accepted Aunt Claire despite the fact she was human. Maybe, just maybe, I could rebuild a life here.

My first week, Lucas began training me immediately. I, along with the rest of the pack, got up every morning at five a.m. to go running, then breakfast, and after that we sparred in the gym, which I discovered was in the subbasement and had once been where the maids washed clothes and stored cleaning supplies. The washing machines and cleaning supplies were now replaced by padded floors, weights, and exercise equipment.

Each of us had to partner up and have a go at one another while Lucas supervised, telling us where to dodge, hit, and kick. As it turned out, I was a terrible fighter. Jake and Eva usually paired off together, while the twins and Sophie took turns with one another, which left me with Isaac. I wondered where Caden was during training. He would run with us every morning, but he disappeared after breakfast. I asked Isaac during one of our spars. He said Caden preferred to train alone but wouldn't say why.

After Isaac wiped the floor with me and Lucas gave me so many tips, tricks, and directions that I could no longer remember or keep track of them, we stopped for lunch. Aunt Claire had made it one of her sole duties to cook for all of us and make sure no one left the table hungry. Caden always joined.

After lunch, Eva and Isaac were free for the day while the rest of the group had "school," which usually involved open books on the kitchen table while they studied. A woman, who I assumed was their teacher, would come by and help them. I stayed behind with Lucas to practice shifting.

"I will teach you to change without thinking. You will be able to shift while in midjump, while fighting, while running, while swimming, as soon as you wake, and right before an attack. It will become second nature to you, as it has with all of us."

I was embarrassed to find that Lucas wanted me to shift in front of him, human nakedness and all.

He smiled kindly at me. As if he realized my unease. "Everyone here is very open with their nudity. We don't think twice about it. Fear of the naked body is a human emotion. You and your pack will be like family and there will be times when you'll have to shift with them. There's no avoiding it."

I was still hesitant, but Lucas eased me into the process. He sent Sophie and Eva to shift with me so that I'd be more comfortable with the idea. I was wary at first, given Eva's obvious dislike toward me, but she didn't balk or laugh at my nakedness. I had to remind myself that she had been human once, too, and was the only one I knew who'd also had a late start in this new life.

While I trained, Aunt Claire spent her time at the greenhouse. Lucas didn't like the idea of letting the only human in the community out in the open, but Aunt

Claire wouldn't take no for an answer. She wanted to show them she could be of some use. Not to mention she was in her element among plants.

Lucas and I agreed we should accompany her the first few days, just in case. The others in the greenhouse were cautious of her at first. Though polite, they gave her a wide berth while she worked and only interacted with her just long enough to answer her questions. The whole time they would glance up and stare at Lucas, either in fear or annoyance.

But soon enough, they warmed up to her. She knew a great deal about plants, and their curiosity outweighed their distrust. By the end of the week, she had a whole group of horticulturists and farmers following her around. They asked her questions about certain plants, soil, and the right organic pesticide, and she taught them everything she knew.

Aunt Claire had loved gardening since high school. It all started when she had to take home a plant for science class. She'd become obsessed with everything there was to know about hers. How much water and sun it needed, what soil was best, and when other students' plants started dying, she'd find herself wanting to help and learn about theirs.

Growing up I rarely caught her reading anything that wasn't a horticulture book. I even caught her in the middle of the night researching on her computer or just sitting on the porch with all the plants she'd horded over the years. Now here she was again, helping others keep their plants alive and thriving.

Once my training and lessons were done for the day, I was almost too tired to function, but I forced myself to venture into the community and learn what I could. I was welcomed with open arms. Some people would stop me in the streets and tell me how much they admired my father and how happy they were to see me. I'd never met these people, but it felt like visiting long-lost relatives.

It was amazing to see the way everyone interacted with one another. Wolves and human shifters walked side by side. Pups played in the streets with kids. Some wolves even carried heavy packs on their backs filled with groceries or materials needed for shops.

Even human forms had an air of wildness about them, as if they were still wolves, just in human shells. They rubbed noses, showed teeth, and snapped at one another, just as they would as wolves. It was so fascinating to watch. I wished I'd grown up here. These people were so connected to their wolves, something they were taught before their first shift. This was something I hadn't quite developed yet.

It got me thinking of "Which came first? The chicken or the egg?"

I laughed at my own version.

"Which came first? The wolf or the man?" I whispered and continued to laugh under my breath.

I tried to get to know the pack I was staying with too.

I got to know Isaac first. He was so kind and gentle, an open person by nature. It was probably why I was usually placed with him during our spars. I was grateful for that. He was incredibly patient and never got angry, which is why I found it so strange that he was secretly in love with Evangeline. He hadn't admitted it, neither had the rest of the pack, but it was obvious. The way his eyes always drifted toward her when she entered a room or watched her when she left.

It was made clear one day while we were sparring and running drills for how to swipe someone's feet out from underneath them even in wolf form. Isaac was the wolf. It was the first time I'd ever seen him in wolf form. His coat was a shaggy brown and black. He was, of course, outmaneuvering me, as he always did in human form, but somehow, I was able to get his feet out from underneath him before he could fully jump out of the way.

He let out a grunt as he hit the floor on his back. I raised my hands in triumph, thinking I was finally getting better at this fighting thing, but when I looked down at his face, I realized I'd bested him because he'd been distracted. As I threw my leg out to swipe Isaac's legs out from under him, Jake—also in wolf form—started besting Evangeline. Even though we were only running drills, Jake was sitting on top of her, using his weight to hold her down while he snapped at her face. Her arms were crossed over his throat to keep his teeth at bay.

Jake could be brutal during sparring session, and Isaac and I knew it, but Lucas was always there and never let him go too far. Besides, Eva really knew how to handle herself. She was by far the best I'd seen at fighting in human form, yet, for some reason Isaac got up and ran over to Jake, grabbing him by the coat with his teeth and tossing him off Evangeline.

He didn't growl or show his teeth at Jake, just looked at him with wary eyes. Eva said nothing. She just got up, brushed her hands on her pants, and left the room. I wondered if she knew Isaac loved her, or if she even cared. The two of them were complete opposites, but she was always kind to Isaac and Sophie.

Sophie loved Evangeline. She clung to her every chance she got, and Eva, instead of being annoyed or frustrated with Sophie—like I would have expected—would dote on her as if she were her mother or big sister.

A few times, I had walked by and saw her helping

Sophie do her hair or playing with her in the living room. Before Aunt Claire and I arrived, Eva was the only other girl in the house and Sophie looked up to her. She needed someone to do girlie things with her and I think Eva knew it too.

Still, it was odd to watch such a fiery, anger-filled person become so loving and gentle. She'd caught me watching her with Sophie a few times and would always snap at me and then leave the room, Sophie hot on her heels.

The twins were exactly what you'd expect two eleven-year-old boys to be like. They were absolute trouble. Usually unable to sit still for more than a few minutes at a time, they'd be zooming around the house or outside, to either torment Sophie or get into something they weren't supposed to. The boys loved to play pranks on people. I found them in wolf form more than any of the others in the pack, catching them running around completely naked more times than I could count.

It was creepy when the two of them spoke, because they would sometimes say the same thing at the same time or finish each other's sentences. I had heard of twins being able to do this; however, Lucas said they also had a strong telepathic bond as wolves. They could completely close the rest of the pack off while they spoke to each other in wolf form and, even in human form, they were still telepathically linked. I thought of Caden speaking to me as a wolf while I was human and wondered if that was something similar. If so, why?

Jake was edgy, pessimistic, and cynical. He liked to start fights and I'd caught him and Lucas in a few screaming matches more than once. It usually resulted in Lucas having to use his alpha voice, which he admitted later that he hated to do. Jake had an addiction to pain, which he satisfied with tattoos and piercings.

I sometimes found him and Eva hanging out together. The two didn't talk to each other much, but they had a lot in common and viewed the world the same way. I'd find them outside, taking drags of the same cigarette, out of sight from Lucas and the others. Jake smoked like a chimney when Lucas wasn't looking.

He was also known for being incredibly promiscuous. He'd sleep with or date several of the girls in the community but never tied himself down to one girl. Despite all his shortcomings, I saw the lighter side of him too. Usually while he was with Isaac, who seemed to bring out the best in everyone, or when he thought he was alone. Jake was funny. He knew how to make everyone laugh without being cruel—if he wanted—and he was pretty talented musically.

The first time I'd walked past his closed bedroom, I thought he was listening to music. It wasn't until later when he'd opened his door that I realized it was him *making* the music. He had an entire music set in his room. There was an acoustic and electric guitar, an amp, a small drum kit, a keyboard, and what looked like a mic set connected to a computer. There wasn't even room for his small futon to be pulled out to make a proper bed. He didn't seem to mind, though. I didn't think Jake slept very much anyway. I could hear him practicing late into the night until someone would yell at him to cut it out and go to bed.

I was happy for the opportunity to get to know Caden a little better too. When training was over, usually after dinner, Caden and I would go for a short walk in the woods, just before dark. The first day we walked together had finally given me the chance to ask him what had happened that day they played football outside.

Caden sighed, rubbing his neck with the palm of one hand. He was silent for a long time, I suspected he was looking for the right words, but after walking in silence for several minutes, I thought maybe he wouldn't say anything at all.

Finally he said, "If I tell you something, you have to promise not to tell anyone and don't mention it to the pack. I know Lucas told them the truth, but we try not to talk about it."

I was honored that Caden felt he could trust me enough with a secret so few knew about. It must be something important, something he either couldn't or wasn't comfortable sharing with anyone.

"I promise," I said sincerely.

We came across a worn-down log. Caden gestured for us to sit, then he spoke slowly, as if each word pained him to say out loud.

"I'm not…like other shifters. I wasn't…I wasn't born human. I was born…a wolf."

I'd admit, that surprised me. I didn't even know that kind of thing was possible, but I figured it was no different from not knowing shifters could be made, like Evangeline. I could just attribute it to something else I hadn't known about the shifter world.

My thoughts suddenly went back to my earlier question.

Which came first, the wolf or the human?

I guessed, as it turned it, it was both.

"I'm a very rare case. The only one of my kind in fact. There have been others, but…they don't live long."

I was silent for a moment, gathering my thoughts.

"So, what does that mean exactly?" I asked. "You are human now, obviously."

"It means, I'm more sensitive to my instincts. As a wolf it's harder to control, but unlike most shifters, I feel it all the time."

"Wait, you mean you feel the pull even when you're human?"

"Yes."

It all started to click into place. Suddenly David's words made sense.

He's more wolf than human.

That was why Caden felt so awkward talking about his childhood, why he preferred to train alone, why he had to be careful as a wolf and why sometimes, when he was angry or upset, his face would take on an eerie animalistic expression.

"That must be really hard, having to always be in control."

I now knew why he'd been so jealous to discover I didn't feel the pull of instincts. I was his opposite. He had to deal with it all the time, while I didn't have to deal with it at all.

He looked down at his hands, as if trying to memorize the shape of them.

"As a human I'm pretty good at controlling it, but as a wolf I lose control much faster than the others, especially when my emotions are high."

"Why were they?" I asked. "When you and Jake fought, I mean?"

He shook his head. "It was stupid, something I shouldn't have gotten upset about."

"Tell me. I won't think it's stupid, I promise."

He sighed heavily. "While Jake and I were on the

ground, wrestling for the ball, he mentioned how fun it would be to…wrestle with you like that…in bed."

We were both silent.

"Oh" was all I could say. To think Caden almost lost himself because of me made my heart clench.

Caden continued. "I knew he was baiting me. He's always trying to start something with someone. I don't think Jake hates me; I just think he likes to fight. He can't get a rise out of Isaac, so he usually aims for me when I'm around. Not to mention, he probably would like to get his grubby little hands on you."

There was that look in his eyes again. The same one I'd seen when he talked about Ross. Now that I knew the truth, I realized that it was his wolf staring back. It was him at his most primal, right on the edge of losing himself. It was dark, wild, angry, and…powerful. It was scary and alluring all at once. The wolf in me called to it.

I touched his arm and suddenly he was back. The look was gone, and that one blue eye and one brown eye were Caden's again.

"I don't think any less of you, Caden," I said softly. "If anything, I think you are the strongest person I know."

He gave me a weak smile. "I don't feel strong. I feel…tired."

I gave him a sympathetic expression, looped my arm through his, and laid my head on his shoulder.

I looked forward to our walks. We'd talk about trivial things like books, paintings, and school. Sometimes we'd philosophize on heavier subjects and then other times, we wouldn't say anything at all, just walk side by side. He even started holding my hand.

After dinner on Friday, I was far too tired to do much of anything. Aunt Claire was tucked into Lucas's arm as they sat on the couch, picking a movie to watch. My heart filled with joy seeing my aunt this way. Caden and the other boys decided to go outside and play a game of football before dark, and I guessed Sophie was with Eva upstairs. Lucas yelled at the boys as they ran for the door, warning them not to fight. I waved at Caden and smiled as I headed upstairs to my room.

I tried not to let on that I was a bit worried Jake would try to start a fight with Caden again, but I reminded myself that Isaac would be with them and if anything should happen, Lucas would be there to stop it.

I took a quick shower, then collapsed on my bed and decided to call Molly. She hadn't been answering my texts lately and I was worried about her. I called her cell, but there was no answer, so I called the house phone. I hoped someone would recognize my number.

On the second ring, Molly's mom picked up. We exchanged pleasantries. She asked how my aunt and I were holding up, and I told her we were doing okay. Aunt Claire was taking time off work, and we were staying with friends for a while. I asked her about Molly. She told me that she'd started her physical therapy, but it usually left her tired after. She promised she'd let Molly know I was trying to get ahold of her. We said our good nights and hung up.

I curled up on my side, hugging a pillow to my chest. I let out a shaky breath, holding back tears. Maybe this was for the best. Maybe Molly was mad at me for abandoning her when she needed me the most. It would be easier to let her go if she was angry with me.

It was still ripping me apart to imagine her not in my life, though. All our plans didn't seem possible anymore. We were supposed to graduate together, then go on a big road trip like they do in the movies. We'd get matching tattoos, go to college together, move in together until we graduated and then live in the same neighborhood. We were supposed to always be close, but how could I when I had this whole other life now? Molly would never forgive me, she would never accept me, if she knew I was the reason she was attacked, if she knew I was like the thing that had attacked her. I cried uncontrollably.

Someone gently nudged my shoulder and jerked me awake. I hadn't even realized I'd fallen asleep, and for a split second, I thought I was in my room back home, with Rob hovering over me. I bolted upright. Caden stood by the bed, a concerned look on his face.

"Are you okay?" he asked.

I shook my head no. My heart was hurting, and memories of Rob still left me with a sick feeling.

Caden sat on the bed. "You want to talk about it?"

I shook my head again. I didn't want to talk about any of it.

"Okay. I'll leave you alone then. Sorry to wake you."

He got up to leave. I realized I didn't want to be alone.

"Wait," I said softly, my voice cracking from misuse and crying. I patted the empty space on the bed beside me. "Can you just stay with me, for a little while?"

He nodded and walked across to the other side of the bed. He lay on top of the covers. I slowly turned so I was facing him. I inched my way closer to him until my head was on his chest, then he wrapped an arm around me. I sighed.

"I'm sorry," he said.

"For what?"

"I'm just sorry you're hurting."

I looked up at him. His eyes boring into mine. There was so much affection there I thought my heart would break in two. I laid my head on his chest again, just over his heart.

"I'm sorry you're hurting too," I whispered.

AFTER NEARLY TWO WEEKS AT CRESCENT PEAK, I HAD yet to see or hear from any of the council members. Lucas had warned me it would be difficult to get them to agree to an audience, but with every passing day, I found myself getting restless and angry. I was starting to think the council was nothing but a group of selfish old men with a God complex. How could they possibly be so busy they couldn't take the time for something so important?

I tried my best to be patient and keep busy. I became fully immersed in my daily routine. Every day I trained and every day I found myself getting stronger, running longer, and shifting faster. Spring break was over and public schools had started up again, but I was no longer going. Instead, Lucas and Aunt Claire both agreed I should be homeschooled with the others for the rest of the year. I tried to argue that it wasn't necessary, but Aunt Claire insisted.

"You've spent this long in school, honey, and you're so close to graduating. You should finish in case you still want to go to college," she'd said.

Conner called and asked when I'd be able to come back to work. I didn't have the heart to tell him I may never be going back. He'd been so understanding when I used Rob's death as an excuse. He told me to take all the time I needed and that the bookstore wasn't going anywhere. I missed working there, though. I missed the smell of books and coffee and the sound of the old antique register. I missed quietly reading behind the counter when there weren't any customers, and I even missed lugging around heavy boxes of books for restocking. A small part of me hoped I could work there again, but I knew the chances were slim.

Molly still hadn't called. Part of me was happy she hadn't. I knew when she did, I would have to keep her at a distance, but I missed my best friend and I just wanted to hear from her. I called her house at least two more times since I'd last spoken to her mom, and each time her mom picked up, she would tell me Molly wasn't there or that she was sleeping.

Caden and I were too busy to go for our daily walks now. I was either studying or training, and Caden was usually helping around the community, mostly running errands in town, but sometimes we'd sneak out of the house at night and go for our walks then.

It was easier for us, we found, to be more open with each other while we were outside. Caden seemed more comfortable and at ease, but there were still some things he didn't like talking about. I never pried because there were some things I didn't like to talk about, either, but we somehow always found topics we both enjoyed. We grew a safe space between us.

Despite my growing anxiety and anger toward the council, I was happy to be at Crescent Peak. I missed working at the bookstore and I missed Molly, but I found myself slowly healing from all my past traumas and I knew Aunt Claire was doing the same, but my happiness felt temporary. Like the calm before a storm. I knew I could never fully move on with my life until Ross was out of the picture.

CHAPTER

TWELVE

I woke to the sound of Aunt Claire calling my name softly. When I opened my eyes, I found her sitting on the edge of my bed, a big smile on her face and a cupcake in her hand. She began to softly sing "Happy Birthday."

Oh my God. Today's my birthday.

So much had happened over the past few weeks. I'd completely forgotten.

When Aunt Claire finished the last verse and told me to make a wish and blow out the candle, I wished for the same thing I wished every year. I wished my mom could be with me on my birthday.

I used to hate my birthday. When I was old enough to understand it was also the same day my mother died, I told Aunt Claire I never wanted to celebrate another birthday again. I didn't deserve to have them. How could I when my mother had died on the same day? How could I when I was the reason she'd died?

"You are not the reason she died, Hazel. She was sick and likely would have died even if she weren't pregnant

229

with you, but that's not the point. The point is, I know your mother was happy to give her life to bring you into this world, and it is your job to make sure it's a good life. So, you have to celebrate your birthdays because your mother would have wanted that. Celebrating your birthday is the greatest thing you can do to honor her."

I took that to heart and from then on, I always thought of my mom the most on my birthday. I imagined what she'd say and do if she were here with me now. I pictured the three of us eating cake together and spending the day celebrating. In that imaginary world, the three of us would live together in the same house. My aunt never needed a man in her life. She would have her sister by her side, and they would raise me together.

I shared my cupcake with Aunt Claire, and we laughed at the fact that we were eating a cupcake for breakfast. When we finished, she went downstairs to cook a real breakfast for everyone. As she left the room, I pulled out the note my mom gave me and reread it over and over again before hugging it to my chest. I breathed in a heavy breath and closed my eyes.

"I'm here. Mom. I'm here and another birthday's gone by. I hope you're proud of me."

My phone buzzed from the nightstand. It was Molly. My heart gave a lurch. We hadn't spoken in two weeks, possibly the longest we'd ever gone without talking. I worried about what I'd say. I worried about what she'd say. I took a deep breath and answered the phone.

"Hello?"

"Happy birthday!"

I smiled as relief flooded through me.

"Thanks," I said, "but you know you could stand to pick up a phone every once in a while."

"I'm sorry. Between physical therapy, regular therapy,

and the drugs they have me on, I've either been busy or totally out of it. I wish I could be there for you on your birthday, but I have school today. My first day back. When are you coming home? I really miss you."

My heart ached. I hated that I wasn't there for her.

"I really miss you, too, but I don't think I'll be going back to school. Aunt Claire wants to homeschool me the rest of the year."

"But it's senior year!"

Molly cared far more about school than I ever did. She was always the one to drag me to functions and school dances. She claimed they were important memories that needed to be made, and I would thank her later when I looked back and reminisced about high school. I doubted I'd ever "reminisce" about high school.

"I know but after everything that's happened, she thinks it's for the best. I think she just wants to keep me close for a while."

"Well, I disagree, but maybe that's just me being selfish because I wish you were here right now. Hey, maybe I can come up and see you after school. Mom said you were staying with the community at Crescent Peak, right?"

"I don't know if that would be a good idea."

"Why?"

"Things are still kind of crazy right now. Aunt Claire isn't exactly up for company."

Another lie.

"I see," she said, sounding a little hurt.

We were both silent for a long time.

When Molly spoke again, she sounded sad, defeated.

"Hazel, are we still friends?"

I heard several feet running up the stairs and then rapid knocks on my door. "Hazel! Hurry up! Breakfast is ready and everyone's waiting!" Sophie and the twins yelled together. I could hear them pushing and shoving one another.

"Be down in a second!" I yelled back, hoping they would go away. They did, scurrying back down the stairs.

"Everyone, huh? Sounds like you better go then, wouldn't want to keep you from your company."

There was no mistaking the anger in her voice.

"Molly, it's not like that. Where we're staying…lots of people live here."

"But Aunt Claire can't handle the company right now?"

"No, it's just—"

"I don't know why you feel the need to lie to me, Hazel. I thought maybe you and Aunt Claire were up there staying in some secluded cabin in the woods to get away from everything and everyone, trying to put your lives back together, but now you say a bunch of people are living in the same place."

"I never said we were living alone."

"But that's what you implied!" she yelled.

There was a pause, then she released a heavy breath. "My life is a disaster. My parents walk on eggshells around me. I can't stand or walk for too long without a cane. I can hardly eat or sleep because when I do, I dream of that demon attacking me. I'm depressed and addicted to pain meds, and I have to deal with everyone looking at the stitches on my face and either avoiding me like the plague or pitying me, which I don't need. What I do need, is my best friend, but she doesn't want to see me, and I have no idea why."

"Molly, I'm trying to be there for you. Why do you think I called so much?"

"Yes, but calling and actually being here are two

totally different things, Hazel. And don't tell me this has anything to do with Rob's death, because you've been acting different ever since I got home from the hospital. I never see you and you won't tell me what's going on. You just keep lying and giving me vague answers."

This was it, a way out. Molly wasn't safe as my friend. I couldn't tell her the truth. I had to let her think I'd abandoned her. I had to make her think I didn't want to be friends with her anymore.

But the words just wouldn't come. I couldn't be that intentionally cruel to my best friend, even if it was for the best, so I said nothing at all.

"Hazel?"

Silence.

"Hazel, say something."

"There's nothing to say," I told her.

I could almost feel my words stab her. I could feel them stab me.

"You know what? Fine. If this new life is more important to you than your oldest friend, then I won't hold you back anymore. Enjoy your birthday, Hazel." She spat the last words and then hung up.

I spent the rest of the morning in bed crying. I spoke to no one when they knocked, except Aunt Claire and even then, I only told her that Molly and I had a fight but gave no reason as to why. I think she knew, though.

When I finished crying, I still didn't want to leave my room. I didn't care that it was my birthday. I wanted to pretend it wasn't. I dug through my bag and found the book I hadn't finished. The one I'd been reading in class all those weeks ago. It was silly, but now that I was holding it, I felt it was important to know if Gabriel really did kill his own brother.

Spoiler alert, he did and it's the saddest scene in the

whole book, which only left me crying again. Gabriel's sorrow for the loss of his brother mirrored my own sorrow for the loss of my best friend. I didn't stab her with a sword like Gabriel had done to his brother, but I might as well have, metaphorically speaking.

By midafternoon, I figured it was time to leave my room. I'd cried so much I no longer felt anything, but I was getting hungry. I showered, did my hair as best I could, and headed downstairs. There didn't appear to be anyone in the living room, but when I rounded into the kitchen, Aunt Claire was there. She looked like she was getting ready to start dinner. When she turned in my direction she gasped, holding her hand up to her heart.

"Hazel! You scared me." She composed herself and smiled. "You okay?"

"Fine."

"You missed lunch. Lucas decided to let the kids out early from their studies. I think everyone's out doing their own thing."

I nodded. That was fine. I wasn't much in the mood to see anyone anyway.

I went to the fridge and found a pear. This would have to do till dinner.

"Oh, hon, I hate to ask this of you, since it is your birthday and all, but Lucas knows a woman here who makes amazing cakes and she offered to make you one."

"Aunt Claire, you really didn't have to do that."

She waved her hands in a dismissive gesture. "Nonsense. It's your birthday and besides, it's already done. I just need someone to pick it up. Would you mind? I have to get dinner started."

"This isn't some trick to get me out of the house, is it? Does anyone else know it's my birthday?"

"I told no one but Lucas, and that's only because he already knew."

"Okay good. Can we keep it that way? I'm not in much of a celebratory mood."

She held her hands up as if in surrender. "Understood, but I do need someone to get that cake and who better than the birthday girl herself?"

I agreed to do it, taking the last bite of my pear. She told me the cabin number—every building had one here—as I put on my shoes and then I headed for the door.

If I didn't already know the cabin number, I still would have easily found it. You could smell baked goods from four cabins down. As soon as I walked into the house-turned-shop, a kind, older woman greeted me at the door. Cake flour covered her apron, face, and hair, but she didn't seem to mind.

"Afternoon," she said, a slight southern accent in her voice.

"Good afternoon. I'm here to pick up a birthday cake, possibly under the name of Lucas?"

She beamed brightly at me. "Hazel, right? My, my. You have your father's eyes and hair color, too, but that face is all your mama, ain't it?"

My face heated, a little shocked by her words. Most of the shifters here only commented on how much I looked like my father. They rarely spoke about my mother. I assumed it was a taboo subject because she was human. The old woman ducked under the counter and pulled out a pink cake box with a blue ribbon on top.

"Here you are." She looked at me intently, still smiling as she taped a plastic cake cutter to the side of the box and then handed it to me.

"I know not many people here probably talk much about your mother, but I knew her. She was the sweetest woman I had ever met. She loved this community and cared about the people in it, even though they shunned her. She'd come here often to buy my cakes and pastries. She said they were the best she'd ever had. She definitely had a sweet tooth, that one." She chuckled and then held out her flour-covered hands. I smiled shyly and took one with my free hand. She placed her other hand on top of mine.

"I see the same light in you as I did your mother. You have a lot of your father's strength and stubbornness, but your mother's forgiveness is there too."

I wasn't sure what to say to this old woman. I didn't even know her name, and she hardly knew me, but her words rang in my head, and I knew she was being sincere.

I asked if she required any payment, but she said no, it was already taken care of. I thanked her for the cake, and she wished me a happy birthday as I left.

As I walked back, the woman's words were still heavy on my mind, until I heard someone call my name. I turned to see David jogging up to me. I was taken back for a second. Even though I knew David was a shifter like me, it still felt like he was very much a part of the human world I'd left behind. I never would have expected to run into him here, but it made sense that we would. His pack likely lived here at Crescent Peak as well.

"David, hey."

"Hey, I heard you were staying here. I've been looking all over for you. How are you?" He touched my shoulder.

The last time I'd seen David, Rob had been alive, and I was on my way to see Molly. A lot had happened since then, but I didn't feel like going into it with yet another person. So I simply said, "Fine. How are you? I'm just glad to see you." He smiled, but it didn't quite reach his eyes. David didn't look well. Sweat covered his shirt and his hands and bare feet were covered in dirt, mud crusting the bottom of his jeans.

I was about to ask if he was okay when he glanced down at the cake.

"Mrs. Sandra makes the best baked goods in all of Crescent Falls. I'm surprised she hasn't tried opening a shop in town. Guess she likes to stick close to the community, like most of the shifters here, I suppose."

I only nodded. So, her name was Sandra.

"Happy birthday by the way."

I cocked my head, eyebrows drawn together in confusion. He pointed at the cake. "It says 'Happy Birthday, Hazel.'"

"Oh, thanks."

We stood in awkward silence.

"David, is everything okay?"

He flinched and his eyes squeezed shut like he was in pain. He didn't open them as he spoke.

"Actually, there's a reason I've been looking for you."

He stepped closer to me, his head hanging low. He moved his head from side to side, scanning the area, but the street was empty. He looked me in the eye.

"I came to warn you. Ross is planning something, and you and your aunt need to be careful. He knows you're staying here in the community."

"How do you know anything about Ross and his plans?"

"Just trust me. You and your aunt might not be safe here for long."

How could I trust him, though? How could he possibly know anything about Ross's plans if he wasn't somehow in on them. Could he be a part of Ross's pack? Was he a spy sent to keep an eye on me?

All those questions started stirring in my head, sending my caution walls up. Something wasn't right. I backed away from him, but he closed the distance between us in a few short strides. He grabbed my face with both his hands. Tears filled my eyes. I was embarrassed, angry. I tried to jerk away, but he held firm. A growl rose in my throat. I would fight him if I had to.

"Let go," I said, locking eyes with him, getting angrier by the second. That would be his only warning.

His face softened from serious to sad.

"I know you don't trust me. I know you'll probably hate me soon, but I'm on your side, Hazel. I will always be on your side. Just like we promised."

Let's promise to always be on each other's side. No matter what. Us against the world. Hazel and David.

The memory was like a punch in the gut.

He leaned in.

"What are you…" I began but suddenly his lips were on mine, stopping my question.

The kiss was quick, so quick I didn't even have time to pull away. When he let go of my face and leaned back, I did the only thing I could think of. I slapped him.

His head jerked to the side, his hand coming up to cup his cheek. When he turned back to look at me again, I expected to see shock or even anger on his face, but he only gave a sad smile and walked away, his left cheek red. I was too stunned to call after him and make him explain himself.

I regretted not doing so on my walk home. I ran through his warning and that kiss repeatedly in my head. Was it a coincidence David came back into my life when all these things started happening to me? I was surprised how hurt I felt by the idea. Part of me knew I didn't really know David anymore, but he had, at one point, meant a lot to me as a kid and now I felt betrayed.

Should I tell someone about his warning?

I touched my lips. They felt bruised. I'd never been kissed before. I was angry my first kiss was stolen…and I had every right to be. I was sick of men thinking they could just take what wasn't theirs. David didn't know me anymore. He didn't know what I had been through and perhaps he thought his kiss was innocent, but it still didn't give him the right.

I was nearly back to the cabin and my anger hadn't diminished. I stopped for a moment to take a deep breath and calm down before I walked any farther. David's warning came to mind. If he was working for Ross, then why would he try and warn me of his plans? Unless telling me was somehow a trick. I decided it was best to ignore it for now. Aunt Claire and I were safe with Lucas for the time being and I wasn't sure I could even trust David. I would look for him again and get the answers I needed, even if I had to beat it out of him, but for now, it would have to wait because I had a surprise birthday party to get to.

I knew Aunt Claire wouldn't be able to resist throwing me a surprise party. She hinted at one every year, but I never had enough friends and family to make it happen.

Now she had her chance.

I caught on to her plan as soon as I had come down the stairs earlier. She had made sure no one was in the house and then she'd sent me to get my own cake when she could have easily made anyone else go. My aunt was good at a lot of things, but lying and keeping secrets wasn't one of them.

Even though my fight with Molly and the anger I still felt over David's stolen kiss left me in no mood to celebrate, I couldn't deny my aunt's opportunity to give me a party. I knew she was trying hard to make the best of our situation and she deserved to have something go right for once.

As I walked up to the house, I noticed a set of balloons hanging from the front steps. I smiled. *Real subtle, Aunt Claire*, I thought and opened the door.

"Surprise!" everyone yelled.

They all stood by the door, balloons in their hands and silly party hats on their heads. Even Evangeline had a party horn in her mouth, though her expression was still one of disinterest. I took in the scene before me and was suddenly overcome with emotion as I realized the gravity of the situation.

I had friends. A real group of friends who took the time to throw me a birthday party. A group of people who actually cared about me, and I them.

And as I looked at them all: the twins and Sophie running up to hug me, Jake blowing a party horn in Eva's face, Isaac giving me a silly thumbs-up, Lucas with his arm draped over Aunt Claire's shoulders, and Caden, who was giving me an almost shy smile, I thought maybe, just maybe, they could be family too.

We had an amazing dinner. Aunt Claire made all my favorite foods, and everyone laughed and joked, even Eva was smiling. When we finished dinner, we moved outside to a bonfire Lucas had set up. We sat in broken lawn chairs and made s'mores, using sticks we had found in the woods to roast the marshmallows. It would have been the best birthday…if Molly were there to celebrate too. I tried my best not to think about it and to just enjoy the company I had.

Caden came and sat next to me. He wore a strange look on his face, almost like jealousy or anger. He kept glancing at my lips. Did he know David kissed me? If so, he said nothing about it and instead, he skewered a marshmallow and held it over the fire. "So, how's it feel to be eighteen?"

"About the same as being seventeen, I suppose."

He nodded. "I don't even remember my eighteenth birthday."

I glanced at everyone sitting and laughing by the campfire. "I'm not likely to forget."

He smiled. "Good."

He scooted closer to me, so close that our chairs touched. He took the marshmallow and placed it between two graham crackers with a piece of chocolate, then handed it to me. "I've been meaning to ask you something."

He sounded hesitant.

"Okay, shoot." I looked up at him. He stared so intently at me that I nearly dropped my s'more in the grass.

"Hazel, would you like to go on a date with me?"

My heart hammered in my chest. "Like, a real date?" I sounded like an idiot, but I'd never been asked on a date before.

He smiled. Oh God that smile. It made my thighs clench.

"Yes. Like a real date."

I said nothing at first. I just stared at the s'more in my hand, the chocolate now melting onto my fingers.

"I've never been on a date before," I admitted.

"It's okay, neither have I," he confessed.

I found that hard to believe. I gazed up at him,

expecting to see the joke written on his face, but he looked serious.

"What about Evangeline. You two weren't a thing?"

He glanced over at her. She was sitting next to Isaac, handing a s'more to Sophie.

"Not like boyfriend and girlfriend. No, but we were something at one point. It was a long time ago, though."

I couldn't help but feel a little jealous over Evangeline and Caden's past. Did he love her then? He said it was a long time ago, but sometimes feelings still lingered. Eva obviously still had feelings for him.

He placed his hand on my wrist so I'd look up at him. "I care about Evangeline, but not like that. I don't think I ever did. That's why I ended things."

I looked Caden in the eye. He sounded honest. I could trust him; my gut was telling me I could. "Yes."

"Yes?"

"I'll go on a date with you."

I would have said yes a thousand times over just to see that smile on his face. It was infectious. He held my hand the rest of the night. Aunt Claire noticed and smiled, looking up at Lucas and then back at me like we shared something special together. Like we'd found our happiness.

Eva looked like she just ate something sour. I wanted to tell her Isaac loved her, but that wasn't my place. That was something Isaac would have to do on his own. Maybe I should talk to him about it, perhaps figure out why he hadn't already confessed. I would soon, but for now, I leaned on Caden's shoulder and enjoyed the rest of my birthday. If happiness was a moment, it was this one.

CHAPTER

THIRTEEN

I took one last look at myself in the mirror. I wore my best clothes: a gray spaghetti strap crop top with a red flannel shirt—hung open and loose over my shoulders—my favorite black skinny jeans, and Chucks.

Okay, so maybe that wasn't someone else's idea of a date-worthy outfit, but I wasn't even sure I should wear a crop top. I'd never worn one a day in my life. This particular crop top had been sitting in the back of my dresser drawer for God only knew how long. It had been a present from Molly. She'd hoped by me wearing it, I would come out of my shell a little more, but I'd never even taken the tag off until now. How it had gotten into my bag while packing was beyond me, but I was grateful all the same because the rest of my clothes were either baggy T-shirts, hole-ridden cutoffs, or running clothes. I didn't have a nice skirt or dress. Weren't those the type of things you wore on a first date?

I wished I could call Molly and ask her. My heart hurt all over again just thinking that I couldn't. If she were here right now, I think she would be proud of me. I was finally going on a date with a guy I liked, and I was wearing the top she gave me.

I pulled my hair up into what I hoped to be a fashionable high ponytail. It was so long now, and even though it was up, it still hung over my shoulders. I left two pieces of hair hang loosely in front of my face. I had no makeup of my own, but Aunt Claire let me use her eyeliner and lip gloss.

I stared in the mirror at my handiwork and hoped I didn't look like how I felt—like a kid playing dress up. I was so nervous my chest was blotchy. I put a cold cloth over it and silently prayed it would go away quickly.

Caden said he'd meet me downstairs at noon. I looked at the clock. It was just after twelve. I took a deep breath, removed the cloth, and headed out of the room. He stood waiting for me by the front door.

He wore a light button-down sweater, dark jeans, and Nikes, but honestly, he could have been wearing an old ragged T-shirt and basketball shorts and he would have been heart stopping. Still, I was glad to see he hadn't over- or underdressed for the occasion. I hoped I didn't look like I had either.

His expression was unreadable as I came down the stairs. When I reached him, he pulled his hands from behind his back and handed me a dozen roses. The gesture was so cheesy I laughed. He was smiling and leaned in to whisper in my ear.

"You look amazing. I'm loving all this extra skin."

His words set said skin ablaze and I worried the blotches would reappear. I held my hand up to my chest to cover it just in case.

"Thank you. You don't look so bad yourself."

He winked, seemingly pleased by my reaction as he

opened the door and then we walked out. I was surprised Aunt Claire wasn't lurking nearby to see us off. Lucas must have convinced her not to. I'd have to thank him for that later.

I asked Caden where we were going as we got in his car, but he told me it was a secret.

After driving down back roads for ten minutes, Caden reached behind him to the back seat, pulled out a blindfold, and handed it to me.

"Seriously?" I asked skeptically.

He laughed. "Yes. Trust me. It won't be a surprise if you don't."

I narrowed my eyes at him, but then gave in. I tied the blindfold behind my head.

We drove like that for what felt like an eternity. I was antsy and desperately wanted to find out where we were going. He turned on the radio and I laughed as we sang to whatever upbeat song was playing. I felt silly with this blindfold on. Caden held my hand and I just knew he was smiling at me.

After a while, he finally pulled to a stop. I heard his door open and close, then mine. "Keep the blindfold on," he said. He held my hand to help me out of the car. Once I was out, he rested his other hand on my lower back as he guided me in the direction he wanted to go. When I almost tripped, we both let out a nervous laugh. He told me to stop. I was giddy as he removed the blindfold.

When I opened my eyes, I realized we were at the lake where Caden and I first met. A large plaid blanket was laid out with a pizza box and a bottle of wine sitting on top. There were flower petals of assorted colors strewn around us. Everything was so neatly placed, it looked like it came from a candid photo or movie.

I looked at Caden. The affection on his face mirrored my own.

"Caden, this is amazing. Best first date ever."

He laughed. "The date hasn't even started yet. Come on."

We sat on the blanket. I took a slice of pizza as he pulled out wineglasses from the wicker basket beside him. I'd never seen a wicker basket in real life and the thought almost made me laugh for some reason. The absurdity of it all. I almost felt like none of this was even real, like I'd wake up and realize I was dreaming about some book I'd read.

I must be nervous.

Caden glanced at me, a sheepish expression on his face. "I'm nervous too."

I stared at him in shock. I'd nearly forgotten our shared thoughts. I still wasn't sure how it worked exactly. It seemed to only connect every so often.

We ate pizza, drank wine, and talked, finally opening up and sharing things we'd been holding back. I told him about Molly and how we'd gotten into a fight. I told him about Rob and what he'd done to my aunt and me. I wanted him to know what he was getting into and how deep the damage was.

As I told my story, Caden just held me against his chest. My throat felt choked, but I didn't cry. There was no reason to anymore. Rob was dead, gone from our lives forever. I felt the anger roll off Caden in waves. I was certain if Rob hadn't been dead, he would have been soon.

Caden returned the favor and bared his soul to me as well. He told me about the deaths of his parents and how close he'd come to losing himself. I think he wanted me to see the extent of his damage, too, and to make me feel like I wasn't alone.

"When I left the hospital and came back to the charred remains of our home, I just couldn't take the grief. I'd never see my mother's smile again, never watch my father paint another painting, never get to witness my sister grow up. So I shifted, and I let instinct take over. I wanted to forget…and I did…for a time. I was a wolf for the better part of two years. I don't remember much then. Every day was the same as the last. I just remember how simple it all was. I was alone but never lonely. I hunted when I was hungry, slept when I was tired, and I never thought of the death of my family. I was free.

"But Lucas searched for me. He set a trap and stuck me in a cage, determined to bring me back to humanity. I don't know why, maybe that's just the kind of man Lucas is. Always trying to help the ones who don't want to be helped.

"He came to me every day and showed me pictures of my family, telling me stories about them, and every day he'd end his story with how they'd died. I knew he didn't want to hurt me, but I think he also knew that it was the only way to bring me back. It took him months to get me to remember, months to make me human again, but when he finally did, I hated him. I hated him for a long time.

"But I let him ease me back into humanity. I'm not really sure why. I think the guilt of forgetting my family was too great. I wanted to be punished for even forgetting them for a second and I felt my humanity was punishment enough. He offered to help me rebuild my family's home. I accepted, but once it was finished, I just wanted to be left alone. I think Lucas had hoped I'd join his pack like the others, but I couldn't forgive him for bringing me back. I couldn't forgive him for ripping me away from my peace."

We were now lying on the blanket. My head was on his chest, listening to his heartbeat while he spoke. I had no idea the torture Caden must have gone through.

"I'm so sorry, Caden. It must have been hard, but I think Lucas knew that you couldn't stay a wolf forever. You couldn't heal as a wolf."

I felt his sigh.

"I know and I've made my peace with him now, but a part of me might always hate him. Just like a part of me will always mourn the loss of my family."

We were silent for a moment. I let the weight of his words sink in, thinking about all he'd been through.

"Hazel? Can I ask you something?"

"Anything."

I gazed up at him as he looked down at me, those beautiful two-colored eyes gave me their full attention.

"I know it's none of my business, but since you agreed to go on this date with me, I thought I should ask."

I gave a nod, urging him to continue.

"Are you seeing someone else?"

I furrowed my brow in confusion.

"No, why?"

"I could tell someone kissed you. His scent was still on you when you came home."

His voice was calm, but I could see the tension in his body. He was fighting his anger, fighting the wolf inside.

I sat up so I could look him in the eye.

"It's nothing like that, trust me," I said sternly, letting him see my anger. "The kiss was as much of a surprise to me as it was to you."

I told him about David and explained our meeting yesterday and the unexpected kiss.

When I finished, I released a heavy sigh.

"I don't know what I was thinking. I guess I just let the nostalgic feelings of our old friendship cloud my judgement. Or maybe David really is trying to help us. I don't know. All I know is right now I don't have many people I can trust. He had no right to just kiss me like that."

I furrowed my brow, angry all over again.

Caden looked at me and sat up so we were eye level. His gaze was intense, almost possessive. It gave me goose bumps. He pulled me into a hug, his lips touching my neck. For one hysterical moment, I thought he was going to bite me, but then I realized what the gesture meant to shifters. I'd seen others in the community do it.

Wolves exposed their necks to another wolf's teeth as a sign of good faith. They were showing the other wolf that they trusted them not to bite. As a shifter, it was also a metaphor to symbolize that you were willing to be open and honest with someone, and that you trusted them to do the same.

"You can trust me," he whispered into my neck.

It made me shiver.

I leaned my head to the side, exposing my neck farther so that he knew I understood, and I pressed my lips to Caden's exposed neck too. I wasn't sure when it had happened, but I knew I could trust Caden with my life, and maybe with my heart. I hoped he felt the same way.

"I know."

When he pulled away, he was smiling. "You're catching on to our customs quickly."

I smiled back. "Thanks."

He reached into the basket and pulled out a small box. "I have a surprise for you, for your birthday."

"Caden, you didn't have to get me anything."

He let out a small laugh. "Trust me, I've been holding on to this for a long time."

He handed me a plain gray box, wrapped in a golden ribbon. I untied the ribbon and opened the lid gently. I let out a gasp.

Inside the box sat a necklace. A gold necklace with a golden wolf charm. It stood tall, head back, like it was howling at the moon. It was the necklace I'd been eyeing all those years ago outside the storefront. I felt tears prick my eyes as I looked up at Caden.

"How did you…" was all I could manage.

"I was the one who bought that necklace all those years ago. I hoped I'd get the chance to give it to you myself someday."

I couldn't understand why anyone would do such a thing. "But…why?"

He only stared at me.

"Because I knew," his mind whispered so faintly I thought I'd imagined it.

We stared into each other's eyes for a long moment, neither of us realizing we were both leaning forward slowly. I really wanted to kiss him, and I could tell he did too. I was about to meet him halfway when my phone rang. I pulled it out of my back pocket. It was Lucas.

I answered it, giving Caden an apologetic face. "Hello?"

"Hazel, the council has finally given approval to meet with them, but we need to go today. How fast can you get here?"

"I can be back there in forty-five minutes."

"Okay, hurry, the council doesn't like to be left waiting."

"Oh sure, right. The council can't stand to wait but what have I been doing this whole time?"

"Hazel," he warned "I expect you'll keep that tongue in check in front of the council."

"I'm on my way."

Caden looked at me knowingly, but before we got up to leave, I asked him to help me put on the necklace. Once it was clasped around my neck, I couldn't help staring at it the entire way back to Crescent Peak. It looked like it belonged around my neck. I'd thought about the necklace so often, picturing the wolf charm sitting on my chest, it almost felt like it had always been there. I glanced at Caden. A small voice whispered in my head a truth I wasn't sure I was ready to face yet. A voice that said Caden might be my mate.

As soon as we drove up to the Orphanage, Lucas was standing by the front door. Caden volunteered to go with us, but Lucas told him the council only requested Lucas and me. I gave Caden a hug and a quick kiss on the cheek, thanking him for today.

"Be careful," he replied. "The council isn't known for being fair."

I looked at Lucas. He only nodded sullenly.

"I'll be here when you get back," Caden said, then took a seat on the front steps, as if he really did intend to wait right there.

Lucas and I set off toward the main hall, where the council had agreed to meet with us.

When we walked inside, each member was sitting behind a long wooden table. They each greeted Lucas but did not ask us to sit. I almost felt as if we were on trial. One of the members addressed me.

"Hazel Lowell. Welcome to Crescent Peak."

I gave a small bow of the head, just as I'd seen Lucas do.

This seemed to his satisfaction. He continued speaking. "Your father was a great alpha in this community and a well-known shifter. We were sad when we heard he'd lost himself in favor of a human."

"And to die a human death," added another member. "Such a shame."

I looked at Lucas, remembering to control my anger. I knew I'd have to watch what I said. Lucas warned me on our walk here that the council would be a bit crass toward humans, believing them to be below shifter kind.

"Yes, well, if it wasn't for the both of them, I wouldn't be here today," I replied politely.

"Yes, yes, I suppose that is true," said another council member.

Each member looked the same to me, just as they had in the photo Lucas showed me.

"You are a rare thing, aren't you? Not many half breeds are able to survive their first shift, especially those raised by a human."

I stayed silent.

"Nevertheless," said another, "you are here now, and we are happy to welcome you into our community. Have you joined a pack yet?"

I glanced at Lucas again. I hadn't mentioned I was considering joining his pack and he hadn't actually offered.

He spoke first. "Hazel is still getting used to shifter customs, but I'm hoping in time, she may agree to join me and my pack someday."

They all nodded and mumbled in agreement.

"Very well. Why have you summoned us here today, Hazel?"

This was it. Finally, my chance to convince the council that Ross needed to pay for his crimes. I only had this one chance.

"Alpha Council, I came here to Crescent Peak under grave circumstances, I'm afraid. An alpha by the name of Ross attacked my friend, a human girl, and killed a young boy in the process. This was all for the sake of scaring me into joining his pack. When I refused, my uncle, a man named Robert Lloyd, was murdered in our home by that same alpha. When my aunt and I came here to seek refuge, I was told you had the power to help me receive justice for the wrongdoings Ross has inflicted upon my family and friends."

The council members leaned into one another, whispering among themselves for several minutes. When they were done, they each sat quietly, staring at me. The council member who sat directly in front of me spoke.

"Though it is true that it is a crime among shifters to kill humans, it is, in truth, only due to the exposure we might face because of it, not the act of killing the human. If Ross has threatened our secrecy, then we will have no choice but to bring him to trial, but, if his actions have gone without notice and no one has been made aware of our kind, I see no reason why we should condemn a shifter to die, especially an alpha, just for killing a couple of humans."

"Humans *are* becoming more aware, though, because of Ross's actions they are more cautious now than ever."

"And this too shall pass. Do you realize how many of us die each year at the hands of humans? Husbands, wives, daughters, sons, sisters, brothers, grandparents. They all must watch as hunters shoot and kill their kin.

As they strip away their loved ones' furs and tails to be turned into coats and trophies and watch as their heads are mounted on walls to forever stare through glass eyes. Why should we care if there are fewer humans left on this earth?"

I stood shaking with anger. I could not deny what was happening to shifters was unjust, but that did not justify Ross's killings. Two wrongs did not make a right. I didn't understand how they could be so cruel to humans. Were shifters not half human themselves? Or did they think that because they had the ability to shift that it somehow made them superior?

I tried to appeal to their better nature.

"What about Caden's family? What about my father? Is there no justice for them? They were shifters, like us, and Ross murdered them. He gave them human deaths, as you say."

"There is no such proof that Ross killed Caden Ulrika's family or Clark Lowell in such a dishonorable way. If, however, some proof was brought to light, then we would gladly take him into custody and punish him accordingly."

"Would you? Or would you give him a slap on the wrist and send him on his way for killing his own kind the way he killed these humans?"

"Hazel…" Lucas warned.

"Enough. We did not come here today to debate such questions of morality. These are the facts, girl, and if you wish to be one of us and be a part of this community, then you will have no choice but to follow the rules we have set and accept that our word is law."

I pointed at Lucas.

"He should be the one in charge. He's the one who

founded this place, not you, and as far as I can tell, you're all doing a shitty job of running this community."

"Hazel, stop," Lucas said sternly. "It is not your place to decide whether I should be leader or not. That is a choice I've already made."

Lucas's words sounded confident, but his face looked like he was questioning his decision.

I glared at him and then back at the council. "Do you think you are safe? Ross wants power more than anything, and he will stop at nothing to get it. One day he *will* turn on you all, and you will be sorry you didn't deal with him sooner, but by then, it'll be too late."

"Enough!" the middle council member shouted.

"You will not threaten us here. We have made our decision. If I were you, I would be more worried about your aunt. She is a human and not welcome here. You have broken our most sacred law. She should not even know about us, let alone be allowed to live in this community. This is a coveted space for shifter kind. We should have you both killed."

A few of the council members leaned in and whispered to the middle member. He waved them away like flies and spoke again.

"But you are a rare case, Hazel. You are new to the shifter world and not fully accustomed to our laws and way of life, so we are willing to let this slide. However, your aunt cannot be allowed to stay here. She has until tomorrow morning to get her things and leave, or she will pay the consequences. Lucas, you should have known better than to let a human stay in your home. If she is not gone by tomorrow morning, you, too, will be punished accordingly."

I stood there in shock and fury. The wolf in me

howled with frustration, begging to be set free. I wanted to tear out the hearts of every single council member in that room, just to make sure they had one. I glanced at Lucas. He looked heart-stricken but said nothing. How could he just let them exile the woman he loved like that? Didn't he have any say? I was starting to think Lucas really was nothing but a coward.

I looked each member in the eye, showing a sign of disrespect. "I will be leaving then as well. I hope you enjoy what little time you have left with your power," I announced.

"We do not fear Ross," said the one in the middle.

I guessed he was the ringleader as he had spoken the most during this meeting, so I looked him square in the face. "It's not Ross you need to worry about anymore."

I sneered at them all and walked out of the room without a second glance.

When I reached the house, I was seething. Caden was sitting on the step, exactly where I'd left him. He got up and pulled me into a hug. He already knew it didn't go well. I wanted to pull away from his touch. I was too angry to be near anyone, but he held on tight.

"I can feel your anger, and your hurt. I'm so sorry, Hazel."

Tears pricked in my eyes, which only made me angrier. I didn't want to cry, I wanted to get even. He held me at arm's length.

"What do you want to do?"

I gazed up at him. I hoped I looked fierce—strong—despite the fact that my eyes were burning with unshed tears. It was not the time for weakness. I meant what I said to the council. I would get even with them, just as soon as I took care of Ross myself.

"I think it's time to have a talk with the rest of the pack. They need to know what's going on."

"I agree," said Lucas, who had just walked up behind me.

I turned on him, ready to let loose a string of curses, but he held up his hand.

"Save your words for the rest of the pack, Hazel."

He walked inside, calling everyone to his office. Caden and I followed. Everyone, except the twins and Sophie, joined us. Aunt Claire looked at me, then at Lucas. She knew something was wrong.

"What happened?" Isaac asked.

"Your alpha is a coward, that's what happened." I sneered at Lucas.

He ignored my comment and addressed the rest of the room. "The council has decided that Ross is no threat. They felt it was more of a concern having a human among us, so they banished Claire from the community. She has until tomorrow morning to leave."

Everyone glanced at Aunt Claire. She had her hand over her mouth, her eyes were firm, eyebrows drawn together with worry.

"I think you all know Claire is my bond. I did not want to make our relationship out to be so serious, but this is a serious situation that needs to be weighed carefully."

I was the only one in the room who appeared shocked. Even Aunt Claire didn't look surprised.

"You two are mates?" I asked, turning to Lucas.

He nodded. "I explained it all to your aunt. She knows."

I looked at Aunt Claire, feeling a little betrayed. "Why didn't you say anything?"

"I was waiting for the right opportunity, honey. I wasn't expecting this to happen."

She took my hands in hers. Despite the situation and my feelings of betrayal for not telling me sooner, I was happy for my aunt. She looked like she'd never been surer of anything in her life. Of course, she did, she'd found her soulmate, at least that was the impression Caden had given me when he explained it.

Lucas let out a sigh, bringing our attention back to the group.

"I am giving each of you a choice. It is obvious that I will not abandon Claire, therefore I, too, will be leaving the community. You can choose to join me or to stay and join another pack. I will not force you to come. Without the protection of the community, Ross will likely try and attack while we are vulnerable. His obsession with Hazel will not waver, just like it did not waver with Hazel's father. He will never stop until Hazel is a part of his pack, or dead."

I was looking at Lucas in a new light. I never imagined it would come to this. I thought Aunt Claire and I would be on our own. I felt shame for ever thinking he was a coward.

He looked at me.

"I'm sorry I let you believe I'd given up on you and Claire. I couldn't let the council know what I was thinking. They would likely try to strip my pack from me without giving them a choice and"—he looked at each of us—"I want you to have a choice."

Everyone was quiet for a moment.

"I'm with you," Isaac said. He looked at me and Aunt Claire. "Hazel and Claire are family now, a part of this pack, and we protect our own."

He focused on Jake, who only nodded in agreement. Isaac then turned to Eva. She looked angry, but when she glanced at Caden her face softened. She finally looked at Lucas, letting out a long exhale through her nose.

"This pack is all I have. Lucas took me in when I had nothing and no one. If he really is bonded to Claire, then Isaac is right." She looked at me, and although there was still no kindness on her face, for once she did not sneer. "You're both a part of this pack now, and I'm not going anywhere."

"And Caden?" Lucas asked, looking up at him from behind his desk. He'd said nothing the entire time. He looked only at me, a fevered expression on his face.

"I go where Hazel goes. Always."

My heart swelled.

"Thank you all, so much." I offered a small smile as I acknowledged each one of them.

"What about the kids?" Evangeline asked.

"I suppose they have a choice in the matter as well, but if I had to guess, I'd say they'd want to stay with us too," Lucas said.

"I'm gonna go down and talk with them." And with that, she left the room.

Lucas turned to Caden. "Can we move into your lodge?"

Caden gave a small nod. "Of course. It was always meant for a pack."

Lucas smiled. "Good. Good. Thank you, Caden. I'll have both you and Hazel sworn into the pack officially as soon as we get there. We'll need all the strength we can get, should Ross really decide to attack. Let's get everyone packing. I intend to be out of here before morning, just as the council requested." Everyone nodded in agreement. I was about to tell Lucas about the warning David had given me when suddenly a scream and a crash echoed from inside the house. I was closest to the door, so I was the first one out as we all rushed down the stairs to see what had happened. The twins were in the living room, crouched over a mass of fur. Evangeline.

"They took her! They took her!" The twins pointed at the broken window.

Caden rushed over to look outside. "There's two of them. They're heading into the woods." He looked at everyone. "They have Sophie."

Isaac crouched over Eva, pressing two fingers to her fur-lined neck, then sighed with relief. "She's breathing," he said, pulling her head into his lap.

"Why Sophie?" Jake asked.

Eva let out a whine through her nose and suddenly she was human again. Lucas draped a blanket over her naked body. She let out a cough, her voice making a croaking noise as she started to speak.

"She was the closest one they could get to. The boys were in the other room. They snuck up on me when I wasn't looking. I couldn't do anything. I couldn't save her." For the first time, I watched Eva lose her cold and angry composure. Tears were streaming down her face.

"This is Ross's doing," I said.

Lucas nodded in agreement. "It could likely be a trap. Ross could be trying to lure you away from the pack."

"Or lead the pack away from Hazel," Caden countered.

"We have to go after Sophie. We can't leave her with Ross and his pack," I stated.

"I agree," Lucas said. "Caden, Isaac, and Hazel will

go after Sophie. If you can catch the two shifters before they reach the rest of the pack, there might be a chance we can save her. Jake and I will stay here and protect Claire and look after Evangeline."

"I'm fine," Eva croaked.

"Then you can help Jake and me look after Claire while the rest save Sophie," he said sternly. There was no room for argument. "Hurry, go!"

Caden, Isaac, and I each climbed out the window. It was faster than going out the front door. There was no time for modesty as we removed our clothes quickly and shifted. We immediately shot toward the woods, spreading out so we covered more ground. I ran as fast I could, only stopping every so often to sniff the ground for Sophie's scent. She smelled like sweet pea and lavender.

My nose was so trained to the ground I nearly ran right into a rushing creek. The scent stopped abruptly and for several frustrating minutes, I thought I'd lost it, but then the wind picked up and I caught her scent again. It was across the creek. I jumped into the freezing water and half paddled, half padded across. When I reached the other end, I shook the water from my fur and took off running again, her scent was getting stronger. I howled, letting Caden and Isaac know I was getting close.

The trees suddenly gave way to a clearing. I slowed down, crouching. Something was wrong. It was the same feeling I had gotten when I walked into the house and found Rob dead on the kitchen floor.

Instinct was telling me to be cautious as I scanned the area. I spotted a small mound of white fur lying in the tall grass. I knew it could be a trap, but I had to be sure Sophie was okay. I got up, prepared to run toward her, but suddenly two wolves emerged from either side of the clearing, hair raised and teeth snapping.

I bristled and released a low warning growl, prepared to fight. They wasted no time. As soon as they were close enough, they lunged for me. I dodged the first wolf, but the second one hit me on my side, digging his teeth into my back. I let out a yelp, bucking him off. I looked over at Sophie.

She still wasn't moving.

I was distracted and the wolves took advantage of my mistake. Both pounced again. This time each of them landed on top me, pinning me to the ground.

Stupid. My worry for Sophie was making me panic, but I had to keep a level head. I had to make sure I lived through this, for both our sakes. I couldn't help Sophie if I didn't help myself first.

I let out a growl as I pushed one of the wolves off me, then I bit the other on the front leg. He yelped and staggered back, giving me the opportunity to slip out from underneath him. I jumped away from them. The wolves were circling me again, looking for a weakness. I tried to remember Lucas's training, tried to remember what was most important.

"You likely won't have as much experience as your opponent. They will have been training to be shifters for most of their lives, even before their first shift, but you have something they don't. You are in total control. Half a shifter's strength is used to keep their wolf at bay, half their focus will be on trying not to lose control, but you don't have that problem. So while your instincts are important, just remember your biggest advantage is your ability to think clearly. Your advantage is the ability to think more like a human."

I looked around the clearing, trying to figure out a

plan. I knew one wolf didn't stand a chance against two, but as a human… I took off running toward the edge of the clearing, away from the wolves. They were stunned at first. A second later, they ran after me, reveling in the chase.

I shifted mid-run, picked up a large rock at the edge of the clearing, and began climbing the nearest tree, one-handed. When the wolves reached me, they seemed almost confused. I positioned myself on a sturdy branch and gave them no time to think about shifting to try and climb after me. I braced myself, rock held over my head, and I leaped, landing on the nearest wolf and smashing the rock as hard as I could onto his head.

He didn't get up again.

My legs had pins and needles in them from the fall, but I forced myself to get up immediately.

The other wolf circled me. Something was off about him now. I could see there was no human recognition in his eyes. The shock and loss of one of his pack members must have thrown him over the edge. There was only a wild animal circling me, and it was furious.

I shifted back and let out a long howl. I hoped Caden and Isaac would find me soon. Someone needed to get to Sophie, and fast. I lunged at the wolf first, digging my teeth into the side of his neck. I could feel his growl rumble through my teeth.

He pushed me against the tree, repeatedly, but I held tight. I tore through flesh and tasted blood—metallic and hot—in my mouth. He pushed again, this time with all his strength. My head cracked against the trunk so hard I saw black spots in my vision. I had no choice but to let him go, my jaw was no longer doing what it was told. My eyesight blurred as I sank to the base of the tree, unable to stand.

The wolf's teeth pierced my flesh and held me by the throat. I scanned the area frantically for something that could save me. I reached my paw toward a large branch lying next to me, but I needed to shift for it to work. I couldn't completely shift into a human, the wolf had me by the throat and my weak human skin would be torn to pieces within seconds. Lucas hadn't taught me how to use selective shifting, but he said it could be done. After all, I'd been able to shift my teeth before I'd even become a full shifter.

I concentrated all my thoughts on my front paw, willing it to be a human hand. Slowly my claws turned into nails, my paw into fingers, until I was reaching with a full set of fingers and a thumb, but the shift didn't stop there. It gradually crept up my arm. Soon I would lose what little control I had and become entirely human again. I had to be quick. I grabbed the branch and with all the strength I could muster, I bashed it against the side of the wolf's head.

With a yelp and a shake of his head, he released me. I quickly shifted, fully human now. Using both my hands and a pointed end of the broken branch, I let out a yell and thrust it into the wolf's eye. A deafening howl erupted from him as he tried to pull away. I thrust deeper, grunting with exertion. I felt like I'd been pushing for an eternity, when finally, the wolf stopped howling and slumped forward, dead at last.

I pushed him off me, the branch still stuck in his eye. I glanced down at my naked body, covered in dirt, leaves, and blood. I wanted to cry, to pass out from exhaustion, but there wasn't time for that now. I had to get to Sophie. I didn't shift again. I didn't think I had it in me, so I ran on two legs.

I called her name, but she didn't stir. They must have

knocked her out, left her unconscious. I couldn't let myself believe that someone would—that something so horrible could...

When I reached her, she still wasn't moving.

She was so small. A tuft of white fur against a sea of green.

"Sophie," I whispered so softly I barely heard it myself.

I crouched down slowly and lifted her up. Her fur was so new, so soft.

She wasn't breathing. Her chest didn't rise and fall.

There were no marks on her to speak of, but...she wasn't breathing.

She.

Wasn't.

Breathing.

This couldn't be happening. The world couldn't possibly be so cruel. Not to a little girl. Not to someone so small and innocent.

This couldn't be happening.

This couldn't be happening.

I repeated this over and over again in my head, my face a blank mask, staring down at her unmoving form, willing her heart to beat, willing her eyes to open.

"Wake up, Sophie. Wake up," I whispered.

I must have sat that way for an eternity. Hoping against all odds that she would wake up.

And then the weight of what had happened finally set in and I let out a scream of rage and anguish. Misery and heartache gripped me so tightly I thought I would choke on it. I leaned my face into her fur, whispering her name repeatedly as I sobbed.

"I'm so sorry. I'm so, so sorry, Sophie. This is all my fault." I breathed between sobs. "This is all my fault."

I heard Caden and Isaac coming through the clearing, but they didn't approach. They moved no farther than the tree line. They must have heard my scream of anguish. When they shifted into human form, Caden fell on his knees, his hands in his hair, a look of despair on his face. Isaac was crouched on one knee, a hand over his eyes, his body racked with sobs.

I held her close to my chest, rocking her back and forth as I wept. I thought of nothing but the pain I felt. The loss of someone so young and beautiful. How alone and scared she must have been, hoping someone would come and rescue her.

We stayed like that for a long time. The boys came no closer, battling their own pain and loss.

When I was finally able to see past my own grief, I lifted my head and looked around the clearing. My eyes settled on the two dead wolves by the tree. I released a growl and smiled cruelly. At least some justice was had. At least Sophie's killers lay dead by my hand.

But they were not Sophie's real murderer. It might have been by their hands, but it was Ross who had killed Sophie. This was Ross's doing.

The guilt of Sophie's death left me paralyzed, unable to continue, unable to carry on, but anger was replacing the ache in my heart. Fury was giving me the strength, if only till my goal was met.

Only one thing mattered now. Only one thing drove me.

Revenge.

Ross could not be allowed to live on this earth when he had taken something so precious from it. I would see to that, and if he killed me in the process, all the better, because this was my fault too. I should have ended him sooner. I shouldn't have relied on someone else to solve my problems. I led him to this pack. I led him to Sophie's demise.

I would never make that mistake again.

I stood with Sophie cradled in my arms. I was naked, covered in dirt and blood, but I didn't care. I stood there like a wild, vengeful forest god, looking at Caden and Isaac. "Does she have a family?"

Caden nodded. "Her father lives in Canada." His voice was soft, broken.

"We'll have to tell him what happened." I tried to sound stern, but my voice shook.

"What should we do with…with her?" asked Isaac.

I looked down at Sophie, her violet eyes forever closed and then looked at the clearing before us. Patches of wildflowers lay scattered in the tall grass, butterflies landing gently on their petals. Sophie loved butterflies and flowers. She loved anything that was beautiful and full of color. This clearing had plenty of that.

"I think we should bury her here," I said, sounding less broken than I felt.

Isaac and Caden nodded in agreement.

They shifted into wolves and began digging a hole in the middle of the clearing where I'd first found her. I knew I should probably help, but I couldn't bring myself to put her down.

When the hole was dug, I began to cry again. I knew she was gone, but the thought of leaving her alone in that hole ripped me apart. In the end, Isaac was the one who took her from me, gently laying her to rest.

I picked wildflowers and quietly laid them on her body. The boys and I, in human form, covered the hole with dirt. We fashioned a makeshift grave marker from two small sticks, and I silently promised we'd get her a real one soon.

When the job was done, I sat there broken, my hands covered in dirt—all our hands were covered in dirt. Caden reached out to touch me, but before he could, I stood up and began walking back toward the community. I couldn't let him touch me, couldn't look him in the eye. I knew if I did, I would lose it all over again.

I had to steel myself. There was no room for feelings right now.

I shifted into wolf form and took off running into the trees, Caden and Isaac followed.

We returned to the place where we'd left our clothes and dressed quickly. We said nothing to one another, saving our strength for the hard task of telling the others what had happened. No one came outside to meet us. We walked up the front steps, so engrossed in our grief that none of us realized there was something wrong till it was too late. Caden pushed a hand in front of me as the door burst open.

Three naked strangers stood behind the door, their teeth pulled back, growling. They lunged, each of them restraining us before we could run, holding large knives up to our necks so we couldn't shift. They led us into the house, closing the door with a slam. Fear gripped me tight as we entered the living room.

Ross sat on the couch, his arm draped casually over Aunt Claire's shoulders. Her hands were bound in front of her, her mouth taped shut. Lucas was kneeling on the floor, hands bound behind his back, mouth also taped shut. Two guards stood on either side of him, each holding a knife against his neck. There was murder in his eyes at the sight of Ross touching Claire.

Evangeline and Jake were also on their knees, bound similarly, a guard standing over each of them. Eva gave us a worried look as we entered. A silent question was there. One I couldn't answer right now. I looked away from her, but that was all it took. She began silently sobbing on the floor. Her cries muffled by the tape. Jake, also realizing the meaning, slumped his head forward, his eyes closed tightly shut.

I heard banging and scratching on the basement door. Brandon and Brian must be locked away down there. The guards behind us pushed us to the floor. They tied Caden's and Isaac's hands and bound their mouths with tape. Caden let loose a growl, but it was cut short when the guard pressed his knife harder against his neck.

"Nice place you've found here, Hazel," Ross said casually. "So…quaint." He looked at me and smiled. He was dressed in a suit and tie, looking as put together as ever. His posture was calm and casual, as if he were sitting in a business meeting and not in a living room filled with naked shifters holding knives to people's throats.

I growled, giving him my most menacing look.

"Don't pretend, you bastard. Tell everyone what you did! Tell them how you murdered Sophie!"

Eva began to wail through the tape. Ross glanced at the guard closest to her, and he smacked her across the head. She made a muffled, pain-filled sound as she slumped over on her side, still crying but more quietly now. Jake tried to lean toward her, but he was held back by the knife at his throat. I looked over at Lucas, tears streaked down his face. His eyes were wild, chest heaving.

Ross had the gall to look shocked. He placed a hand over his heart.

"I did not kill her. I only told my boys to kidnap her. Are you sure she's really dead?"

"Yes, you bastard!"

I was screaming, eyes burning.

Ross looked like he was deep in thought. He placed a hand over his shortened beard, stroking it with two fingers.

"That is a shame. I didn't wish to harm the girl. Where are my pack members now?"

"I killed them." I growled with satisfaction.

He only nodded solemnly. "I suppose that's for the best. I would have done the same had they returned to me. I can't have members disobeying me."

He stood then, gripping Aunt Claire's arm and pulling her up with him.

"You had your justice for Sophie. You killed her murderers. Now it is time to get to the matter at hand."

"You sent them after her. It's your fault she's dead," I sneered. The guard holding my arms growled, giving me a swift blow to the head. I hissed in pain.

"You will not speak to your alpha that way."

"He is not my alpha," I said, looking Ross in the eye.

I spat blood on the floor. I must have bitten my cheek.

"Ah yes, but that is why we are here today, isn't it? If anyone is to blame for Sophie's death, Hazel, it is you. You are the reason things turned out the way they did. If you had accepted me as your alpha in the beginning, Sophie would still be alive."

"What about Molly? The boy you killed? Rob?"

"Oh please. I didn't kill your friend, did I? And the boy was just an accident. If he hadn't gotten in my way, no one would have died, and don't pretend that killing Rob wasn't doing you a favor. He molested you and beat your aunt, did he not?"

"How do you even know all this?" I shouted.

"I told you. I've been looking for you for a very long

time. When you first started showing signs, I had people watch you, to see if you'd live through the first shift. I believe you've already met my son, David. Why do you think he was there the day you climbed out your window?"

I stared in shock. I knew there was something about David that I couldn't trust, but I had thought the worst-case scenario would be that he might be a member of Ross's pack, not his own son.

I looked Ross in each eye and realized what an idiot I'd been. David had his father's eyes. That golden hue I'd found so unnerving. Now I knew why.

"I'll admit he's pretty taken with you. He nearly ruined my plans, the disrespectful little brat, but he's home now, learning his lesson. I *was* going to let him take you for a mate, but now I think I might keep you for myself."

His smile was sinister. I heard Caden growling again. I tried to give him a warning glare, willing him to calm down, but he was nearly unrecognizable, the look in his eyes was all wolf.

Ross took a knife from a pack member closest to him and held it to Aunt Claire's throat. I sucked in a breath, panic rising within me.

Not her too. Please not Aunt Claire.

"I'm done playing games, Hazel. You have two choices. You accept me as your alpha and become a part of my pack, or your aunt dies and I kill everyone in this room, including you."

I had no choice. My life had come full circle. Once, Rob had made me feel trapped and helpless. Then over the past few weeks, I felt that maybe I had risen above that, but now I was caught in the hands of a man far worse, feeling trapped and helpless all over again. My life wasn't much, I knew, but the rest of them, they were everything. They deserved a chance.

And Ross was right, in the end it was my fault Sophie had died. It was my fault they were in this mess, but now I had a chance to make it stop. I couldn't let anyone else die for me.

"You will let everyone here go and you will never come near them again."

Ross released a slow smile. "You have my word, but only if you swear yourself to me, right here, right now."

I looked at Caden, gripping the golden wolf necklace now hidden under my shirt. I wished I could give him a proper goodbye, but he wasn't quite there anymore. His eyes were like a wild animal, darting from me to Ross, his face a mask. I hoped he'd realize that I was doing this for him, for everyone. I hoped he knew how much I had fallen for him.

I then looked at Lucas. His cheek was bruised, eyes red. He stared back at me, but I couldn't read his expression. I hoped he knew I wouldn't blame him if he wanted to trade me for Aunt Claire's life too. It was the way it should be. Aunt Claire was his bond, his mate.

And then I finally looked at Aunt Claire. Tears were streaming down her face. I tried to give her an apologetic smile. I was breaking my promise. I was going to save her again, at my expense. I wished I could tell her it was worth it, and that I knew she'd do the same for me. I wanted her to live a long and happy life with Lucas, her soulmate, the one she was meant to be with.

I steeled myself and turned my attention to Ross.

"What do I have to do."

"Kneel," he commanded.

I did as he said, already feeling the pull of his authority.

"Hold up your wrist."

I lifted my hand to him. He was still holding the knife to my aunt's throat. He leaned forward, and with his free hand, he took my wrist.

"Now accept me as your alpha. Say it out loud. The words do not matter so long as you say your name and pledge yourself to me."

I swallowed, a tear streaking down my face.

"I, Hazel Lowell, accept you…as my alpha." My words were slow, painful to say.

Ross smiled. Bending my wrist to his mouth, he gave it a lick, looking me in the eye. And then, with fangs extended, he sank his teeth into my wrist. I cried out. The pain was like fire. The effects of the bond were immediate, like a rubber band being snapped into place. My life was his, my will, his.

He released my wrist, blood streaming down his mouth. I gripped the wound tightly to my chest to stifle the bleeding.

"You made me wait a long time, Hazel."

I stared at his chest, no longer able to look my new alpha in the eyes, unless told to do so.

"I should punish you for fighting me, for thinking you could win."

He took Aunt Claire by the neck and pushed her against him, the knife held closer to her throat. She gave a muffled shout.

"Please!" I begged. "Please don't hurt her. You promised to leave everyone alone. You got what you wanted!" I choked back a sob.

His eyes were dead, his face expressionless. There was no humor. His casual, businesslike demeanor was gone. He was no longer playing games, because he had already won.

"Maybe you should have thought about that before you disobeyed me. I told you, Hazel, I don't take lightly to being disobeyed."

He then took the knife and thrust it into Aunt Claire's stomach.

Someone screamed. It was so loud, so piercing. I didn't realize it was me until my throat turned raw.

Aunt Claire sank to the floor, her back leaning up against the couch. The knife was still embedded in her stomach as she looked at it in shock. Blood quickly soaked her shirt. There was a roar, then bodies began crashing through furniture. Lucas had gotten free and was in wolf form now, the largest I'd ever seen. He tore guards apart, trying to get to Aunt Claire. I went to get to her as well, but before I could reach her, Ross's remaining members dragged me away.

I screamed in anger. I could feel Ross's bond, telling me to go with them. My body was trying to obey, but I resisted it. All that mattered was Aunt Claire. I reached for her, fighting desperately to get to her. She looked at me with weak eyes. Dying eyes.

I heard Ross yelling commands. The bond was growing stronger by the minute, but I kept fighting. I would never stop fighting. Nothing would keep me from her. The more I pulled my focus away, the more his commands loosened, causing the bond to break. Ross either began to panic or lose his patience, because he commanded someone to pick me up.

Someone grabbed me and lifted me off the floor. I shifted, hoping it would weaken their hold on me, but it didn't. They only gripped me tighter, their hands digging into my fur. I snapped and growled, trying to bite whoever had me. I'd nearly twisted myself around, ready to sink my teeth into flesh, but before I could get the chance, something heavy hit me on the side of the head and my vision began to fade.

The last thing I saw was Aunt Claire, lying in a pool of her blood, chaos reigning around her…

And then everything went dark.

The End

EPILOGUE

I ran through the trees, my four legs quick and silent. I could sense the others near me. My pack, my family. I felt our strength, a force to be reckoned with. and I was proud to call them mine. We stopped in front of our makeshift home—an abandoned cabin. It was small, but most of us preferred to sleep outside anyway. I shifted, not worrying about modesty. Why waste time with such trivial, human thoughts.

Today had not been a successful day. I was angry and frustrated. I heard the door of the cabin creak open and I smiled when I saw him step out.

My friend, my savior, my everything.

He ran to me, sweeping me in his arms. I buried my face in his neck, breathing him in, digging my fingers through his hair.

When he set me down, he took in my face, reading my expression. "The hunt didn't go well, I take it."

He handed me a shirt and pair of shorts. I threw them on quickly.

"They are sneaky. Shielding themselves among

humans whenever we gain on them. It's hard to keep track of their scent." I gathered my hair up in a ponytail with a frustrated tug.

He gripped my shoulders and forced me to look at him. "We'll find them. They can't hide forever. Nowhere is safe from us."

I nodded and released a heavy breath through my nose, my shoulders sagged. "I just want it done. It's been months. I want the justice she deserves and the revenge I crave."

"And you will have it," someone said from behind. I turned to see who'd spoken.

The alpha walked toward us.

We kneeled before him, eyes down. He placed a hand on both our heads, signaling for us to rise. When we did, he took my chin in his hand and brushed a strand of hair from my face. I involuntarily shivered.

"Their betrayal will not go unpunished."

A stray tear fell down my cheek. He wiped it away gently. "I know you miss her."

I did, more than anything.

"We'll try again tonight."

I gave a small nod as he walked back to the cabin. I would forever be grateful for all he had done for me. He took me in when I had nothing, gave me a home, and a promise to help me get revenge on the pack that had killed her.

"I'm going to take the next sweep of the perimeter." I started walking toward the tree line.

I had to stay busy. Idle hands meant idle minds, and my thoughts were something I just couldn't be left alone with. Visions of blood, death, and the bicolor eyes of someone I didn't know but hurt to think about plagued my dreams. Feelings of anxiety, despair, and longing weighed heavily on my mind throughout the day. If I sat around for too long, a sense of wrongness would settle within me and I'd develop an anxiety no one could save me from.

No one but him.

"Hey," he said softly, feeling my growing unease.

I felt his hand intertwine with mine as I looked up into golden-colored eyes. He raised his other hand, pinkie extended. "Always on each other's side, right?"

I laced my pinkie with his and smiled. "No matter what."

We leaned in till our foreheads touched.

"Hazel and David," he whispered.

"Against the world," I finished.

ACKNOWLEDGMENTS

This book has been years in the making. While it's practically a different story entirely now, the things that matter most are still there and the people that made it matter are still there.

Thank you to my middle and high school friends for getting excited to read when I'd write a new chapter in my spiral notebook (sorry, teachers, for disrupting class).

Thank you, Mrs. Hensley, for being an incredible creative writing teacher. You always steered my stories in the right direction when I needed help and ignited my love for novel writing. Also, Mr. Petersen for being such an amazing high school English teacher. You helped me appreciate the classics.

Thank you to my family and friends for all their support. Especially my brother, Matthew, for all the times he listened to me bounce ideas off him and let me get excited when I accomplished all my writing goals. He doesn't know it, but he is the person I go to when I need to reignite my creative spark. I will always be grateful for that.

Thank you to my Instagram writer friends. You guys are one hundred percent the reason this book is finished and out in the world. You are my cheerleaders, my teachers, and my inspiration. I would not be where I am without you and your support. It has meant more to me than you will ever know.

Thank you, Laura, with Tulip Editorial Services for being an amazing and patient editor.

Thank you, 100 Covers, for designing an amazing cover design. You perfectly captured what I wanted and gave my book a face I love.

Thank you, Maggie Stiefvater, Stephenie Meyer, and LJ Smith, you not only shaped my writing, but you also shaped me into the reader I am today. My love for books runs deep because of you.

Lastly, thank you to my readers. Whether you loved it or hated it, I appreciate you for taking the time to invest in my story. I am honored.